Burning Issues

An Australian Story

Leah MacGuire

Linellen Press
265 Boomerang Road
Oldbury, Western Australia
www.linellenpress.com.au

Disclaimer

Burning Issues is a work of fiction. Names, characters, places and incidents in this story are the product of the author's imagination. Any resemblance to any real person or place is purely coincidental.

Contents

Acknowledgements

Thanks to Helen Iles of Linellen Press, who helped tirelessly with editing and ideas.

Thanks to Shirley Eldridge, who gave advice early in the book's development.

Thanks to The Society of Women Writers WA for their guest speaker programme and for helping to hone a writer's craft.

Chapter One

The Meeting

2018

The afternoon sun shone with all its might as he tried to ascertain the presence of smoke in the distance. Ross squinted as he drove around the corner in his recently purchased utility, towing his caravan. Was that a dark cloud up ahead? Yes, he could see the black swirl in the sky now, and as he sniffed the warm, still air, his old fear of fire heightened. He'd been a farmer when he was young, and now the hair on the back of his neck prickled as he realised that a shed ahead was burning. He pressed his foot harder on the accelerator; wound down the window to cool down as the fear-induced sweat collected on his forehead. It didn't work – his window stuck tight, and the temperature in the cab climbed quickly.

As Ross continued along the road, an ambulance came from nowhere and swerved to miss him and his utility. He could now hear the siren blaring, and he realised the noise of the emergency vehicle had been sounding for some time. With a thumping heart, he pulled over, drew to a halt and took stock of the situation. As a veteran who'd survived a world war, he recognised the imminent danger and felt panic washing over him. He needed to take a break and calm down.

Opening the ute door, he stepped out onto the side of the road, steadied himself as he leant on a nearby tree and gazed ahead. In the distance, an old man was walking down the now deserted road, and, as Ross looked harder, he thought it was a heat mirage. But logic kicked in as the man's features materialised, and gravel crunching underfoot came to his ears as the figure came closer. The man carried a water bag and appeared exhausted. It had been a particularly long, hot summer, which was unusual in Carson in the southern part of South Australia. The parks in the town now looked dry, and the buildings in the main street threatened to soon shed their paint. Usually, there were enough showers of rain to sustain the grass all summer long for the dairy farms, but global warming was raising its ugly head, Ross thought. Carson, near Murray Bridge, was suffering. Only a few dairy farms remained, most farmers moving south where there was more rain.

'Come and sit here in the shade,' Ross called out.

The man with the waterbag took heed, and as the two old-timers sat on a fallen tree trunk near the roadside, nothing needed to be said. The walker's breathing slowly returned to normal, yet he still looked hot and bothered. He was dressed in khaki working gear and a dirty old tennis hat that was covered in dust and sweat, and his furrowed, weathered face looked as though there were many stories, all probably untold, beneath his unassuming demeanour. His bloodshot eyes looked in Ross's direction.

'Wretched fires in this weather. Then the wind came up and we were really in trouble.'

'But that ambulance? Clearly, someone was hurt!'

'Nah, I'm not worried about it. Boss can relax now.' He paused for a long time and closed his eyes. 'We managed to get the machinery away from the hay shed to bare ground. Then we just let the fire go – it was pointless trying to save the hay shed once it was alight. Think he'd let the fire go even before that. Good on him, I say. In fact, here's the boss and his sister coming now in the green ute. He's going somewhere. Don't know where but he'll think I've walked home. I live just up here on the hill.'

Unsure of the old man's ramblings, Ross looked towards the hill and noticed the green vehicle approaching, dust billowing out behind it. It slowed as it approached the two men sitting near

Ross's ute and caravan. Dust swirled to the front and sides as the ute drew to a halt. A tall, slim man dressed in dusty working clothes alighted from the driver's side, but the woman kept looking straight ahead, a wisp of curly grey hair blowing slightly across her face in the feeble breeze. Ross expected them to look exhausted, particularly given their age, but they both wore a slightly smug look that couldn't be hidden by their hats and sunglasses. Calmly, the boss said, 'See you in the morning, Sandy. It's the end of it all.' Then, as quickly as he had come, the boss opened the driver's door, pushed his dog aside, and slipped back inside. Without another word, he and his sister slinked off into the distance in their surprisingly new ute. The sister had not looked sideways.

Ross frowned at the indifference towards the ambulance and the boss's comment. *What did he mean 'It's the end of it all?'* Perhaps he'd spent too much time driving and he should have stopped sooner. Perhaps old age had caught up with him? Had he imagined it? But surely, his eyes *and* ears couldn't be wrong.

He stood contemplating this, as he often did these days, and decided to offer the waterbag man a cup of tea. He was pleased when his offer was accepted with 'strong black with two sugars.' Of course, that's how an old Australian bushman would have his tea. So, Ross set about boiling some water on his gas stove in the caravan. It was too hot for flies, which was some consolation. This was what he loved – lots of time and a big shady tree – and ultimately, Ross and the waterbag man enjoyed their beverages.

Ross assumed the man, Sandy, would not be much of a conversationalist, living alone in the bush with nothing to think about except the flies and the weather, but he was wrong.

'So, I suppose the boss and his sister have been living a very conservative life here in rural Australia, watching the seasons come and go over their lifetimes?' Ross mused, easily imagining the dullness and the routine the two of them might have endured until now. Here they were, almost ready to meet their maker without a single significant event ever happening in their lives.

'Mate, have you got a few hours for me to fill you in on some important details?' He glanced around and gave a twisted little smile. Then he took a deep breath, wiped away the sweat running down his face and shifted to find more comfort. It wasn't easy, given his generous size. 'Actually, it might take more than a couple of hours, so you go and get your caravan off the road and park it inside the fence when we've had this tea. No hurry now.'

Waterbag Sandy perked up a bit, revived by his tea and the coolness of the shade. He had a captive audience in Ross, who was still intrigued by the ambulance and the total ambivalence of the bush characters towards the daily happenings.

'Bring over two folder chairs, old fella, from that flash caravan of yours and fill up your kettle again. I've got a story to tell.'

Astonished and with his interest spiked, Ross obeyed without question, and the two men settled in for a yarn.

'Firstly, it was someone with bushy, straggly hair who was carted off in the ambulance, but they were wasting their time. It looked like a woman, but I could be mistaken. Who would know these days, but I do know what a dead person looks like after they've collapsed,' said Sandy, whimsically.

Ross nodded – he did too – and he continued to listen. In the late afternoon heat of the day, the bush stayed silent; no leaves rustled. The ambulance noise faded in the distance on its way past Carson – *probably on its way to Murray Bridge by now.* The boss and his sister were long gone in their ute with the dog, and so, too, was their dust. Ross watched, intrigued, as Sandy took out some cigarette papers and a pouch of tobacco, his brown-tinged fingers deftly rolling a smoke.

Sandy frowned as his mind took him back to when he was young. His Irish accent hadn't diminished over time, but the edges had softened slightly as he took on the Australian vernacular. He loved reflecting on when he was youthful, a mere slip of a boy. They all were then.

Sandy began his story.

Chapter Two

The Young Parents

1970

Sandy took Ross back to 1970.

'Ernie, as a young man, had been lucky enough to purchase his farm in the dairy area of South Australia sometime after the war, and it certainly helped if one's father was a farmer who could then finance the next purchase. In true form, after a few years, Ernie and his wife had children – they were who you saw in the ute today, the son Ian and his sister Bonnie. I arrived on the farm as an Irish migrant looking for work when I was in my twenties, and at that stage, Ian was in his early twenties, as well. He was a good looking fellow, full of life, and intent on becoming a farmer.

'Little Bonnie, who was quite a bit younger than Ian, was away at nursing school, learning to be a nurse, so she didn't really feature much in my early days on the farm. Don't get me wrong though. She came to be a major player later, but she was mainly silent on the Trevilly farm in those early years.

'The two children looked quite different – he had blue eyes and blond hair while she had brown eyes and brown hair. The family originally came from Truro and inherited the genes for intolerance, and, just like those smugglers from Cornwall, they didn't take any prisoners!

'One day the family came home early from tennis and a workman, Toby, was milking a cow. Now this was forbidden, as milking was strictly twice a day, in the milking shed, by the milking machines and the milk would be ready for collection by the tankers, which came to the farm each night. It was serious business. Pat collected some of the milk and distributed it to all the workers, including Toby. Needless to say, poor Toby and his wife had to pack their bags and leave … …

'Trust is important, Pat,' Ernie said. 'We cannot employ people we cannot trust, and we need to instil this in all our workers who live here. What Toby has done amounts to theft. It's theft from the business because now the cow, milked by Toby, will be dry at milking time.'

'I know you're right, Ernie, but it seems hard on those two little kids. Why should they suffer because of the parents?' Pat said quietly, as if deep in thought. Her brow set tight as she thought about the wife and children. It was some time before she could wipe her hands on her floral apron and set about other tasks in the kitchen. She liked to keep busy as she put the freshly cooked biscuits into their own specific tins.

Jobs were allocated and a high standard was expected, without any sneaking of extras. Ernie was rather ruthless, but so was the whole family. With this toughness came resilience. The seasons were kind in those days, and winter rains fell regularly in the 1960s. The oat crop was sown and hay was made. However, there were risks taken and accidents narrowly averted at times.

One winter, when the tractor was working at full capacity and workmen were tired, there was a cold and frosty night when the boss worked the late shift. To beat the forecast rain, they operated into the night. Around and around the paddock the tractor groaned, only stopping when it was necessary to load with seed and superphosphate fertiliser. Occasionally, Ernie could feel his eyelids droop, and he was known to fall asleep while driving. But on this particular night, he noticed a continual gouge in the freshly tilled soil ahead. *It must be a stump or a large stone caught in the harrows*, he thought. Mesmerised by this gouge, he decided to check it out the next time he loaded the combine seeder. Minutes crept slowly past.

Then it was time to fill up so he stopped the tractor and waited for the workman to move the truck next to the combine seeder. Ernie soon began to feel annoyed, as the truck was nowhere in sight, which meant the driver had fallen asleep. Despite woolly gloves, Ernie's hands were stiff with cold, and it was difficult to move himself to dismount from the tractor. His legs had become immobile due to the long period of idleness and the cold. It was dark and still, with the only light coming from the tractor projecting just enough light to see and guess what was ahead. He felt slightly irritated as Gerry, his best workman, feared the dark. Ernie could understand this as the dark could be rather scary for anyone.

With trepidation, he slowly descended the tractor ladder, going down step by careful step. Then he heard the noise. And stopped to listen! It sounded like a groan, but Ernie rejected this notion even though the hairs on his neck started to bristle. Then he heard it again and this time it sounded human. His heart started thumping.

His annoyance rose as he strained to hear, and he stopped moving to listen. It definitely was a groan and it was out there in the dark. Ernie reached for a torch in his pocket and hoped the battery was not flat. Normally, the truck lights would be enough to provide light but without the truck, darkness prevailed. Further, in the moonless night, any noise seemed exaggerated. There it was again! This time Ernie used his torch, pointing it in the noise's general direction.

'Oh my God! What happened? Gerry, is that you?' screamed Ernie. Gerry was trapped behind the seeder, in the covering harrows, leaving a drag mark in the freshly tilled earth as Ernie had driven around the paddock. Suddenly the cold and darkness seemed immaterial as Ernie felt for Gerry's legs and arms. His ankle had become caught and trapped in the harrows, dragging his body behind.

Ernie's eyes had now become accustomed to the dark, and he

managed to extract him from the cold, metal harrows while poor Gerry groaned. This had been an incredibly lucky moment in only one of many farm mishaps. Gerry was lucky to be alive with no broken bones and minimal lacerations, and it had been fortunate the paddock was relatively bereft of stumps and rocks. They sat on the soil and slowly the two men regained their composure, realising how Death had paid them a visit but had gone away empty-handed.

'I was attempting to free a blockage and, as the machine moved forward, I slipped. I was going to clean the seed tubes but this didn't happen. I know the safest way is to check everything when the machines are stationary, but I thought I'd save some time and do it while the seeder was in motion. Oh well, I think I stuffed up.'

Ernie, sitting silent, now realised why the truck hadn't moved.

It was freezing cold sitting on the ground, yet they sat still until Ernie felt able to retrieve a thermos and pour them a hot drink.

Pat, too, was a key player on the farm, but no way would Ernie allow her to drive farm equipment. Well, at least, in the early years of their marriage when the children were young. During these years, she was happy growing vegetables near the swamp, close to their house, where past inhabitants had dumped rubbish of all kinds, including dead animals. All consumers of the vegetables were oblivious to the reasons for the tastiness or the extraordinary size of these swedes, turnips and carrots. Leafy green vegetables, too, delighted in the spoils of the old swamp on the farm. Only later did Ian refuse to eat the 'yuk from wastewater sludge', as he relished in telling all who would listen. But fruit trees continued to delight in what the swamp had to offer.

Ernie and Pat's generosity was felt by their neighbours who came to visit, knowing there was always a bonus at the end of a chat. Old Derrick, with only one arm, regularly came in his flash car, and Ernie would gently tease Pat about any old bachelor who came to the house. Old Derrick would always give a long toot of the car horn and Pat was expected to go out and talk to him. Only when the children pestered for tea could Pat give him an armful of vegetables and expect him to be on his way. Ernie dared not leave the shed and go to the house in that time, otherwise, he too would be drawn into the long conversations epitomised by the loneliness of isolated living during the post-war decades.

But toil on the land and the promise of good returns from the soil ensured happiness for Ernie and Pat Finch. Their lives with their two children on Trevilly, as the farm was known, served them well. Their social needs were met by sport in the local community of Carson, and, luckily, family members proved talented in this field. Sporting results and an individual's physical prowess ensured lively conversations in the shed that continued from one week to another.

However, life wasn't all jolly. Occasionally, tragedy struck and fear penetrated their hearts on realising how quickly disaster could strike. One time, when Ernie was driving home after a night out at the local pub, he discovered something that consumed him for many months – years really. On driving around a corner, he saw an upturned car ahead that had failed to take the bend in the road. Of course, he stopped to render assistance but soon realised he was too late. On the side of the road, near the spoon drain, a prone shape lay with its head at right angles to its back and shoulders. The head was slightly tilted upwards but flat on the dirt, as if in sleep. The angle of the neck immediately told Ernie this was disastrous. Before he turned the head over, he recognised it was the man he'd given a haircut to only days prior – his neighbour George, who also happened to be his brother.

Ernie tried to straighten the head to align it with George's body and brushed the dirt off his face as best as he could. He felt coldness as he touched George's face and his neck also felt cold. He felt for life and warmth but to no avail. George's spirit had left his body. Ernie put his head on his brother's chest and let out a loud moan of denial as this was not the George he once knew and loved. He could hardly believe what had happened! His beloved brother, a stalwart of the community, was dead.

'He's been thrown out of his car,' Ernie muttered to himself as he drove back into town, trying to rationalise what had happened. He felt numb, though his heart pounded and sweat ran down his back as he battled to focus on his driving. Luckily, his car knew the road and soon Ernie saw the lights of the town ahead. *Thank God for long-formed habits*, he thought as he drew closer, the lights twinkling randomly and providing light. Ernie opened his door and tumbled out, mindful of the alcohol blurring his vision. He stumbled towards the noise and soon the raucous sounds drifting to his ears became louder. He managed to subdue his nausea, realising what he would soon have to say.

'There's an emergency out on the south road about two miles out,' he yelled as he stormed into the pub. But the noise was too loud. He bellowed again, and gradually people started to look at him.

'What is it, Ernie?' they kept repeating but Ernie could barely speak. 'Out there on the south road. It's George!' He wanted to shout more but the words somehow became stuck in his throat, hampered by a sob.

'Righto! Who is sober enough to drive out there?'

'I'm going home,' became the general word around the bar.

'Ernie, come with me,' someone said. 'You get into the car and I'll drive.'

When they arrived at the accident scene, Ernie muttered incoherently. 'Please take me home.'

So, he was taken home. He could only imagine what must have transpired there on the dust as he told Pat. There wasn't any blood at the accident scene but, being people of the land, they recognised Death when it stared them in the face.

A few days later, as they all sat around the kitchen table, Pat said 'I hope this isn't an omen for our future.'

No-one spoke. They were still in shock and feeling grief. Ian spent a lot of time supporting his cousins, Ron and Mal, as well as Uncle George's wife, Aunty Enid. They thought about selling the farm but Ian talked them out of it, despite his own nightmares about what must have happened and Uncle George's last moments. Regularly he woke in a sweat and found he needed to make a hot drink before he could erase the images from his mind. Ernie refused to drive past the accident scene for years. Each Sunday, the family went to tennis or golf, but the early model Falcon had to learn a new route to Carson, where the sport was played. It didn't matter that the gravel made driving more dangerous or that the wildlife featured more prominently at night, thus increasing the danger. Hitting wildlife was an occupational hazard while driving along these lonely, unsealed roads and Ernie made a conscious decision to drive more carefully. He wanted to keep his family safe and there was no more speeding around corners either on Trevilly or into Carson.

Chapter Three

The First Wedding

1975

Ian lay on his bed on his wedding night, feeling relieved – relieved that he had someone next to him to stop the nightmares he'd been enduring ever since Uncle George's accident so many years ago. He could now roll over and touch another human being and find comfort. Indeed, it was more than merely comfort and he thought that, if the last few hours were any indicator of married life, then may there be much more of it! The pleasures of the flesh had been a real source of absolute delight for him and his wife June. She knew where to touch and how to touch. Indeed, the trick was in just how much pressure to apply and then when to stop the touch! And soon it started all over again. Clearly, she was well practised at this game and Ian gradually learnt the meaning of a woman who was experienced. As he listened to his wife's breathing, he smiled inwardly at the many nights ahead, and the many days too, if nocturnal activities were on the agenda. Life was good!

Often at the shed, Bill would notice the grin on his face. Sandy noticed too. 'Ian, there's a smile on your face that any man knows about! It is so broad, mate, it'd be impossible to wipe it right off your dial.'

'It's okay for you, old fella! Why aren't you married? Then you'd have a wide grin too.'

'Not for me. Nah. Women are too much trouble. They're like a lamb chop. Fantastic when it's fresh and new but pretty awful when the meat goes rotten.'

Ian was determined his meat was not going to go rotten! He loved the games June played. Often when he got home after a day's work, June would have little notes all around the house depicting the human sexual anatomy in varying states of arousal. Often, she cooked dinner naked, and the game was to assume normality for as long as possible before succumbing to the whims of the flesh. Then one day, the game ended quite abruptly when June announced she was pregnant. The grins on Ian's face were less common at the shed and even Bill noticed the difference. He was subtle enough not to ask if the meat was deteriorating, and even the milk truck drivers commented on the lack of spring in his step. It had gone. He now moved like his father.

'Come on, Ian! Keep those cows up!' was called out regularly in the milking shed. Usually, the cows didn't have far to walk to the dairy and each one ambled into its bale to enjoy the fresh hay. Ian began to work hard at something that had been quite natural in the past, but the heifers in the nearby paddock had also become a burden for Ian to feed. His father commented how he must be getting old and slow at running, but Ian blamed his slowness on sporting injuries. He had learnt about morning glories and even lunchtime glories, but these slowly stopped as June increased in size with each month of her uncomfortable pregnancy. He hoped that their fantastic nightlife would begin again after the baby came, but he was to be disappointed.

The bonus from the pregnancy was June gave birth to a daughter: Sheila. Ian had hoped for a son, who he'd wanted to call Wallace because he had Scottish ancestry, as well as his Cornish past. He delighted in anything historical and academic, despite June's indifference. Part of his story included being related to William Wallace from Stirling in Scotland, and he loved telling anyone who'd listen. June grew bored with history and didn't share a passion for cerebral activities or reading, unlike Ian, who could really turn his hand to many things, much to his father's delight.

'Come on, Ian, let's go and knock out a tune,' was Ernie's

regular parting comment at the end of the day and the two of them would often play their musical instrument – Ernie on the piano and Ian on the mouth organ. As little Sheila grew up, these soirées became more regular and neither Ian nor Sheila were keen to rush home. Sheila, of course, loved the music!

The novelty of the bedroom had clearly waned and one day Bill said, 'Come on, Ian, old son. Where is that cheeky grin? You know the one I'm talking about?'

Ian started the pump engine so he didn't have to respond but Bill had noticed Ian's reluctance to acknowledge him. The loud banging sufficed for some time but Bill didn't move away. He waited until the engine had run its course and the shed fell silent again.

'I don't know. I think I'll have to work a bit harder.' Ian went home early that afternoon, but there were no little notes now, no naked chefs, and indeed no one at all at home, which was not unusual. Disappointment reigned as he'd planned some time alone with his wife and had left Sheila with Pat.

*****

Pat loved her time with her much-loved grandchild, and she and Sheila became immersed in the garden and the miracles of nature. She loved the cyclical aspect of plant growth and marvelled at the bloom of flowers and fruit. She explained how the nitrogen and carbon cycles worked to naturalise the miracle of chemistry in their world, but this abstract notion evaded Sheila. She understood how all animals died and how decay was connected to the cycle of life but she lacked the curiosity of truly intelligent children. Pat had realised their son, Ian, was a bright boy early in his childhood when she remembered his interest in abstract ideas with his endless questions. However, Shelia had a darker side too. She tended to take coins she found and other things of value around the house and put them in her pockets to take home. Pat gently told Sheila if she ever wanted anything then she only had to ask, but to take without asking was a violation of trust. She wasn't quite sure Sheila understood, and occasionally June returned objects she found in Sheila's pockets, including Pat's wedding rings. Well, she thought, perhaps Sheila wasn't going to be as bright as her father, but she dared not think about the qualities she could have inherited from her mother. Pat liked her daughter-in-law well enough but was concerned about how easily she raised her hand to Sheila at the slightest misdemeanour. Pat sometimes wondered if the smacks on the legs were to mark a position of power – *she* was Sheila's mother and Pat Finch was *only* the grandmother. However, Pat tried to dismiss these thoughts as quickly as they came into her head. She needed to show support for her son's marriage to June.

*****

'June, where are you?' Ian called, but she was out again with all her boozy friends, and a note had been hurriedly scribbled and left on the kitchen table. He had become accustomed to this and, now that an outsider, Bill, had noticed, Ian was keen to try hard at being a good husband. He plopped down on one of their nice new dining chairs, with the dogs at his feet licking his toes, waiting for June. Being summer, she was probably at the local swimming pool, he thought as he began cooking their dinner. He began whistling as he cooked their steak on the barbeque thinking about the green salad and tomatoes. He prided himself on being a good cook and, as a child, had often helped his mother in the kitchen when workmen needed feeding, this role lasting for weeks on end. *Ah*, he thought, as he wondered about the reason why he often had trouble with the spring in this step, *I'm just a bit tired.* He consoled himself with this idea for many years. June was out more and more so Sheila spent time with Ian and the men at the shed, or with Pat. Ultimately, the great morose set in and everyone at Trevilly just waited and waited.

Seasons came and went. Birds continued their constant cacophony in the trees, stripping all the leaves and creating ghostlike limbs deprived of life as they gradually died. Christmases with family, including Bonnie, who'd become a nurse by now, continued at Trevilly. Working men came and went but faithful Sandy and Old Bill stayed. The football seasons, or some other sport, continued to create a marker in the week and rains created a regular pattern of nature interacting with the environment, just as it should. Pat's garden continued to thrive, and milk production met targets for markets and contracts. But the heaviness in Ian's heart continued as he realised that he and June had nothing in common. The sex had become mundane and boring, eventually ceasing to exist. Ultimately, June moved into the back room on the south to enjoy some of the feeble sea breezes.

'Are you going to come back inside, June, now the house is air-conditioned?' But she didn't.

'The painters have created a toxic paint smell. Think I'll stay out the back.' And so excuses for a lack of intimacy continued. Ian eventually gave up.

One summer, when Sheila had turned twelve, June just left. Ernie and Ian heard the car start up, heard the accelerator at full throttle and heard June shouting that she was taking Sheila too.

'And I'll be back for everything else as well. You just mark my words!'

The dust hung in the air and even the noisy cockatoos were silent. The bush knew when tragedy struck and, although no one had been killed or hurt, a turning point started for the folks of Trevilly as life was never the same again. True to her word, one day, just as they were about to commence seeding the oat crop, the removal truck crunched on the gravel and backed up, ready to be loaded.

This time Ian acted like a man possessed.

He slammed the door of his truck and pushed the dog off its seat in a bid to move fast. His dog yelped in surprise and Ian realised the extent of his wrath so he took a deep breath as he patted the faithful animal. He stood behind the loaded truck gathering his thoughts as he realised his house was about to be emptied.

'She's taken Sheila, but she's not going to take the rest of my life,' he said aloud to no one in particular. He managed to stop the removal men from achieving their task and surprised himself with his civil tone when he requested they leave. He had to pay them and swallowed hard as he realised there was payment of some form or another for everything. In this instance, it came in the form of a sizeable cheque. At least June was gone, though he knew he'd have a battle ahead.

Luckily, he wasn't aware then just how huge the battle would be. In the future, he would have to assume the persona of his Scottish ancestors when they battled the English. He needed to be tough, but that was difficult for him with his gentle nature.

Later the same day, Bill patted him on the back, and with no words spoken, Ian remembered his comments describing women. Pat grew quiet and withdrawn as she missed Sheila. For Ian, his lamb chop had certainly gone rotten, and it stuck in his gut, making him feel physically ill. There was no respite either and Old Bill, an Aboriginal worker who'd been working on the farm for as long as Ian could remember, understood the complexity of human relationships. Ian wondered how these men could be so wise.

Painfully aware he was blundering through life making mistakes and feeling pain, poor Ian found an upturned four-gallon drum and sat down. He looked up at the sky and shouted, 'Uncle George, those old blokes at the shed know everything!'

To say it aloud felt cathartic, and with that utterance, he decided to stop being morbid and think only in the moment, so he could embrace some peace.

'Come on, Ian, let's go and move the mob of heifers,' Old Bill called out as he clearly read the situation. There was nothing like physical activity to relieve a tortured soul. Old Bill had walked into the shed many times to save the children from awkward or dangerous situations. 'We need to do it before dark as there's no way I'm staying out after dark!' He knew this would evoke a good reaction from Ian, who smiled and responded in the way Old Bill predicted.

'No boogie man out there, Bill. I reckon we could stay out in the paddock all night.'

Ian respected the beliefs of different cultures but there was no way he was staying out late during the dark, just in case Old Bill was right. He didn't want a visit from Uncle George's spirit in any form!

Deciding they were all safer at home, out of the dark, he rose and joined Bill so they could return to the shed in time for dinner. He enjoyed the banter with this wise old man, and he loved the way he'd always been given respect, despite being a 'young fella'. Many times, Ian, mindful of his youth and inexperience, appreciated that Bill and Sandy treated him as an equal in the world of men, and this fulfilled a need in Ian as he navigated his way through the world of human nature in a melting pot of work and play.

Chapter Four

The Nurse

1980

Nurse Bonnie couldn't help her brother. No one could as numbness slowly set in and his melancholy became a permanent feature. To connect with him, Bonnie warily offered her opinion as she gently pushed her wavy brown hair away from her face. 'If I ever get married, I'm going to marry a doctor. I know I keep saying that but it's true.'

'Bonnie! I've heard it all before. Go on and marry a doctor,' Ian teased her gently.

'Well, I need to find a decent one first, and honestly they aren't really particularly good at slowing down and having a meaningful conversation. They are all so work-focused and serious. Most are really old fuddy-duddies.'

They sat together on the beach, enjoying the warmth of the day and the scent of the ocean, in Glenelg, a genteel area of town, but that didn't stop drug dealers and crooks from inhabiting the fashionable environment when they chose to do their deals. And they weren't easy to identify from other folk who spent time on the beach. Today, there were mainly family groups gathered and Ian and Bonnie both stared out at the long jetty, with its swimming platform at the end. There, busy, excited children jumped into the water and splashed about in delight.

'Do you remember when you used to jump off the big jetty? A little kid surrounded by big boys, wanting to be just like them?'

Ian smiled as he, too, remembered. It seemed a lifetime ago and so much had happened.

'I've asked Vern to join us as I heard he was in town. Poor Vern, and the pain he's in. It must be shocking,' said Bonnie, keenly moving the conversation to the present to lessen Ian's melancholy.

'I'm glad you asked him here today so we can all catch up. Not quite sure how he'll navigate this slope on his crutches though,' Ian replied wistfully.

They stretched out onto the lush green lawn beneath the pine trees. Sunset in late January still held the day's heat as evening strolled towards them- and they reflected, in one of their rare meetings, on the year that had passed. They looked towards the lowering sun while she sipped her Chardonnay and he swallowed his beer; the cheese platter Bonnie had prepared lay largely untouched.

'I'm sure he'll manage, though I know what you mean. If anyone can survive, it's Vern.'

A farmworker had run over Vern earlier in the year so Vern had been fighting for his life ever since, for which Ian had felt totally responsible – he'd employed a druggie and had been ready to have an altercation with him, but was waiting for the right moment. Unfortunately, the right moment never came and the accident happened while Vern was working in the shed. Ian could not even say the worker's name, he felt so much anger and disgust – he just called him the druggie, as farmers were incredibly good at devising nicknames for everyone. It happened that the druggie put his foot on the accelerator while Vern was working underneath the light truck, adjusting the brakes, and Vern had spent the next six months fighting for his life, the truck wheel passing right over his body, partially disembowelling him in that instant.

Bonnie remembered Vern telling her how he heard a bang as his tummy popped and the next thing he knew he had to put his gizzard back. He was always a great storyteller and, being a nurse, Bonnie wasn't quite sure how much was fact and how much was fiction. All she knew was Vern was lucky Death hadn't claimed him.

'Gosh, you've had a bit to deal with during the last few years, poor brother,' Bonnie said as she looked out over the ocean with its smooth patches and its rough waves. *Rather like life*, she thought. She knew there was no way anything in Ian's life could be put in a kind way, but she had to verbalise information as she knew her pragmatic brother would see it.

'Yep, life can be a bitch. I know this is a cliché but then you marry one and she tries to destroy you. She got nothing from the divorce coz Mum and Dad own the dairy, but she took our daughter.'

Bonnie knew this was painful and didn't want to spoil their precious time together, but she had to acknowledge little Sheila somehow. 'How is she?'

'I don't know. I ring but June won't take my calls. I haven't spoken to Sheila for years. She's all grown up now but she probably blames me for her mother's failed marriage. She would have told Sheila I've abandoned her.'

They were entering into Ian's pain, even though Bonnie had wanted to avoid this thunderous roar that took up space in Ian's head. Thankfully, as she glanced up towards the car park, she saw a man struggling with his crutches.

'Vern!' she called out and waved her arms wildly in a bid to fling off the pain of human relationships. As she rose and looked towards the trees, the sight of Vern lifted her spirits. She focused on his broad smile. In another time and place, she may have felt attracted to Vern with his larger-than-life personality, good looks and positive spirit. He was fun and had the ability to make anyone laugh. But he was a country man through and through, just like Ian. That was why she'd asked Vern to the beach: she wanted someone to make them laugh. *Definitely pleasant to the eye*, Bonnie decided, but she was a city girl, not interested in the bush, with its relentlessly vicious weather, flies and dust. A thought flicked through her mind and the reference to Ian's wife, June, sent a shiver down Bonnie's spine. While she liked the idea of a companion, she was all too aware of the pain that accompanied the joys of male company. She was going to keep them all at a distance.

'Great you could make it,' Ian said as Vern tried to settle himself on the grass, all the while trying to make his crutches look invisible. Vern then focused on trying to open his can of beer and even that was difficult. Still, they sat enjoying the company and the moment, with the sunset preparing its best for them as if to make the occasion incredibly special. The hours passed without reference to Worksafe visits to the farm, police reports about what had happened on that fateful day and other challenges they had all faced throughout the year. Soon it was time to leave but each looked forward to their next meeting when they could, hopefully, spend more time together.

After a few weeks, on Ernie's birthday, Ian and Bonnie visited their parents for dinner. They stayed up late and around midnight, decided to stay overnight. Bonnie and Ian had their own separate accommodation at the large family house in North Glenelg, the red brick, Californian bungalow-style home with its old-fashioned front verandah a sanctuary for the Finch family. It was the home of Ernie and Pat since they'd retired from the farm.

At breakfast the next morning, Bonnie verbalised what she'd been thinking for months. 'Mum and Dad, while the four of us are here, I thought I would tell you something. I'm thinking of joining a medical team that practises medicine in Africa. Remember my friend Thelma?'

'If you think you've got news, well, I'm thinking about getting engaged,' Ian interjected. 'I'm only thinking at this stage. There's probably a long way to go.'

'What? Did I hear correctly?' Bonnie screamed. 'Here I was thinking that our poor parents were going to have single adult children forever.' She blinked for a moment to absorb this new information which was, indeed, life-changing.

'Too funny! Sarah White and I have been seeing each other for a while, so now I'm going to make an honest woman of her. Mrs White could become Mrs Finch. And do you know what? Her son adores me and I love his company. They are both easy to be around and fun. This time I'm marrying for love, not lust. I can't wait to be a married man. Perhaps I might be too set in my ways, I don't know, but I'm going to give it a go and make this work.'

In his excitement, Ian felt an urge to blurt out more but stopped himself. He hadn't even asked Sarah yet and the relationship was still in its infancy.

'Great news, Ian. I'm sure it'll work. Sarah's a local girl and she knows farming. She's a teacher, isn't she? If you love her, my boy, it'll work,' his mother reassured him. 'And a grown son too! That's a bonus to have the family you've always wanted.' Pat, a big woman who had clearly enjoyed a lifetime of good home cooking, sat up straight in her chair, trying not to become over-excited.

'Your mother's right. Sarah's a good sort. You'll make a great team,' Ernie said. As wise as ever, he'd become almost serene since his retirement from the farm; he loved to walk down to the beach, along the popular precinct, along Jetty Road. Sometimes he'd reach the beach but quite often meet up with someone he knew and have a long chat; sometimes he'd read the paper in his local café. He enjoyed his new life away from the farm, playing bowls at the local North Glenelg Bowling Club, and his solitary walks gave him a time for reflection. Ian knew he'd given his father a lot to think about on his next morning walk. If this new prospect of marriage came to fruition, then Ernie had some serious succession planning to consider regarding his precious dairy farm. Now that he was approaching old age, or at least he thought he was, his mind was in a whirl.

Now, with their two adult children on the brink of new adventures, life was treating Pat and Ernie Finch kindly. They didn't need to worry about climate change and the new technological age of computers – that was Ian's role on the farm. Like all retired people, they listened to the News each night and adjusted their days to accommodate social outings, gardening and naps.

Just as he was starting to drift off in his thinking, Ernie remembered how his daughter had dropped a bombshell too.

As he moved his chair out from the table to get himself a second cup of coffee, he said, 'Bonnie, did I hear you say something about going to Africa? What's that all about?'

'Yes, Dad. Do you remember my friend Thelma? The girl, or I should say woman … we're all over forty now … who married the Zimbabwean farmer?'

Ernie scratched his head and worry crossed his face. He sat down in his comfy chair, which needed to be replaced but he was a frugal man who liked to think he was modern and saved money by not being extravagant. However, he spared no expense when it came to spending on the farm. Pat had nicknamed him Scrooge, but he told her that his tastes were modest and when he died, she would be rich. They liked this kind of banter and laughed readily.

'His name is Craig. Anyway, as Thelma and I were looking at the church noticeboard, she asked if I'd like to come to her place later in the day for a drink. So I said I'd be there closer to early evening after tennis. When I arrived, this stately gentleman was sitting on her front verandah sipping Scotch from, of all things, a crystal glass. As I stepped up onto the verandah, he opened the front window and called out, "Thelma, there's someone here to see you and she's not from the church. It's someone in little white shorts".' Bonnie smiled at the memory.

'Then he put his glass down on a rickety table nearby as Thelma came to the door. She looked at him, then at me and said, "Craig, I want you to meet my friend Bonnie – from the church." It took a couple of seconds before we all roared with laughter and so began my wonderful friendship with Thelma and her family. I love them to bits! Craig always teases me about my little white shorts and my church connection.'

Ernie laughed. By this time, Pat and Ian had settled in to listen to this African story.

'Look, I won't be going for a while yet and now with this wedding on the horizon, I'm not going to miss it for anything!' Bonnie exclaimed, still unable to stop smiling. 'This is going to be a great year. The future is looking good. And who knows what the next decade will hold. Perhaps I might even get myself a doctor to marry.'

'Let's get the champagne out, Pat. Bugger the coffee! We have a lot to celebrate.'

Ernie made a move towards the cellar for his prized drinks while Pat reached for the crystal glasses in the lounge room cabinet. Four glasses were plonked down on the jarrah dining room table with a thud, and a lot of contentment and joy in the family. They proposed a toast to the longevity of happiness.

Chapter Five

The Second Wedding

1985

In October, Ian and Sarah were married in an old church on a beautiful sunny day and became Mr and Mrs Finch. The grey stones in the walls had seen many couples come and go through its huge wooden front doors and a sense of happiness flowed over the small crowd and the newly married couple. The bells chimed to conclude the service and the smell of fresh soap and hairspray mingled in the air as the guests shuffled out through the doors to stand on the grass to wish the newlyweds good luck. As people socialised, Ian turned his head and looked up the street. He squinted, then squirmed. A black ute parked facing the church and, although it was some distance away, he could make out the silhouette of a large person with a cap on slouched in the driver's seat.

A shiver ran down Ian's spine as he thought about his absent Sheila. He still hadn't been able to make contact with her for many years, and she would be a young adult by now. Of course, he'd wanted to invite her to his wedding and make her part of his new family but June's ability to be difficult had continued over the years. She'd simply shut him out and in doing so, effectively shut out Sheila as well.

Gradually his sense of rationality returned, and the shiver left him. He was being paranoid about his daughter, who he figured would feel she'd been abandoned. He looked at his new bride and a natural smile spread over his face, and soon it was love he felt, and the dreaded trepidation left him.

Sheila sat sullenly in the black utility, parked like a demon, just far enough away to ensure its anonymity, the temptation rising to start the engine. Dearly, she wanted to plant her foot hard on the accelerator and speed noisily past the bridal group, then brake hard at the last minute and do a burnout to create a fog of thick black smoke. She just wanted to cover her father and his bride in smog, which would serve them right. *How dare that woman take the place of her mother. How dare that rotten father of hers abandon her.*

She felt sick with rage just thinking about it and seeing the joyous occasion outside the church made her seethe. The black ute proved good camouflage as no one would expect a girl to drive such a beast, and she pulled her black cap down on her forehead, strengthening her disguise. Sometimes she even put on fake glasses and thought about doing so now. But instead, she squeezed the steering wheel hard and turned the radio volume to its maximum.

After a few minutes, she realised the only person she was hurting was herself and remembered what her psychologist had told her. She turned the music off and released her vice-like grip on the steering wheel. Slowly, she started counting to one hundred and shut her eyes in an attempt to disgorge the image she had just seen. Her psychologist had also told her to simply walk when she felt enraged like this, but Sheila wasn't leaving the sanctuary of the dark ute.

He's quite a good bloke, this psychologist, Sheila thought, *but sometimes he has weird ideas.* She had only started seeing him when her mother had threatened to dump her onto her father. But instead, her mother had labelled her as a kid with anger management problems. Soon after, she'd left home after yet another argument with her mother. *She's such a control freak,* Sheila thought. *All she does is scream and shout so why shouldn't I scream and shout back?*

She pulled herself up abruptly from her reverie when she realised the crowd she had focused on had started to disperse. *Look at them all there,* she fumed. She watched as Ernie and Pat, all dressed in their fancy clothes, kissed and embraced the newlyweds. *They're traitors too. In fact, they're all traitors!* Sheila wished she lived in the past where individuals were simply disposed of during the night. She loved fantasizing and playing roles! Regularly she would plot the demise and disposal of enemies in both real and imagined life. She loved the idea of revenge, despite her psychologist advising her not to embrace these demonic thoughts. At times, she felt like disposing of her damn psychologist too but reasoned that he was easy enough to ignore.

But other things were not easy for her to ignore: the need for money always loomed largely ahead of her. But she was not going to think about money at this point in time. She strained to see ahead so she could decipher and identify individuals she knew. There were only a few people left in the group and Sheila kept staring at her grandparents. She assumed they would be driving to their home and wouldn't be attending a party of any sort. Sheila decided to follow the old people, just out of curiosity and boredom really.

She started the engine and tailed the vehicle her grandparents drove, keeping a discrete distance behind. After a short distance, they pulled up in their Glenelg home driveway, and she was impressed with the grandeur of the house in this leafy green suburb. Ernie took a long time to unlock the front door and while he did, Sheila took a photo of the fancy letterbox with the number '9' clearly defined. She then turned and took a photo of the street name, realising she now had her grandparents' house address. She knew she should have a feeling of connection but all she could feel was the difference between the 'haves' and the 'have nots.' She felt cheated, being in the latter group, and soon felt the familiar tightness of anger in her chest, so she turned her ute around and sped noisily away.

Driving around in a daze, taking time to restore some sense of calmness, she still felt unsettled as she neared her humble rental on the outskirts of Adelaide. This was all she could afford and if there wasn't a letter from that chemical company offering employment, she'd need to do another burglary run tonight and all week. *Phew!* The letter *was* in the letterbox, but this was quite a different letterbox from the one she'd photographed several hours ago – this letterbox was rusted tin propped up on an equally rusted metal pole.

Everything about this rental reeked of poverty, but it was all she and her house mate Rodney could afford. She was definitely going back to a leafy green suburb later that night in the hope some rich old fool had forgotten to lock his front door. She didn't like the look and feel of poverty and today she had seen how the other half lived. She hated her father and his family even more and what her mother said was right: they had too much money for their own good and June believed she'd been unfairly treated by the legal system in her divorce from Sheila's father. June believed she had been entitled to half the dairy, but this view was not accepted by the Court.

Both June and Sheila knew a lot of people who believed rich people deserved to be 'taken down' wherever possible. *Well, I'm going to pay a visit to a couple of them tonight to see what I can get hold of to make a few things even.* Staying busy would take her mind off what she knew her father and his new wife would be doing in their luxurious accommodation on their wedding night.

She helped herself to one of Rodney's bottles of wine from the fridge, rearranging the contents to disguise that one was missing. She looked for some loose change on the benchtop but Rodney knew she was adept at making loose change disappear. She wasn't actually short of money; she just enjoyed the thrill of the chase where money was the reward.

She sat on the old wicker chair, forgetting to check for spiders before she did, but she did not care that night: if one appeared she would squash it and watch the runny contents ooze from the spider in its death throws. After sipping her first mouthful of wine, she put her glass down on the grimy side table. Some day she intended making lazy Rodney clean up his joint so it was organised and tidy; it had a damp, musky unpleasant smell about it. He owed her that much, she figured.

Half an hour later, not even the alcohol could settle Sheila as she tried to sleep for a few hours, knowing she had a busy night ahead. She put her black coat and beanie near her bed so she could dress in dark clothing for the nocturnal event. She didn't expect to be seen by the old fools she would visit later in the night. However, she didn't want any unwelcome surprises either.

The following morning, Ian and Sarah enjoyed morning tea with Ernie and Pat, where scones with jam and cream were served as part of the tradition. Always on the farm, Pat had produced the most amazing scones and, when complimented on her cooking, she replied that she'd had a lot of practice, which was true enough. The Anzac biscuits, too, were part of Pat's specialty. The kitchen, wherever Pat lived, smelt of fresh baking.

'Mum, you've done it again! I think *you* should have catered last night. Your cooking is so much better than these fancy hotels. You would have done a sterling job.'

Pat's smile beamed as she wiped her hands on her apron. 'Enough about the scones. What are you two doing today? I know you'll be in a hurry to get back to Trevilly.'

As Ian watched his bride help herself to a second helping of cream, he marvelled at the way Sarah did everything so nonchalantly. *This is what I want*, he thought, *someone low maintenance who will fit in with farming life.* She seemed oblivious of the conversation, more intent on the scone. He chuckled in his mind as he formed a response to the question.

'Well, last week I decided to invest in solar water pumps to replace the windmill. So, guess what, Mum? If you were still on the farm, you would not have to wait for the wind to blow and pump the water for the garden. Actually, it was a bit more serious than just replacing pumps. A few weeks ago, I was on the windmill platform, up thirty feet on the sandplain mill, ready to climb into the cradle when the wooden platform gave way. It had perished. I fell backward and was forced to reach out and grabbed part of the framework. Luckily I had a harness on. Not a pleasant experience, I can tell you. So, I was hanging on to the windmill halfway down. My descent from there was with very shaky hands and legs. It scared the living daylights out of me!'

'Hmmmm … you were very lucky, son. I am pleased you had the forethought to have a decent harness.' Ernie helped himself to a second scone, telling himself his diet would start tomorrow. He liked to keep in shape, unlike Pat.

'Well, Dad, remember when Bill fell off the windmill a few years ago?'

Ernie remembered only too well. He was incredibly lucky it was the windmill near the front road, which was only about twenty feet high, a common height for old windmills. As Bill was about to step into the cradle from the platform, he made the fatal mistake of looking up and seeing the clouds move. This was lesson number one for heights and windmills, as the moving clouds led one to believe the windmill was moving, and the blades, therefore, were coming towards the frightened person on the platform. To avoid the blade, or what Bill thought was the blade, coming towards him, he moved and slipped. Startled, he'd lost his grip and fell. Luckily, his flimsy harness had swung him towards the frame so he could regain his grip. Naturally, he became terrified of heights, knowing he'd been extremely lucky to escape unharmed.

Ian realised he should not expose his staff to risks and all the complications where risk was involved. Farming life was embedded with dangers of many types, and it took a lifetime to learn them all, and new problems were always arising.

'Good on you, son. You've always been one to embrace technology. New ways make life easier and safe. Are these solar pumps expensive? Not an issue really as I can see the good sense on many different levels. I just wish we'd had solar pumps for your mother's garden. It would have made my life a whole lot easier.'

'Yes,' Pat intervened. 'I wish we'd had instant water. So, tell me, Ian, while the sun shines, these solar pumps churn out the water?'

The flies buzzed outside the kitchen door reminding Pat of her farming days when cattle dung attracted flies by the hundreds and created putrid smells. There were some things about the dairy she didn't miss.

'As you know, in the sandplain country, there's plenty of underground water, so the answer, Mum, has to be yes. Your old swamp is still there, and this year I will try to clean it out so the spring water is fresh. It's starting to smell awful. We need a pump on the swamp too.'

Pat looked wistfully out the window, realising she was about forty years too late to embrace this incredible technology. How she wished she'd had access to instant water via solar pumps during her time on the farm. But her years on the land were finished now. It was over to her son and his new wife. She liked the energetic and friendly Sarah, and so did the whole family.

'Bonnie's visiting later today, Ian. Are you able to stay and hear about her plans for working in Africa?'

Like all mothers, Pat was keen for a closeness to exist between her children. She'd come from a large family and so had Ernie, but she and Ernie only had two children. She'd wanted more, but somehow things didn't work out that way, despite the local doctor telling her she was fit enough to have half a dozen more children.

'No, Mum. I think we'll leave soon and head back to Trevilly after we've bought the pumps. We're newlyweds, but the cows come first. And we still have a few hours of driving. You know how these things go.'

Indeed, Pat knew better than anyone how work was paramount in farming life. She felt pleased that her new daughter-in-law was a local girl with a grown son, who also loved animals and the farm. Life was looking good for the whole family.

Chapter Six

Preparing for Africa

A decade later: 1995

Bonnie settled into her comfy seat on the plane, heading to Johannesburg, her thoughts still on her brother and his ten-year anniversary party that had been held just prior to her departure for Africa. It had been a real reason to celebrate. Ernie and Pat were thrilled the dairy was in good hands and were content their two children had established themselves with happy lives.

Bonnie had given up looking for a doctor to marry and was comfortable with a circle of friends who provided companionship for her. She had thought she would feel a twinge of jealousy seeing the happiness on her sibling's face, but it was quite the opposite; she was relieved to see Ian and Sarah were a happy, middle-aged couple. They had a few lines on their faces and hints of grey hair but clearly, they were devoted to the idea of family and each other. Ian even had a hint of baldness creeping in but it only added to the appearance of strength that came with advancing years – such was the story he loved to tell. Bonnie had nearly married but she hadn't allowed herself to commit to any permanent relationship – and he was a doctor! They loved each other but were just too set in their ways. This had been the standing joke with Ian as he often teased her about her commitment phobia. He was probably right, she reasoned.

Ken practised as a surgeon and Bonnie worked shifts in the theatre at the local Adelaide Hospital, close to Glenelg. Their shifts regularly coincided so they worked on the same days and regularly she was the theatre nurse when Ken was the surgeon. They began having meals together after her shift finished, and then going to concerts together. Eventually, they became a couple and Bonnie had even invited Ken to the family home for Christmas. However, Ken's relationship with his ex-wife and children complicated his life and Bonnie found herself stalling on the connection she enjoyed with him. She'd seen what had happened with blended families and she wished she'd met Ken before they were middle-aged with encumbrances. Slowly she'd felt herself drifting away and making excuses. Gradually they became good friends, rather than a couple.

She had taken Ken to Trevilly Farm to meet Ian and Sarah one Christmas. Afterwards, Ian voiced his approval one evening while they were alone sipping drinks on the old verandah. 'He's a keeper, sis. Clearly, he adores you.'

'I just wish he didn't come with family baggage,' Bonnie had replied wistfully. She'd never met Ken's wife, Rhonda, but after listening to Ken, it was clear she could make unreasonable demands. Ken called her 'high maintenance, always wanting this, that and the other.' However, the two daughters were just like ordinary kids, and she warmed to them when Ken introduced her to them at a party. *But I don't really want a ready-made family,* she'd thought wistfully. *It'll be too hard trying to appease all members.* She had felt a frown spreading on her face and had shifted uncomfortably to avoid the nail in the wooden verandah. It needed replacing or at least some kind of repair so the white ants didn't spoil it completely and she remembered thinking life on the dairy had many demands so verandah repair didn't rate highly for Ian or Sarah.

'Just look at us,' Ian had said. 'If anyone had baggage, Sarah and I did, though Sarah's baggage really was non-existent. It was mine that was the problem. Sarah gave me an awesome son. Adam's a great farmer and the same age as Sheila, who I haven't seen or heard from for years now. Adam understands cattle and the dairy and he's made friends with Aunty Enid and Ron. We all see a lot of each other. As for Ron's brother Mal, it was good when he left the farm and became a lawyer in the city. He wasn't really an outdoor type and who knows when one might need a lawyer in the family! There's always someone around here threatening to sue someone about something.'

'Why would that be?' Bonnie, so cocooned in the medical world, often had to pinch herself to realise other worlds existed. One day she'd do something about her situation but for now she was comfortable sitting on the verandah with a trusted soul, listening, from time to time, as the silence penetrated through the trees and garden. She'd felt relaxed totally and purred with contentment. The sun had slowly set and the sky had turned red, promising another warm day ahead. The sleepy old farm dog had moved and positioned himself next to Bonnie to enjoy the warmth of her feet, oblivious of the odour from her smelly socks.

'There are the issues of contamination of genetically modified crops and ensuring that chemical drift doesn't peep over the neighbour's fence. Old Ted and his son are still being difficult. Chemicals of all sorts are a problem. Then the use of veterinary medication leaving residue in milk is a big problem. Oh yes, and then there's litigation about workplace processes. Cannot afford having someone fall over a log and break a leg. Honestly! The insurance is horrendous, and Vern's case has been an ongoing nightmare in court. It took years for a financial settlement and Vern had to live with all the pain and pressures of the legal system. That's why I want to minimise the number of my employees. I don't know – it's a new era really, and I have to deal with all the complexities involved. One can't be just a farmer nowadays. Thankfully, Mum and Dad lived simple happy lives but these days someone's always ready to turn to a lawyer about something. It's a bit scary really. I hope our visits to Mal continue to be social and family-orientated, not business.'

'Lucky there's a strapping young man to help you with the farm and of course Sarah, who loves the farm and the little kids at her school. She's a great teacher I'll bet. Oh yes, and there's Ken to advise us when we get sick. Lucky, too, Bill, Gerry and Sandy are still here for milking each day. I think we've got all bases covered.'

Bonnie had laughed, taking the seriousness off the situation. It was Christmas and there was noise and good cheer coming from the house. 'Let's go inside before this wild party starts getting out of control. We need to stop Aunty Enid drinking all the good wine. She bought a few bottles here but she's probably drinking the good stuff.'

'Good idea,' Ian had replied and it was the last conversation she'd had with him for some time.

Bonnie had decided to sell her home before going overseas. The real estate agent had obtained a good price for her unit, which had originally started out as an investment. Living at Glenelg in the big family home with her parents had suited her well but as the years passed, she'd decided to buy an investment near the hospital, with the intention of moving in after a year or two. So now was the time to finish that chapter in her life and prepare for a global adventure. She knew she could always move in with her folks when she returned and perhaps, they may need looking after by then. But she wasn't going to think about it for now. She felt excited about her trip to Johannesburg and working with Thelma. Life in Africa was going to be exciting, and she looked forward to seeing wild animals and working in an African village with Thelma and Craig.

The plane continued its whirring noise and Bonnie allowed her eyes to shut, yet sleep eluded her. She'd always enjoyed daydreaming or reflecting. She was good at compartmentalising her life, too, and now that she was heading for Johannesburg, then Harare, she put thoughts of her parents, family and friends behind her. Her parents were safe and secure which allowed her to look ahead. She thought about stretching her legs and moving out of her seat, which was so restrictive. At one point, she had thought about flying business class, albeit fleetingly, as the cost was phenomenal and, with an uncertain future ahead of her, she wanted the security of a healthy bank balance. Suddenly a steward appeared at the front of the aisle and the drinks trolley began its rattle towards her. *I'd better stay seated*, she reasoned.

She put thoughts of Ken behind her too. He had a successful career, and he would not leave his home or his position in the hospital. She knew they were good for each other, and she'd even wanted him to join her on her African adventure.

'Why Africa, Bonnie?' he'd said. 'It's a third world country and is so politically and economically unstable. Actually, the unknowns are outright dangerous.'

'With Thelma and her family there, surely I should be safe. They are going to provide work for me and are encouraging me to establish a medical clinic on their farm on the outskirts of Harare. It is so secure, and my salary will be paid into my local bank account. From their pictures, it looks quite civilised, though I'm aware it's like any country, only the best parts are shown. Ken, it's time for me to make a move and have an adventure.'

He'd accepted this, albeit with some misgivings. Ken, the voice of common sense, security and comfort. For this reason, she loved him. He was so stable and sensible, as well as tall and attractive. But she valued her freedom and so she'd left the comfort of Australia. She'd promised to write regularly and keep in touch, so he'd decided to be content and satisfied, clearly recognising he didn't have a lot of choice with their relationship. He loved routine and Bonnie loved putting her feet up on his couch while he cooked her a meal. His house and his life were comfortable, but his family situation was sometimes complicated. While his daughters had always been accepting of her, now she was off on a global adventure, they could see Bonnie and Ken had a purely platonic relationship and were even more friendly.

It all felt quite strange and she felt relieved to be separating herself from it. She'd always been intrigued and often puzzled by the complexities of human relationships, and flying to Africa meant a welcomed break from the hospital's routine work. All she had to do was choose from the dinner menu on the plane and what to have as a predinner drink. She suppressed a smile as she acknowledged the pleasure in the trivialities of life, despite being thirty-odd thousand feet in the air. She readily embraced her new adventure.

Chapter Seven

Sheila's Work

1995

Sheila, too, had been on a plane, and when her flight landed, she was in Darwin in the Northern Territory. The place was not as rugged as she'd expected, in fact, it featured multi-storey buildings, traffic lights and all the other signs of modern life. The hellish heat and humidity hit her as she stepped out of the plane, and she mentally prepared herself for a long bus ride to the city. It wasn't fair, really, that she had to undertake this menial activity, even though she was well-paid. Her payslip described her as middle management, but she thought she was better than mere middle management. The best part of her work as a systems auditor for a national chemical distribution company was she could tell those bosses to comply with the rules and standards. Later, when she returned to Adelaide, she would have to sort out those dreadful women in the office.

She slowly made her way to the carousel to collect her baggage, then briskly walked through the glass doors for the waiting bus that idled quietly in the afternoon heat. Swinging into the front seat, she shut her eyes to avoid having to talk to anyone coming onto the bus. As her thoughts drifted back to her time in Adelaide, she felt thankful her job was so generously rewarding and that on this business trip, she would be staying in top-class accommodation. Then she remembered how, the last time she was at home in Adelaide, she'd stalked her father, who should have provided a home for her and her mother.

Well, home was still the old rental she shared with Rodney, and she was surprised he had tolerated her for so long, but then again, Rodney's work still entailed long periods away. That's why they never came to grief and argued, though there were many times when he annoyed her. In fact, Rodney had been so annoying last time she had decided to stalk her father just to get away from Rodney. It defied rational thinking really, she acknowledged, but stalking was one of her favourite past times: she liked to imagine she was in the Secret Service or something important, hence, her position of power. Her form of revenge was retaliation for her perceived deprived childhood, which had been going quite well until her parents' self-indulgence and self-centredness overtook their duties as parents. Her mother had left the farm and had to fend for herself in a rental; she had to get a job at the local takeaway shop, one that sold overcooked, soggy food fried in old fat.

Sheila blamed all the processed food for the size she had become now she was an adult. She was big and knew she took up a lot of space. However, her size was quite helpful, especially when dealing with co-workers who underperformed. She enjoyed the authority associated with this role. When those small women annoyed her, she took pleasure in belittling them. Often, she felt like pushing them out of her way, but she knew she had to use her words, not her size, to get whatever she wanted in life. To achieve this, she had become skilled at putting a slightly different spin on her words to make others in her workplace squirm. On the odd occasion, when she was confronted about it, she manipulated the story to make herself appear the good guy so work colleagues went away puzzled.

She liked concocting stories and using her authority as the boss in the chemical distribution company where she worked. Her role as a systems auditor also entailed writing reports for her line managers after checking situations against a series of meticulously detailed standards. She really liked pointing out faults that resulted in others having to correct their actions.

Then she remembered the huge argument she'd had with her mother when she'd left home, her mother having invited her new boyfriend to live in their house. Leaving was a good thing as her mother nagged and nagged. She could still hear her screaming out: 'Keep your room tidy and don't tell lies.' *God, she could go on and on!*

'Goodbye and good riddance,' Sheila had screeched at her mother as she had sped noisily away in her black ute. That was the last time she had seen her.

She'd bought the black ute cheaply some time ago from Metho Mike, who'd told her he needed to get rid of it as it attracted too much attention from the cops. She reflected how, on the odd occasion when she'd been stopped by the law, they had been surprised to see a woman in the driver's seat. She smiled inwardly: the black ute suited her personality! She knew Metho Mike was a drug dealer, but she only used on rare occasions, not wanting to end up a druggie like a lot of people she knew. She didn't hang out with Mike's crowd either – she was too respectable and superior for that. Regularly though she carried out deliveries for Metho Mike, but now, with her recent work pay rise, she wasn't going to risk being stopped by the cops. At least for the time being.

The first time she'd ever used Meth as a recreational drug was with Rodney – he'd told her that the best sex ever was after a snort of the stuff. She thought she'd give it a try, particularly as Rodney was paying, and she was curious to see what all the fuss was about. Rodney had been right about the best sex ever and regularly wanted more, but she'd decided she could take it or leave it. Most times, she didn't want to waste money for a good bonk.

Gradually she had created distance from Rodney and usually managed to spin him a story about how he needed to experiment with someone else. As time passed, she became increasingly annoyed when he always wanted money for rent. Occasionally, she felt like trading sex for rent money, but without a snort, Rodney wasn't interested. Sometimes she felt like leaving him and his rental, but she was wise enough to know she needed somewhere to live, and she sure as hell wasn't going to return to her mother's house.

As for her father … well … she was going to just check him out without him knowing.

The idea of being a super sleuth gave Sheila an adrenalin rush. If it were at all possible, she would love it if she could catch him committing a crime so she could wield power over him. She didn't quite know why or what she would do with this power but she hated him enough to mentally stick a knife in him. After all, he'd told her mother to leave the farm back all those years ago. *That's right! He'd kicked us out!*

Sheila felt the redness rising in her neck; she felt like putting a noose around someone else's neck. She didn't care if she was being paranoid; she just wanted to hunt down someone and watch them! Perhaps even torture them! In films, she'd seen bad guys tied up on trees with a noose around their neck so she knew how to do it, and she was strong enough to hoist someone up, no matter how big they were. *Right up and then let them swing. You are big and strong for a reason.*

She tried to let this image slide from her imagination as she drove her black ute miles south along the highway, ultimately reaching the dairy town of Carson. As she complied with the speed limit and allowed her vehicle to cruise through the sleepy town, she imagined the inhabitants of the dwellings pulling down the blinds and peeping through a little crack to see the unknown visitor. No one would know her now, and no one would remember the circumstances of her leaving the farm called Trevilly. Marriage breakdowns were uncommon in conservative communities, she reckoned as she passed through the quiet town, crawling along the smooth bitumen with only an occasional pothole. She remembered the bakery and the bank, the railway station and the school. Soon she was through Carson and on her way to the farm, hoping she wouldn't pass anyone who might arouse suspicions. But then, she hadn't done anything wrong and reminded herself it wasn't a crime to think horrible thoughts.

Sometimes she had to work hard to keep her mind on the straight and increasingly narrow road as she veered further from civilisation. She needed to think about what her psychologist had told her and started counting in her head until she reached the farm gate. There, she killed the engine and heard a ticking sound as the metal cooled after the long drive. Soon, it stopped and silence reigned. She rolled up the sleeves on her shirt and shifted in the driver's seat as the sweat from the skin on her ample thigh stuck to the vinyl seat. Her shorts were too tight, and the socks in her boots felt hot. She wound down the window as far as she could before it became stuck. The sound of birds became louder. She heard a tractor noise in the distance and realised the seeding program was probably underway. It was only a small dairy with a tiny acreage, but each year a paddock of oats was planted to make hay for their cows. She was tempted to walk down the track she'd walked as a child to catch the school bus. At the time, that two hundred metres seemed a huge ordeal. Now she felt more concerned about being seen from where she was parked.

Plucking up her courage, she put on her black hat and turned the key as she'd now decided to drive down the dairy farm entrance. Slowly, she pressed her foot on the accelerator and the black beast slunk along the gravel track towards the farm buildings. She remembered to put on her glasses to help her disguise. If she saw someone, she would just turn around and drive out but, as she approached, she could see the shed was empty. No one was around.

Phew, she thought. Although adrenalin rushed around her body and her heart thumped, logic told Sheila she wasn't really going to kill someone. She felt less like it now than earlier in the day and she might even be civil if needed. She could be quite charming when she played a role, and indeed playing roles was what she liked to do. But for now, she had to investigate and, if the opportunity arose, she would turn on her charm. She didn't know what to expect or what she would do. She hoped she could find useful items to take home with her.

As she alighted from her vehicle, she heard banging. *A noise in the wind. Was it hammering inside?* Sheila wasn't sure so she stood still, dressed like a man, and tried to identify the noise and its direction. It came from the direction of the old shed and slowly she realised the wind was blowing a loose sheet of iron on the roof. A smile crossed her face as she remembered how that kind of noise very much annoyed old Ernie, her grandfather. He would have climbed up the ladder, hammer and nails in his work belt, and stopped it with a few swift swings of the hammer.

But for now, it was all Sheila could hear as she ventured into the shed. Her eyes took some time to adjust to the darkness and, as they did, she thought she could see a shadow move on her right then disappear behind some chemical drums. She didn't recognise the chemical drums and realised her father bought his products from a company other than the one she worked for. She heard the noise again. *It's probably a cat. This shed was always full of wildlife.*

She plucked up more courage and called out: 'Hello. Is anyone here?'

She thought she would move to the corner in the darkness of the shed so she could easily see if anyone came along. That way, her eyes would become accustomed to the dark. The cat moved again but she wasn't going over to investigate. The last thing she wanted was to be attacked by a wild creature when it was cornered. Her heart thumped loudly in her chest and, if anyone had been around, she felt sure this noise would give her away. She looked over to the house just in time to see Sarah come out of the back door and move around to the side of the house. Luckily, she hadn't looked in her direction.

But Sheila took this as an omen! She was out of there before she got caught snooping around where she knew she would not be welcome. She was not sure how her father would react: indeed, she was not sure if he would recognise her as the daughter who had wanted to milk cows and feed animals. Would she be able to recognise him from the working men? But deep down, she knew she *would* recognise him, despite the many years that had passed since their last meeting when she was little more than a child. Oh well, an adolescent perhaps …

Just as she was about to step out of the shed, she heard an engine start up near the milking shed, only a short distance away. She took refuge in the dark and strained her eyes, looking towards the noise to see if there was any action. And there was Sandy working on some machinery, and someone in working clothes was doing something near the silos. She looked again and figured it must have been Sarah's son, Adam, who was moving an auger near a silo. He looked strong and tanned.

She felt enraged! *That should be me, not Adam, doing the farm work. That is my job!* Despite her being a female, this imposter was taking her place. *He's the one who should be hung on the noose!*

Sweat ran down her back and saliva filled her mouth as her massive body took the fight or flight response, pushed by increased adrenalin. Adam seemed happy and looked like he was whistling or singing! *He's happy! Of course, he's happy! Here he is on a farm, by default, and thinking he runs the show – milking the cows and feeding them oats.*

Sheila's fists tightened. Then common sense prevailed. She hurried back to her ute and drove off. She'd been tempted to fill her vehicle with fuel when she saw the bowser. But was it diesel or petrol? She didn't know and now it was immaterial as she needed to be out of there, quick smart. With the auger engine creating its own bellow, it didn't matter how fast she left and, by the time she reached the front gate, she had calmed down. Indeed, she felt hungry and reminded herself to stop at the next town for a feed. Perhaps she would stop at Mt Barker.

Slowly, the figure emerged from behind the drums. It was Ian, visibly shaking. He didn't know why he felt like this. He didn't know why he remained hidden, but his sixth sense had always served him well. He had a distinct dislike of black utes usually driven by silent, sullen males who looked like they were up to mischief. Of course, he recognised who it was. Years ago, when Ian and Sarah were engaged, Sheila had tried to entice Sarah's teenage niece into stealing jewellery from a shop. From that time on, Sarah was wary, and so, too, was Ian. Sheila had lied about her actions, even when she was confronted with the evidence. In the argument that followed, Sheila spat on her father's face and swore all types of obscenities, so Ian told her to leave and only come back when she apologised. A long time ago, Ian's father, Ernie, had talked to him about trust and lies; and many examples had shown how trust underpinned all human relationships.

Later that night, when Ian and Sarah were just finishing dinner, Ian talked about his visitor for the day.

'I wonder what she wanted,' Sarah pondered. 'I wonder why she was dressed like a man. I guess she wanted money again. Or perhaps she wanted to steal something.'

She cleared the dishes away and sat down in the comfortable dining room chair. Her yellow dressing grown complimented her attractive tanned skin and girlish figure. Sarah would label her night attire as sensible and, now that the nights were getting cooler, it served its purpose well. She pulled the lapels closer as if to block out unwelcome thoughts about the wild Sheila. A shiver jagged down her spine and it wasn't caused by the coolness in the air.

Ian looked over the top of his metal-framed glasses as he read the paper and frowned. 'I'm sure it would have been her purpose. She thinks she's entitled to the dairy farm and, when she got out of her ute, she was dangerous. I thought she was a bloke. She's grown so big it wasn't funny. She had a block of wood in her hands like she was going to use it to knock someone's head off. She had one hand at each end and then just looked around. She checked out the fuel bowsers but then Adam started up the auger at the silos and the noise made her take off. Of course, she grabbed something before leaving.' Sarah felt relieved Adam hadn't encountered her and realised Adam had everything Sheila wanted.

The nurturing mother in Sarah made her fearful for her son's safety, as well as Ian's. She was glad Ian had the good sense to stay invisible in the shed and wished Sheila would develop some feminine traits and perhaps find someone to nurture, particularly someone who would nurture her. Perhaps she would even marry and have a family of her own.

'What did she grab?' Sarah's eyes were red-rimmed, and she felt tired as she looked at Ian.

'She took the nearest things to her – the sledgehammer and a gemmy bar. She'll probably flog them somewhere to get some money. Walking around in her black shirt and scruffy shorts, she looked like a real lout. Honestly! I wish she'd just leave us alone. I'm amazed really that she's got such a good job but clearly, anger is an issue. She needs to find a purpose in her life and settle down.'

Suddenly the airport bus started moving as the engine came more to life, snapping Sheila out of her daydream. She'd almost gone to sleep! The air conditioning began humming, and she started thinking about her work. She needed to get a manicure on the weekend when she returned to Adelaide and perhaps spend some time at the beach after a long lunch. In the interim, she would be auditing another warehouse tomorrow and writing up a report for her boss tomorrow night. *God, I'm going to get even with that father of mine if it's the last thing I ever do.* But even she couldn't work out why she hated him so much. For now, though, she had to focus on her work.

Chapter Eight

Life in Zimbabwe

1995

When Bonnie's plane touched down in Harare, via Johannesburg, she felt she'd reached the end of the earth, but while walking to join the passport queue, her excitement grew about seeing Thelma. The trip had been long and tedious, and even the food trolley arrival hadn't relieved the monotony. Still, the journey was behind her now, and what was in front promised to be a change in lifestyle like no other. Little did she realise how true that would turn out to be!

Thelma waved excitedly to her. As she drew closer, she realised the man next to her was Craig, whom she'd met so many years ago. As she passed through all the officialdom of arriving in a new country, her eyebrows rose when she read the sign: 'PLEASE ENSURE YOU RECEIVE THE CORRECT CHANGE'. *So even the authorities don't trust other people working in the industry. How strange!* But this was just the start. For the moment, though, she loved seeing her friend and being in the company of people she trusted.

The big Mercedes hummed quietly along the deserted streets, the darkness hiding the clandestine activities happening in the shadows. They soon arrived at the gates of Thelma and Craig's home, the car stopping a short distance away. Out of the dark, two men appeared – clearly guards for the very grand house. Some chatter in a foreign language preceded the opening of the gates. The car then slowly edged forward along the driveway to the majestic pillars ear-marking the main house. Straightaway, Bonnie realised the British occupation of Zimbabwe had placed a real distinction of wealth in this country. But even so, the opulence of the house surprised her.

'Thelma, why did the car stop some distance from the gates?'

'If the gates open when the car arrives, bandits use the opportunity to slip through and bypass the guards. A conversation happens some distance away so when the car arrives, it does not stop as the gates have just been opened. Clearly, they shut the gates straight after the car enters the compound. It is just a security precaution, really. It's not a big deal.'

But the answer shocked Bonnie. For her, it *was* a big deal.

The plush leather seats in the luxurious car interior engulfed her, as if reassuring her that wealth and privilege brought comfort and security. This was post-Rhodesia, where Africa operated like a British colony, but she forgot how the civil war in the 1950s had actually been won by the natives of the colony, and now indigenous Africans ruled. Hence the name changed from Rhodesia – the breadbasket of Africa, governed by Ian Smith – to Zimbabwe, an African name. Currently, the political landscapes in the nation were rather ill-defined, and Bonnie took comforted in the friendliness of the natives who were clearly on Craig's and Thelma's domestic payroll.

As she sank into the soft mattress that night, she slept soundly, reassured by the gate guards some distance from the house. Guards also patrolled the grounds, safeguarding them, but from what, she wasn't sure.

Breakfast the next morning made Bonnie think she was in a five-star hotel. There was freshly squeezed orange juice and scrambled eggs made by Cathy, the maid. Craig made his own "oats" from goodness knows what, and clearly liked his meals a particular way. Thelma explained quietly how Cathy was a name the family had chosen for her, as her African name was difficult to pronounce in English. The large, friendly maid didn't mind, according to Thelma. Of course not, Bonnie realised. She was on the payroll and this job suited this kind, motherly soul with her uniform and maid's apron. Bonnie's head reeled at this lifestyle, but she tried hard to imitate Thelma, who sat enjoying her scrambled eggs and tea. *I could easily get used to this!* Bonnie thought.

'Bonnie, Cathy will clean your room and any ironing you have will be taken care of if you just leave it on the bed. At this stage, I can see you in my office at nine o'clock, and I will outline your duties,' said Craig as he finished his second cup of tea and began to leave the table.

Bonnie gulped her tea and answered appropriately. Thelma passed the toast plate, so Bonnie took a piece and prepared to enjoy her time in another world.

'Bonnie, soon we'll go out to the farm and you can establish the nursing post near the school. There are many farmworkers employed here, and all the kids go to our school. Your job really will be to run the nursing post for the farm. I oversee the estate with the help, of course, of someone out there. There is no shortage, ever, of help to administer tasks. How does that sound?'

Bonnie had heard all this before. But now she was actually here in Zimbabwe, she felt apprehensive yet exhilarated at the thought of being so useful to such a large group of people. She'd be ready outside Craig's office, like a good little schoolgirl, right at nine o'clock!

Bonnie suppressed a smile, amused at how Craig took control and Thelma was so compliant in his presence. Soon, she, Craig and Thelma were in the car, this time with a driver, which enabled Craig to point out all the significant buildings in Harare. The car moved past beautiful Jacaranda trees in full bloom, the vista dominated by a flood of purple. Juxtaposed against the beauty lining the streets was the squalor just beyond the footpaths, corrugated iron humpies where poor people who lived. Those inhabitants now stood looking into the cars that travelled past. It was quite eerie, as if the people were waiting for something to happen.

Craig explained how the lack of purpose in their lives led them to merely loiter, sullen and aimlessly, in the streets. Bonnie had never experienced anything like it and tried to look at the floor to avoid making eye contact with anyone. The atmosphere was almost menacing. She felt the spirits of the people and their desperate poverty move in from the footpath, into the personal space of the car, despite its momentum. She smelt fear in the air and felt lucky the driver kept moving. Clearly, he had experienced this before as he looked straight ahead, unwavering.

'We'll be out into the countryside soon, Bonnie, and then we can speed up,' Craig explained. 'Only a few miles to go.'

After what seemed a millennium, a farm with all its associated paraphernalia came into sight, much to Bonnie's relief. As they approached the buildings, children in purple dresses and purple shirts came into view, cheering and running towards the car. Bonnie felt like the queen on a royal tour and waved to the crowd and all their smiling faces. When the driver tooted the horn, it added to the children's excitement and slowly adults joined the row of smiling faces. Clearly, this was a daily routine as, when the car pulled up and stopped, the crowd made way for the occupants to alight. Craig reached for the door handle and Bonnie thought he was going to open the door for his wife and her friend, but this was not the case. Craig straightened his shirt as the door handle released and he eased his way into the crowd.

'Don't mind him, Bonnie. Just look after yourself and, if in doubt, follow me. Here we go.'

As the days unfolded, more surprises came Bonnie's way. Indeed, Craig provided staff for her to work with, and she gradually assumed a role more akin to a doctor than a nurse. She assigned someone to create a list of necessities for a medical centre and a sick bay. It seemed that anything was at her disposal and she was thrilled. This was what anyone would dream of, she later explained to Thelma.

Bonnie soon worked out there were nearly a hundred workers

on the farm, so if each had a wife and family, then there were a lot of people under her jurisdiction. Children were to be her main concern but naturally, farm accidents were treated at the medical centre and so, too, were all the aches and pains of the women and the elderly. The idea of multi-generational took on a whole new meaning for Bonnie. She became known as Dr Bonnie, a title she secretly coveted for years, and she amused herself by imagining Ken's face when she could eventually tell him. They would laugh together over dinner. It seemed in Africa, the old rules of western civilization were moulded to suit a particular niche. One rule of the establishment strictly maintained was white male supremacy and male hierarchy for both the expatriates and the natives. The exemptions were for Thelma, the boss's wife, and for Bonnie, the doctor and master of everything medical. The two friends quickly slipped into their roles of white goddesses and enjoyed all the privileges as well as the responsibilities that came with it. Bonnie wished Ken had joined her as time unfolded and stretched into a few years. She sometimes wondered where the time had gone but these moments were rare.

The weekly supply of equipment, including drugs, powerful ones at that, came to the railway station each Monday, and Craig ensured their delivery to the farm so the medical centre was as efficient as it could be. It was supposed to serve the children's needs, but the gradual increase in medical records indicated how all families on the farm were well served by western medicine. Bonnie was incredulous how supplies were so readily available, given the squalor and unemployment in the town. These people who lived and worked on Craig's farm were privileged.

Working long hours eventually made Bonnie tired, and Thelma also became exhausted and worn out with the constancy of many months, then years, of continual, constant grind. Time passed so quickly as one year blended into the next and then the next. Eventually, Thelma approached the farm manager, who told them he had a team of men who would take their place for a few weeks while they had a break.

'We're going away on a holiday for a few weeks, Thelma,' Craig announced one night after dinner. 'We're off to Victoria Falls and Kariba Dam. We need to show Bonnie the absolute best Zim has to offer. Would you like Elsbeth to make all the bookings, Thel, or would you like to do it yourself?'

'Elsbeth can do it. She knows what to do,' Thelma answered. 'I'm exhausted.'

After Craig left the room to take his whiskey in the drawing-room, Thelma looked at Bonnie. 'If I make the booking, whatever happens, it'll be wrong. Elsbeth will do a great job and we'll have a fun time. You never know, Craig might have to come home early.' Bonnie and Thelma giggled like two schoolgirls. 'It's been a long time since I've had a night out with a few bets at the Casino. Craig watches me like a hawk, and with disdain, when I mention the casino. We'll see how things go,' said Thelma knowingly.

On the day of leaving, Bonnie was checking her clinic and tidying away the last pieces of equipment before handing over to Gaz when a shout went up, and a vehicle crunched to an abrupt halt outside. Bonnie rushed out, accustomed to the sounds of panic in an emergency. Craig and Arno clambered out of the jeep and helped Thulani into the clinic.

'What's happened?' Bonnie asked the worker while trying to stay calm. Thulani, even with his ebony skin, looked pale.

'He fell out of the truck. He got up laughing, but his side now hurts.'

Bonnie knew this could be serious, but if he had stood up laughing, maybe it wasn't so bad. But with her leaving that day, she wanted to take the safer option. 'You must go to the hospital, Thulani. You must go today.'

'I no go hospital, doc-ator. Thulani no trust hospital.'

Bonnie was aware of the time. She was due back at the school to meet Thelma very soon. 'But you must go to the hospital,' she said precisely.

'No.' He shook his head.

Craig looked at his watch and raised an eyebrow.

'But treating this is above my qualifications, Craig. I can only assume it is a crack. He needs x-rays and careful management. He needs a qualified doctor in case it is or becomes more serious.'

But Thulani shook his head again, more determinedly.

Beckoning Gaz over, she asked, 'Are you going to be able to handle this? I think he might have cracked a rib. He will need to rest quietly so he doesn't damage it further. And this must be adhered to. Rest. No work. I can give him painkillers to help him rest but you must watch over him closely. You must insist he goes to Harare if he gets worse. Do you understand?'

'Yes, doctor. I can handle this. You tell me what to do and I will do it.'

Gaz gave her a wide, white-teethed grin and nodded, and Bonnie breathed with relief. After examining her patient more thoroughly and deciding painkillers and strapping would suffice for the moment, she left her patient in Gaz's care, but reiterated that he needed to go to hospital if the pain didn't subside on the drugs.

Then Craig bundled her off in the jeep to collect Thelma. They would be leaving in an hour.

Sure enough though, Craig had to return home almost as soon as they arrived at Victoria Falls so he caught the next plane back to Harare.

'What a shame,' said Thelma, and the two friends burst out laughing as they ordered another cocktail at sunset on the Elephant Lodge verandah. 'Did you know the Queen stayed here at this hotel when she visited Victoria Falls? Well, if it's good enough for the Queen, it's good enough for us. Let's have dinner and then a flutter. If I have a handful of cash, I'm not going to spend any more. That's my target and it's your job to make me obey!'

They laughed loudly and prepared themselves for a big night out.

The next morning, they met for a late breakfast with lots of orange juice before preparing to see the 'smoke that roars'. The loud noise from Victoria Falls could be heard from their hotel and soon Bonnie worked out why the famous waterfall was awarded the name, along with other accolades, within the world heritage listings.

'Don't speak, Bonnie, otherwise you'll be ripped off and have to pay tourists rates. Let me do the talking and the negotiations. Not so bad for our accommodation as Elsbeth has paid locals prices for all our costs. This is how it works. Locals are looked after, and tourists pay tourist prices. I'll speak their language and you just say nothing.'

This was a different kind of environment from life in Australia, but Bonnie more than happily obliged. It certainly helped that Thelma spoke the African language and the lack of tourists was evident by the exorbitant prices non-locals had to pay.

'It's called survival and making the most of opportunities,' Thelma said when she saw Bonnie looking at the prices.

'I call it extortion,' Bonnie whispered back, but she had seen the poverty and understood the reasons. *Not all things are equal across different worlds*, she realised, and the thought unsettled her slightly. However, she put it out of her mind, determined to enjoy special time with her friend. It was even better now that Craig had returned to work so Bonnie and Thelma had to look after each other. Bonnie chuckled – she knew who was looking after who. Soon, Thelma returned, still speaking in the African language, and put a ticket into her hand.

The next day they flew north, to Kariba Dam. Thelma wanted to show her friend the pride of the country, the massive expanse of water dammed to supply all the hydroelectricity for Zimbabwe. They arrived at their luxurious accommodation and prepared for sunset drinks. The slight breeze and warmth in the air promised perfect weather for exploring the next day when they were going on a tour!

The development for tourists in Africa surprised Bonnie. Alongside their lavish lifestyle stood poverty, straight and rigid, where people were surprisingly friendly, even to foreigners. Bonnie and Thelma were no strangers to the colonisation of Africa, having learnt about the British Empire at school, which now left Bonnie feeling slightly guilty and ashamed. Thelma had no issues with this country's history though. She had grown up with this lifestyle. But Bonnie regularly felt unsettled when all she had to think about was the menu for tonight's dinner. She only had to take a few steps outside her cocoon of wealth to see how dinner for others was merely subsistence.

She couldn't dismiss her thoughts in the people's plight and asked Thelma about the elections which would take place in several months.

'The natives will be restless,' Thelma said, nodding. 'They do not like their leader, but hey, he's meant to be controlling the country. There have been reports of take-overs of white men's farms by natives and many white farmers and their families have been reported as missing. They've been killed, of course, but the newspapers don't report information like that.'

'Have these incidents been increasing? Is it due to restlessness about the elections?'

'Yes, Bonnie, on both counts. It is unsettling for people when they are reminded of the poverty and corruption in this country. The whole place is totally corrupt, with everyone trying to make the most of every opportunity to accumulate anything, really, to survive. I don't blame them, but I don't want it to touch me. This is just my opinion, though.'

'How can you prevent it from touching us, Thelma?' Bonnie asked, concerned.

'Double the guards at the house and pay them as much as they want.' Thelma shrugged, her response troubling Bonnie. Suddenly she didn't feel as hungry as she'd originally thought.

They had an early night and, while Thelma reported sleeping like a baby, Bonnie tossed and turned.

Chapter Nine

The Medical Clinic

2000

Craig greeted them with open arms the night Thelma and Bonnie returned home to Harare, and even Cathy smiled widely as she served dinner. Along with dinner came the mail on a silver plate, served in true colonial style. Bonnie felt like she was in a movie, and half-expected Clark Gable to walk through the door. After dinner, Bonnie took her mail to her room, a little disappointed that her holiday with Thelma had come to an end. They'd had such fun and tomorrow she would resume work at the farm medical centre.

She looked forward to seeing Gaz and was keen to hear how the clinic had functioned under his management. Although he didn't have any formal qualifications, he was interested in medicine and was a person Craig trusted. She opened the letter from her mother.

February 2000

Dear Bonnie

I do hope all is well with you, so far away. We hear on the News each day about the invasion of white farmers' farms in Zimbabwe and the subsequent disappearance of the white farmers and their families. Your father and I pray for your safety and for the safety of all the people in Zimbabwe. It sounds like uncertain times are ahead with the elections coming soon, and with political unrest a certainty. Honestly, what is the world coming to we often wonder. Perhaps everyone was happier when Ian Smith was president, but I guess nothing stays the same forever. Since 1965 I guess we could predict that, being an independent sovereign state, would not come easy for any country moving away from British colonialization. The currency is devaluing each time your father reads the paper. As long as your friend Craig keeps paying you, that's all that matters to me! Oh well, not quite all. Just kidding!

Nothing here has changed. Dad reads the newspaper each morning and tells me all the news, particularly news pertaining to Zimbabwe, as I wash dishes and floors. Actually, he's been quite busy in the garden taking out all the roses at the front and just letting the lawn regrow to the road. He's had some help in doing this as Mal has been popping in each day in the last few weeks. He's been helping us update our Wills and ensuring the dairy transfer to Ian went through with minimal cost. Now the dairy transfer has happened, the house and any money left over goes to you. It's quite simple really and it has been made easy with Mal. It's great having a lawyer in the family and he tells us some interesting stories. Often, he stays for dinner too. Apparently, Aunty Enid and Ron are going quite well on their dairy and have received an increase in their milk quota. Mal has been doing succession planning and Wills for them too but he's had to move it to another partner in the law firm, due to a conflict of interest. Office work eh?? Who needs it? But it must happen, I guess. Bit morbid really but you know how your father operates! He likes to know the farm and his money are in good hands! We're lucky to have two great kids!

I haven't seen Ian or Sarah for a while but Dad went to Mt Barker a few weeks ago to play bowls. The town and the farm were looking great which is good to hear, given the dry seasons and strict milk quotas in recent years. However, people are still selling up and moving to the city or further

Bonnie's other letter was an account for the medical supplies used by the farm medical centre, paid for, of course, by the farm. She simply submitted an order and a cheque and, at the end of the month, all the unused supplies were returned. With the last couple of weeks away, Gaz had a lot of responsibility for the clinic, so tomorrow Bonnie would have some paperwork to do, along with her 'normal' day of work. She realised how, although she'd been employed as a school nurse, her role had extended way beyond the one hundred school children, and even beyond their families who lived on the farm. She referred individuals to the local hospital when it was necessary, but mostly, she easily treated those who fronted at her clinic. The locals, bless them, even called her doctor – a term which she secretly, sometimes not so secretly, coveted as part of her African persona.

While Bonnie was the nurse, Thelma was the teacher's aide, helping where she could. There was a principal too, who attended to all the paperwork while Mrs Thomas taught the children, all thirty or so in a classroom. Bonnie often helped in the classroom and this made her think that, if ever she changed her profession, being a teacher would be quite rewarding. The children were so eager to learn and they realised how attending school in this country was a privilege, one that would lead, hopefully, to a purposeful future.

For now though, Bonnie needed to be briefed on all the days she had been away, so a meeting with Gaz was the first item on the schedule. She walked into the office and saw papers strewn across the desk. She assembled them into an orderly pile before heading off to find Gaz, who was probably in the schoolroom.

After morning tea, she started to prepare for the return of the unused supplies that needed to be assembled for Friday.

'Where are the drugs to return, Gaz? I have some drugs, but where are the high potency painkillers … the narcotics?'

She'd been surprised that Oxycontin, Tramadol and other brands of opioid drugs, which were prescribed sparingly in her last workplace, had been so easily obtained on her list of supplies.

'These are highly addictive and dangerous in the wrong hands. Where are they, Gaz?'

Gaz shrugged.

'You didn't use them all on Thulani, did you?'

'No, Doctor Bonnie.'

'Are you sure?'

'I am sure, Doctor. I could not have. Thulani died not long after you left.'

An instant chill ran through Bonnie's body. Her mouth fell open. 'What do you mean he died? Did you take him to the hospital?'

'No, Doctor. He would not go.'

'So what did you do? What happened?'

'Thulani got very sick as soon as you left. Got the shakes real bad. Then couldn't breathe. He dead by nightfall. Authorities not happy with you, Doctor. You did a bad thing, they say.'

Gaz slowly turned his head towards Bonnie. 'And the drugs are missing. Just gone. When I arrived last week, they were gone. I put key back in its right place but when I looked for some antibiotics last Wednesday, they were gone.' He looked away knowing that missing drugs meant he was in trouble.

'They can't just 'be gone'. Let's go over the paperwork so we can determine exactly what was delivered last month and then we'll go through the daily records and see what was used.'

Bonnie's brain quickly shifted into work mode. The death of a patient was devastating, especially seeing she was not qualified to be diagnosing that level of injury nor administering painkillers for it. It sounded like Thulani had had a bad reaction, which could take an hour or so to be apparent. Maybe the rib had punctured the lung and caused internal bleeding which collapsed the lung. She should never have gone away. She should never have left him that way. And now, with the drugs missing too, she was in deep trouble.

Three hours later, she sat exhausted at her desk, her head throbbing from the grief of losing her patient, and the drugs still missing. According to Gaz, the authorities were waiting for her return, and would be checking her inventory so she and Gaz had searched for hours. And they wanted to view her qualifications. Bonnie started to panic on both scores.

'Gaz, did anyone else have the key to the drug cabinet? Did you give it to anyone else at any time? For any reason?'

'Not at all, Doctor,' Gaz replied, starting to sweat profusely. He was in trouble and he knew the doctor would be in trouble too. He wasn't going to say the drug key had been left on the table all day, with anyone coming into the clinic having a view of the keys. He knew the cabinet key was left on the table in the morning and it was still there in the late afternoon when it was time to lock up the whole clinic, including the drug cabinet, prior to going home. With absolute dread, he realised someone could have taken the key for a few hours and then returned it later in the day, making it look undisturbed. An unscrupulous person could have keys cut at the town key cutting shop. This would give them access to the schoolroom, the office, the clinic and the drug cabinet. He knew he had to deny everything. His job was on the line and if he lost his job, he would be on the street with no home and no future. He would be forced to join the freedom fighters as he would be unemployed. His only way to survive was to deny everything to the doctor and somehow, she would have to take the blame for the missing drugs.

Bonnie knew the missing narcotics would be sold on the black market and then repackaged by drug lords to pedal to the poor drug addicts of Harare. Missing drugs constituted a serious breach of trust and someone had to be lying. But she was in charge and she was ultimately responsible, and just as responsible for the death of a patient. She should never have left him in untrained hands. And it would not be possible to blame anyone else. Blaming one of the workers just wasn't a good reason in this country where individuals did whatever they could to survive.

It was obvious Gaz had taken his stance, and Bonnie knew there would be trouble ahead. She left Gaz standing at the table, his head drooping in shame, and wondered what she was going to do. How was she going to tell Craig?

During the afternoon, Thelma and Bonnie travelled back to Harare from the farm, Bonnie finding it difficult to maintain a normal conversation about the trivial events of the day. She had jumped into the driver's seat so she needed to concentrate on the traffic and this way cover her lack of conversation. Soon Thelma drifted off to sleep in the passenger's seat. Bonnie's head was in a whirl. *Should I tell Craig straight away or should I tell Thelma, who might know how to cope with this bombshell?*

She felt some relief when, on approaching the house, she saw a familiar car in the driveway. Craig's brother Pete and his wife Hazel were coming for dinner so at least, for the time being, Bonnie had a reprieve, albeit a few hours. She'd forgotten about dinner and as she made her way into the house, she ensured her footsteps were light as she quietly crept to her room to avoid lively conversation, which would be expected.

Dinner was not as jovial as usual, the upcoming elections putting a blight on life for everyone. In April, it would be all finished, with the expected result of re-establishing the current dictator firmly in his dictatorial government. It seemed when a person was on the side of the government, favours could reign. But being on the side of the government meant corruption and difficult lives for people in Harare and the whole of Zimbabwe.

'Any white farmers who do not support the government can expect to be thrown off their properties, or worse. We have become accustomed to this idea slowly over the last decade. The military is aligned with the government. They all know which side their bread is buttered on,' said Craig. 'Furthermore, the death of Thulani has placed us in a very dubious position. No one is blaming you, Bonnie, but the death of a black African at the hands of a white man or woman will not be taken lightly. I fear our time here is short.'

Indeed, the ownership of farmland had been contentious since the white colonial government had been overthrown and a black majority government was established under Robert Mugabe. The new government had been seizing property and giving it to the natives as compensation for the abuses of colonial rule since Zimbabwe gained its independence. Robert Mugabe had won fame as a guerrilla fighter, fighting against white minority rule. Since then, white farmers had their farms 'reclaimed' by the government, which the farmers called 'theft'. The African people, the rebel freedom fighters as they called themselves, who benefitted, however, called this justice and redistribution, as a result of wrongful European occupation.

Amid the morbid conversation, Bonnie decided to tell the family about the missing drugs.

'What?' screamed Craig. 'Holy hell.'

Everyone was outraged as they realised the significance and probable consequences.

Afterwards, there was silence. Even Cathy knew to stay out of the room. There was no doubt the servants were loyal to the family as their lives depended on the generosity and well-being of Craig and Thelma. Here they all were — five adults at the table contemplating the notion of missing narcotics.

'Clearly, Gaz is lying but that's what happens when we trust one of the locals. Clearly, someone paid him decent money and now he and his family are set up. We could stand by and watch what he does but I don't think we've got time for that. Those hospital thugs, with all their accounting, will take this opportunity to crucify us when they see missing narcotics, not to mention Thulani's family who are already angry and stirring things up. They have called on the police to help, and we know what that will mean.'

Craig continued. 'I should have administered the clinic myself. I'm surprised Gaz sold us out, but I suppose the price was too high and he succumbed.'

'Why don't we double the guards outside and pay them twice as much?' intervened Thelma.

'A short-term measure, my dear. But then again, who knows when we could expect a knock at the door or even worse. They may even strike tonight but my bet is that they'll make us sweat, just like we are now.'

Pete looked worried. 'Don't take it to heart, Bonnie. If it wasn't the death or the missing narcotics, it would be something else. The police, many of them corrupt, will use anything as an opportunity to liaise with the freedom fighters. In fact, it is just an excuse to evict white farmers and force them out. It's lucky you have a base in South Australia, Craig. If the worst happens then we all have somewhere to go. This has been coming ever since the end of British rule back in the fifties. These freedom fighters are violent and angry about their rights. The missing drugs and a countryman's death are just a catalyst.'

Cathy brought in the sweets but suddenly no one was hungry. The metal spoons clinked the bowls and soon the cup of English Breakfast tea signalled the end of the dining experience. At last Craig spoke.

'Pete, I have an idea. I've been thinking for a while of course so this is not some recent hair-brain scheme. How does this sound? If anyone here is in trouble, we will ring your phone three times and then hang up. Don't come straight away but just come over first thing in the morning. I say morning coz trouble is going to come at night. I expect the house guards will be disposed of, and then the house will be the target. What do you think, Pete? And Hazel too, of course.'

No one spoke for some time until Pete said, 'I think it sounds like a plan.'

Dishes rattled in the sink in the adjoining kitchen while the family sat in silence; the dining room was accustomed to long periods of silence. This was where important decisions were made, and currently this decision was as important as life itself. Thelma knew when to remain silent as this was serious men's business. This was no place for women's rights or opinions just now and equality of the sexes fell away by a century. This was a colonial outpost in many ways. Both racism and sexism featured as huge as elephants in the jungle, except they were the elephants in the room.

'Righto,' said Craig with gusto. 'Pete, get the whiskey out, can you? You girls can drink your own stuff but tonight calls for the best of the Irish whiskey I have. It's in the top cupboard.'

'I'll get five crystal glasses from the kitchen.' This was Thelma's cue to extract herself from the tension. Bonnie remained sitting at the table. She needed to use the bathroom but thought it looked like an escape if she left just now. She would have to wait and, at this time, she didn't quite trust her legs would move properly if she moved from her chair.

They each slowly drank their liquor, hoping for the calmness that alcohol brings to kick in quickly. Ultimately, Pete and Hazel said their goodbyes knowing a point had been reached tonight that may signal a different beginning. The old way of life as colonial expats was ending and while other members of the extended family would probably embrace a limited lifestyle under an African regime, extended family members like Aunty Val and her family would have no choice. But it was like a thundercloud approaching for Craig, Pete and their families. Bonnie felt terrified at what could lay ahead.

Chapter Ten

Goodbye Africa

2000

The next morning, the Land Rover taking Bonnie and Thelma to the farm travelled slowly through the traffic, like it knew its occupants were reluctant to reach their destination. The Jacaranda trees were thinking seriously about losing their leaves now that the flowers had faded and dropped. Bonnie murmured almost to herself, 'I'm not going to say anything about the Medical Supply Return sheet today. I'm just going to leave those columns blank. Perhaps no one will notice the drugs are missing. Hmmm, not likely. I'm just going to go about my own business as if nothing is at stake. The courier will come for the paperwork and the returns. He can then take it to the hospital for auditing or checking, or whatever they do.'

'Excellent, Bonnie. Just take a deep breath. Let's hope for a good day.'

They saw the farm and the idealist lifestyle quite differently that morning. The children's singing seemed beautiful and their written work quite incredible. Their lovely crisp uniforms were pristine and worn proudly. They were able to write in Swahili and in English. Perhaps they had an eye for the future, whatever that may be, for Africa. The two Caucasian women were wistful, knowing that if white people were evicted from the farm, then hostile bandits would take over and these loyal farm workers and their families would be dispossessed. Nothing seemed right. All they knew was the political parties wanted white people out of Africa by fair means or foul. Without Craig and his way of running the farm, these workers were at the whim of people like Gaz, who in turn were beholden by pieces of gold or the highest bidder in a world of greed and violence that served to meet the ends of a selfish few.

Thelma knew Craig would be ensuring land titles were posted to his Swiss bank, where he had a security lockbox. He was hopeful this would count in the day of reckoning when he was either dead or alive. He knew the time was approaching when they would have to flee like moths in the night, attracted to light of some form elsewhere. All the uncertainty unsettled him. This wasn't good for his heart which he could feel racing in his chest. Perhaps he'd just have a heart attack and drop dead, he thought, but then again, he couldn't desert Thelma and Bonnie. God only knew what would happen to them if he wasn't here.

He refused to think like this and tried hard to keep his mind on his office work. He looked at his Swiss gold watch, a gift to him from his late father, and wished four o'clock afternoon tea would hurry up. Soon after, the girls – or at least he liked to think of them as girls – would arrive home from the farm – their work. He cast his mind back to the first time he met Bonnie, a girl in those little white shorts from the church. He guessed she must have been close to forty, which seemed quite young then. This was what he wanted to think about!

He looked out the window, hoping they would come home early but was disappointed to see no one coming up the driveway. Oh well, he would just have to wait until Cathy called him for tea.

Two days passed, and nothing unusual happened. Then, on the Wednesday night, all hell broke loose!

They were having dinner and quietly watching the rugby on television when they heard the noise of glass breaking, followed by loud voices shouting to each other.

'Those voices are far too close. Someone has succeeded in moving past the house guards,' Craig murmured to himself. He laid his fork on his plate and moved to the phone where he dialled

Pete's number. Bonnie and Thelma sat still and looked at each other. 'I know our plan was to ring three times but, Pete, I think they're moving in. Can you book two seats on a plane to anywhere for Thelma and Bonnie? If you both come in the morning, then Hazel can take the girls to the airport and I'll be somewhere around. I'll be waiting, probably down near the pool, as I'll try to get out quick and get behind them if I can. Lucky it's a new moon tonight. It's dark out there and they won't be able to see a thing. Best to vacate the house here. Thelma and Bonnie will be waiting at the back gate for Hazel, whatever time she arrives. Must fly. Wish me luck.'

Then Craig hung up and turned around. 'You two go to the guest suite just like we planned. We've gone over it in our heads dozens of times and now it must play out. We knew it would happen like this.'

The banging and shouting noise increased. Then more glass broke. Cathy took refuge in the large kitchen pantry while Bonnie and Thelma moved to the guest suite off the back verandah as quickly as they could. They bolted the door to ensure no one could enter the suite and breathed a sigh of relief because they didn't encounter anyone as they scampered along the verandah. It was only a short distance to the guest suite, which had served as Bonnie's accommodation.

Sounds of big men shouting grew louder as they yelled to each other in Swahili. Soon they could be heard around the back of the house, so Thelma and Bonnie had only just made it to their place of safety in time. The family guessed the hostile natives would ransack the big house, looting as they went. An idling car could be heard near the front of the house and doors opened and slammed shut.

Then gunshots sounded! But no human noises accompanied it so the women assumed that locks were being violated so treasures could be gathered. Craig had tried to secure as much as possible in the cellar of the house, but sufficient items needed to be left to satisfy the robbers. These bandits realised white men's homes housed valuable objects, and the women had even more lucrative prizes, such as jewellery, which could be sold for money. At times like this no one was going to stand in the way of violent, vicious robbers.

Thelma and Bonnie moved into the bathroom of the guest room. It was a tiny space but Bonnie sat on the shower floor and Thelma sat on the toilet. Craig had given strict instructions for the taps not to be turned on under any circumstances, as the running water noise would easily identify their whereabouts.

He had wisely left liquor in easy access as he guessed the bandits would help themselves to expensive booze very early in the robbery. He hoped they drank heartily to become totally drunk and useless. Soon loud music from the record player could be heard as drunkenness raged. Bandits shouted, sang and thumped around, all the time loading up the car with white man's goods. They cussed and abused each other as the hours went on. Towards midnight, the car was heard leaving, but several of the thugs remained. Soon Thelma and Bonnie thought they could smell petrol and kerosene. Craig had anticipated an attempt would be made to burn the house down, and although he was tempted to remove fire accelerants, he left them there as part of his plan for the family to escape with their lives.

This was the women's cue to unlock and climb through the heavily barred window, hidden from outside view by dense shrubbery, and escape into the garden. They pushed their way through the greenery, trampling whatever was in the way, sniffing to identify the smell of something burning.

The move towards the fence and away from the house began quickly for the women. They each had a small 'escape' suitcase containing all the goods they could easily carry. The bath in the guest suite was the hiding place for the cases and served as part of the escape plan. Passports and some clothes had been packed away ever since the medical supplies had been tampered with on the farm. They knew they were in serious trouble and, at some stage, this danger would materialise, just as it had happened. Although terrified, the women were in control as they realised the attack was unfolding exactly as Craig had anticipated. They were unsure of his whereabouts, but he had told them often enough that they were to worry about themselves only, as he could take care of himself. He could act as a decoy, only if necessary, and their behaviour would determine how much of a decoy would be necessary. The less dependent they were on him, then the safer he would be. They had practised their route in the darkness, knowing it would be difficult. Although they each had a torch, they did not wish to use it and alert their attackers to their position and that they were attempting to escape – it would not end well.

They crept about eighty metres in the darkness to the fence. In the rear corner of the compound, again hidden by shrubs, was a double locked personal gate in the high cement brick fence. This gave them access to the street, and they had the keys. Keeping the torch covered by their bodies and clothing, they flicked on the torch long enough to insert the keys. Then they opened the gate slowly to avoid noise, and slipped out into the street.

There, they huddled together, a blanket thrown over themselves so they looked just like any other homeless person on the street. Now they had to wait for Hazel.

Thelma allowed her eyes to become accustomed to the dark while Bonnie wriggled around trying to get comfortable on the hard pavement. The smell of rotting vegetables and discarded human rubbish filled the air. Periodically, the smell of human excrement wafted past and increased their discomfort. They had expected the street to be quiet, but the sound of human habitation consisted of distant sirens and cars. Distressed voices surrounded them, and their rug provided limited comfort. They were dressed in warm track suits and expensive walking shoes, knowing these clothes would suffice for many days. Now was not the time for thinking about first-world conditions. They were in survival mode, and Bonnie suddenly realised that many of the locals lived this way.

She shut her eyes, allowing the moisture to provide some comfort for her. Her head throbbed, and in the quietness under the blanket, she riffled through her suitcase and found Panadol. Breaking open the aluminium foil, she found her water bottle and swallowed down two tablets, knowing she couldn't afford a headache so early in their escape. She had to take care of herself as the road ahead was going to be difficult.

Slowly the hours crawled by. Several cars had driven quickly on the road, passing them a metre or so away. Both women realised that Hazel would slow down so they strained their ears for the familiar sound of an engine decelerating. They could peep out from under the rug, but it was pointless and only served to heighten their discomfort. After what seemed an eternity, they heard the purr of a diesel engine in the distance. It slowly approached the main gate. Visibility was nil so Thelma and Bonnie relied on their ears.

'I think it's Hazel's car. She's slowing down at the front gate but she won't stop. Pete will be behind her and he'll deal with the gate and whatever that may entail,' Thelma whispered. 'Remember not to talk to anyone at all. If it all turns pear-shaped, I will do the talking. You are mute.'

Bonnie felt her heart beat faster, heard it pounding in her ears, and silently told it to stop so she could listen for the car's approach. The purring became louder as the car continued to slowly approach as it came into the back street.

Thelma peeked out of the blanket. 'Yep, it's Hazel. Grab your bag, Bonnie. I'll gather the rug, but you get in first. Hazel will open the back door.'

True to form, Bonnie heard the smooth click of a door opening and made her move. Stiffly uncoiling herself, she hurriedly scrambled into the car and slid across to the other side to make way for Thelma.

'Oh my God, I feel so safe now I'm in your car, Hazel,' Bonnie exclaimed, shivering with fear and cold.

'Well, I wish I could reassure you but we've all got a long way to go before you two are safe. Never mind, so far all is well. There is a thermos and sandwiches on the seat somewhere so help yourself. Don't think about Craig or Pete. This is their land and they understand the locals. They're in trouble all right but they will be okay. Somehow, they'll sort things out. They speak the language and will convince the authorities that an accounting error is not a crime. It's so much better for them if we are out of the way, so hang on tight. Here are your airline tickets. You're on the early flight to Johannesburg and then to Perth. Once you're there, you can relax and book a flight to Adelaide.'

Hazel kept looking straight ahead, using the car headlights to discern any landmarks in the fog. She didn't want to become involved in any traffic delays. 'It's five o'clock now and your flight leaves at seven, with a two-hour stopover in Johannesburg. I suggest you don't use your credit card. Just sit and wait for two hours.'

Bonnie was aware of the tension in Hazel's voice. She would be arrested as an accomplice if they were stopped by the authorities; identity checks were a regular occurrence. However, the car purred on like a lion sneaking up on its prey. There was a lot at stake, just like a lion's kill. At this stage, they were not aware of how 'official' the missing narcotics had become, nor who was involved in the house break in. The country was politically unstable so it could have simply been local bandits with no connection to authorities, or it could have been created by authorities with links to unknown people in unknown countries.

Whatever level had been involved, there was no doubt that crime could be bestowed on Bonnie and Thelma. They were both frightened, and with good reason: the Freedom Fighters for Africa would readily use any white man or his connections as an excuse or as a scapegoat to eradicate individuals who would never be seen again. First world law wasn't recognised in many countries of the world. And this had become not quite the adventure Bonnie had wanted. Her throat tightened as she thought about Ken and the comfort he could provide, but it had been many years since she'd seen him. Then she aptly dismissed these thoughts and tried to live in the moment.

Eating sandwiches and drinking tea became the focus for the two women as Hazel drove. Rubbish littered the verges of the pot-holed road and, occasionally, individual Africans were seen just standing on dusty tracks awaiting the new day. Their lack of purpose and poverty was tragic and hopeless.

Bonnie thought of all the Africans who worked on Craig's farm; they'd had a future with the use of current farming practices and a paternalistic, benevolent white man's management, but if the whole farm was overtaken by the freedom fighters, then all those beautiful people to whom Bonnie had become attached, would be out of work, if not murdered first. It was painful to think about their future and Bonnie was relieved when she saw the airport in the distance. The dark grey buildings stood like soldiers awaiting orders from new bosses, the natives of Africa, who were ready to engulf anyone who didn't comply with the new military regime.

Once inside the building, Bonnie and Thelma took stock of the area. The airport appeared normal. Tired women stood behind desks and young men occupied space as visitors moved about attending to their business or lined up for their flights. The air was cool as they moved to the appropriate line for boarding, both trying to look nonchalant. Once seated comfortably in the plane, awaiting a welcome refreshment, Thelma dropped a bombshell.

'Bonnie, when we get to Perth, I'm going to take a flight to Heathrow and lay low in England for a while. Craig and I both have family there, and I think if we both arrive in Adelaide together, the authorities could be on the lookout for the two of us arriving together. It's not what we want, but I think it will be better that way.'

She was right, of course. Perth was busy enough for anyone to retain anonymity if that's what they wanted, but an arrival in

Adelaide a few hours later could be fraught with unknowns. A momentary wave of melancholy swept over them, but they knew what needed to be done. Tiredly, they lay their heads back and tried to get some much-needed sleep while the plane whirred towards their destination.

Chapter Eleven

The Kindness of Ken

2000

While refilling the kettle for his second cup of tea, Ken heard a loud and continuous banging at his recently-painted front door. *A bit early in the day for visitors*, he thought, and he wasn't expecting anyone. A slight annoyance rose as he'd been checking his shares on the computer and feeling quite pleased that the stock market seemed to be rising. He'd retired a few months ago and was loving the extra hours retirement gave him. *Should have done this years ago*, he thought as he made his way to the front door, but he, like others, used his health as a retirement guide. Arthritis in his hands had diminished his confidence as a surgeon, and his retirement had been an easy and quick decision, one he didn't regret.

He pulled open the front door and exclaimed with total shock, 'Bonnie!'

She immediately fell into his arms, sobbing. 'Has anyone followed me?' she spluttered between sobs. Ken wasn't sure what shocked him most – the state of the dishevelled Bonnie or the question she asked. He'd never seen Bonnie in this state.

'What do you mean? Of course, no one followed you. You're home, Bonnie. You can relax,' he assured her as he led her inside.

Bonnie slumped into the chair Ken had guided her to, feeling somewhat awed that he'd used his 'doctor' tone of voice on her. He didn't say anything for a moment; he didn't have to.

Years had passed since she'd left, and he'd had a strong feeling her adventures would end like this. *What had she been thinking?* But he didn't say anything; he didn't want to upset her in this state. She was now huddled over herself on the kitchen chair. Very pragmatically, he realised he'd refilled the kettle for a reason and took a cup to the table, where he left it within Bonnie's easy reach. Her sobbing continued while Ken reached for the toaster. 'I've made some toast. I assume you still like Vegemite so here we are. It's nice and warm, just how you like it.'

Ken had seen many situations in his life that had shocked him: this was merely another one of those cases. However, this situation upset him because the woman sobbing in total despair was the one he'd at one stage wanted to marry. Not for a moment did he doubt her trauma, but he knew better than to plague her with questions. She needed time to adjust to her newfound safety, so he told her he was going to the shop for some milk, allowing her the space she needed to regain some level of peace. Composure would come later. He shut the front door just loud enough for her to hear he was gone.

Outside, Ken sat in his Toyota Prado, processing what had just happened. He noticed Bonnie's travelling bag was still on the front step so he quietly left the car, opened the front door and placed the bag where Bonnie could see it. He imagined she would be looking for her toiletries so she could resurrect normality for herself when she stopped crying. Despite her trauma and exhaustion, he guessed she'd still be awake on his return. She'd always found the changing hours of shift work challenging and had trouble adjusting to the variation of sleep patterns needed to survive in the nursing game. Theatre shifts had therefore suited her, and Ken remembered how disappointed he'd been when she'd gone gallivanting around the world to work in some third world country instead of marrying him. For a split second, 'I told you so' came into his head but he pushed it out the instant it became a neuron in a brain cell. She needed kindness now, and that was what she was going to get.

He wasn't worried about what had happened and no doubt would listen attentively, saying all the right things at a later time.

She was back in his house and for Ken, that's where he wanted her to stay. While he knew some men wooed their womenfolk with champagne and flowers, there was plenty of time for those conventions later. For the next few days at least, he would need to be at home just pottering around in his garden and being attentive. Later, he could recommend some trauma counselling for her and then, if she really wanted to, she could get her old job back. However, he was mindful of Bonnie's independence; he needed to let her recover in her own time and space.

This time, her space was going to be in his house, if she allowed it, and he quietly acknowledged that he'd let her get away once – he wasn't going to let her escape again! He loved her. Much time had passed without his former wife and daughters, and those memories had faded, so he was better placed to be an independent soul now. He had missed Bonnie in the years she'd been away and realised how lonely he'd become. He put his foot on the accelerator, his heart skipping a beat as he realised this might be his new opportunity for a life with Bonnie. A smile spread across his face as he made a mental check not to get too far ahead of himself. But life had suddenly taken a turn for the better, despite poor Bonnie sobbing in his house.

Why is everyone dawdling this morning? Ken wondered, realising in the next moment that he was in an almighty hurry to get back to Bonnie. *All these shoppers could buy their bread later!* Time seemed to stand still as he shifted from one foot to another in the checkout aisle as an elderly lady ahead of him slowly took the loyalty card from her purse. *Hurry up!* The dawdlers almost made him leave the shop. Then again he pulled himself up. *You need to monitor your own thoughts. Bonnie is probably still drinking her tea … you need to allow her time to recover.*

'Next please,' called the shop assistant, jerking Ken back to the present. The slow lady had left and now he was daydreaming in the shop aisle. He regularly had to adjust to his new identity as a retiree, and now, with Bonnie at home, he felt excited about life again.

Events slowly unfolded as the afternoon wore on. As Ken had promised himself, he listened attentively and focused on saying the right words as the pauses in Bonny's account materialised. She had showered by the time he arrived home and she was looking less exhausted. Her terrified look had loosened its grip as she allowed herself to relax. Ken congratulated himself on having the foresight to take her bags into the house before he'd left.

'When do you need to go to work?' Bonnie asked.

Ken grinned widely. 'Work is something I used to do in another lifetime. I have many other interests now.' But Bonnie and her comfort was the only thing on his mind. He wasn't surprised to hear about faulty accounting and drugs disappearing from so-called locked cabinets. And as for the death of a patient, she should never have been put in that situation! She was way in over her head in a third world country, where incompetence and mistrust of individuals was a great security issue. Ken knew she'd been taken advantage of, and she'd been naive enough to accept a position that had placed her at the mercy of corrupt, opportunistic manipulators, forced to treat patients with needs way above her training. Even in a first world country patients died daily of prescription drugs. All drugs could cause death if used incorrectly. It was a massive problem and doctors were aware of overprescribing. Bonnie was lucky to have made it out of the country alive. And he was glad her friend Thelma had the sense to change her mind and take a different route and fly to London. Any connection with a medical person and 'lost' drugs was a huge risk in any country. He didn't want to alarm Bonnie, but he could see she was terrified of being caught. But he didn't know who was going to 'catch' her.

'Bonnie, you're in Australia. You are out of their country and they're not going to chase you overseas. Apart from the accidental death, it's all very low-level stuff, certainly not enough to involve Interpol and international drug rings. It's a racial issue – the hostility is aimed at the white folk in their own country, and you just happened to be in the wrong place at the wrong time.' He took a deep breath, and watched her face for acceptance of what he was telling her. 'I do suggest you let the Thelma friendship go for a bit though, and after a few months, you can reconnect. In fact, you probably need to wait until you hear from her as she's now probably in London.' This, he hoped, would give the whole situation closure. 'Let's go down to the yacht club. You probably won't believe it, but I have part ownership in a yacht and am a member there. We can have a sunset drink then dinner. Or we can wait until tomorrow if you would like and just have a pizza or something simple for dinner tonight so you can rest. What's your preference?'

Bonnie opted for a simple dinner and an early night, which didn't surprise him. She looked totally wrecked, which was expected after her ordeal.

'Okay, Bonnie. You sit down and I'll prepare a snack.'

Bonnie opted to take a nap until dinner time. Two hours later, the door to the spare room was still closed so Ken ate his pizza and settled in for a night of watching television before he went to bed.

At some point during the night, he heard water running and then heard the kettle making its comforting purring noise as a cup of tea was being made. He smiled, knowing that Bonnie was feeling comfortable enough to move around his house in the pitch black, though, as he opened his eyes to peep, he could see a tiny strip of light coming from under her door. He understood sleep disturbances from international travel, and poor Bonnie had trauma added to that; he imagined her night would be quite disturbed. He was pleased she had sold her house before leaving Australia, so now he was on a mission to convince her to stay with him. Smiling inwardly, he rolled over and went back to sleep.

He let the bacon sizzle for some time, knowing a disturbed night would result in a delay in waking up, and he did not expect Bonnie to come from her room for some time. He read the daily paper and then went outside to water the garden. It was autumn so the soil was still dry despite the reticulation and soil mulching. Soon, a beautiful apparition appeared in the back doorway, taking Ken's breath away. He knew she wouldn't appreciate being overwhelmed with compliments, so he said nothing. Bonnie commented on his attractive garden and moved towards the birdbath near the fence. She looked at peace, he noted as he went inside to serve breakfast, the flyscreen door shutting quietly behind him. Never had the bacon tasted so good for Ken, and Bonnie secretly thought the same thing.

'Today we're going to buy some new linen for your bedroom, Bonnie. There's a huge sale on in town so I thought we could check it out. We need to buy some new sheets and some decent warm rugs, ready for the winter.'

'I like that idea,' Bonnie replied and Ken breathed a sigh of relief. He hoped she wouldn't back off and tell him she was moving out soon. *Baby steps. Take baby steps.* Of course, if she wanted to, she could always sneak across the hallway and crawl into his bed for a cuddle, but it was far too early for a suggestion like that, so he assumed his poker face. Tomorrow, he might suggest some trauma counselling but for today he was quite content to let things unfold, and hoped it could finish with sunset drinks at the yacht club while watching the sun settle over the boats in the bay.

The sound of glasses clinking together that night was a good omen, for them both in their own individual ways. Bonnie continued with details of Zimbabwe and Ken talked about hospital gossip. He still undertook some contract work, supervising interns at two hospitals. He liked casual work: it assured an income and allowed him to keep in touch with the medical world. He did not miss his surgical tasks though, much to his surprise. Only once, away from the job, had he realised the level of stress involved. His contact with young interns made him realise he needed to broaden his knowledge of other aspects of life too. Yes, he'd travelled as a tourist but this, too, had been limited. He told Bonnie that since his association with the yacht club, his knowledge of boats and all things mechanical had increased. He had time to research his superannuation and dabble in some shares that a yachtie friend had recommended. This was a different world from hospitals and all things medical, and he now accepted the arthritis in his hands was rather fortuitous. Someone above was looking after him and an angel had catapulted back into his life just at the right time.

'Bonnie, just let me know when you would like me to make a phone call for your job, or we could arrange lunch for a conversation that may lead somewhere. Just think about what you want to do.

'Or you could do nothing, like me, and enjoy this sight in front of us. Or we could sail off into the sunset in one of those big charter boats. I rather like that idea, but I realise you've had enough adventure for a while. And guess what? I'm not going anywhere without you. I figure you could make a mean cup of coffee if we bought one of those fancy coffee machines. I don't mean tomorrow or anytime soon. Now that you are back, I intend to spoil you for Christmas.'

'Do I really have to wait that long? It's not even winter yet,' Bonnie encouraged him with a smile.

The wine, the setting and the beautiful woman sitting next to Ken made him yearn for more. Slowly, he built the courage to emotionally connect with Bonnie as the conversation flowed easily. As he perused the dinner menu, he fondly remembered their good times in the past. He dared not think of their intimate moments for fear of getting ahead of himself, but currently, he was loving their comfortable companionship. He saw lamb on the menu and figured Bonnie would order salmon as he luxuriated in their familiarity as a couple. He loved the idea of unobtrusively using his bar tab and fondly remembered their earlier dates when Bonnie had insisted on splitting the bill. He smiled inwardly as he thought her tactic was probably to ensure he paid his way.

'What are you thinking about?' Bonnie asked when she thought she'd been talking too much. He dismissed this question by telling her she didn't want to know.

On leaving the yacht club, he took her arm. 'Let's go for a walk on the sand,' so he took her hand and they walked along the beach, embracing the freedom of the moment. A slight breeze fluttered past their faces and the pleasant light smell of saltwater wafted to their nostrils.

'I can't wait to sleep in my new sheets,' Bonnie said when the mood moved in a romantic direction. Ken laughed, feeling amused at being able to predict Bonnie and her movements.

'Righto. Race you back to the car and let's go home.'

Bonnie's jaw dropped open and she smiled at his suggestion to run. Despite her exhaustion, she quickly moved towards the car park and ran too. This dispelled her preconceived ideas of Ken being a bit of an old fuddy-duddy. *Fancy him wanting to run just like a kid!* She had enjoyed the day and her thoughts about Ken were rapidly changing. He was actually quite a catch and perhaps one day she might move across the hallway into his bed, despite her nice new sheets. Time would tell.

Chapter Twelve

The Glenelg Homestead

2005

'Come on, Ernie. The kids are coming for morning tea,' Pat called as Ernie strolled past the kitchen window. He spent a lot of time in the garden these days, inspecting his plants and poking around with a trowel. 'You'd better have a shower and get into some decent clothes.'

'I thought Ian would be too busy with all those cows calving. I didn't think he'd have the time to be coming to the city.'

'No, not Ian. It's Bonnie and Ken,' Pat replied.

'Oh, righto. And Bonnie's bringing Ken? That's awesome. I like the trustworthy Ken. He's good for Bonnie and he's got a great old Irish name. I reckon with a name like Ken, Bon's onto a winner. Hopefully, he can talk her into accepting a ring on her finger. But I won't mention anything. I know she can be stubborn. We don't want her running away from him.'

Ernie chuckled to himself as he knew he was rambling. He admired his daughter's strength; she reminded him of himself. But there did come a time when she needed a soul mate, and it was Ernie's belief Ken was the person who fitted the role. He was a solid bloke who liked football and cricket. Oh yes. And he liked a beer and a good steak too. He lost Ernie, though, when he started talking about medical stuff, but then Ernie realised Ken had the good sense to keep conversations to subjects within the listener's interests. Of course, he was an intellectual bloke, and he must be bright to be a doctor and a surgeon. Ernie made a mental note to ask him today what surgery was his specialty.

Soon there was a banging on the front door. 'What was that?' Frowning, Ernie looked out from the kitchen. 'Oh, it's just Sheila on her way to work. I wish she wouldn't slam the door with such veracity.'

'No goodbye or anything. Just grabs her lunch and off she goes. She's such a rude bugger.' Ernie mumbled his last comment to himself as he knew berating Sheila about her churlish behaviour upset Pat. He made another mental note for today: when Bonnie and Ken visited, he wasn't going to mention anything about Sheila. It would just spoil the conversation. He hoped Sheila would find her own accommodation soon then he would have his house back for himself and Pat. He liked it with just the two of them there. He acknowledged he was becoming a grumpy old man who didn't want anyone in his house, particularly people like this newfound granddaughter.

*****

Sheila reversed her ute out and onto the road, her foot flat to the floor on the accelerator to make as much noise as possible. She headed off to spend her day as an accountant and office worker. Well, this is what she'd told her grandparents, and this was all they needed to know.

Sheila drove through the working-class suburb of Elizabeth, and thought about what she was going to do that morning. This was the day of the week she worked in Accounts to ensure the contractors were paid. She wrote out the cheques, posted them and ensured the incomings and the outgoings balanced or at least were accounted for. She also paid a decent sum into petty cash to ensure that some flowers were ordered for special occasions, or some other trivia, for the HR department. She made sure the cash amount was hefty and kept the weekly change. Sheila felt infuriated that the rich people around town had the means and fortitude to control the lives of the little worker, like herself. *Well*, she thought, *one day I'm not going to be a mere worker.*

At night, she spent time plotting ways to become one of the big names around town. As soon as those thoughts implanted – which was most nights – she thought of her father on the farm, which was worth big bucks. She'd heard the new stepson had assumed his place on the farm and now he, too, was a big fellow around town, splashing all his dough. She'd seen him with his girlfriend, looking as smooth as anything. She kept an eye on all possible bases as one day she would get her revenge … revenge on her father and the family. She would pay him back for not providing her with a place in the family, a position that was rightfully hers! In recent times, Sheila had thought about revenge a lot.

She looked at her lunch in its crumpled brown paper bag on the seat beside her. Each day she binned it. She didn't tell her grandmother this, of course. She told her she liked her lunch and knew it made the old lady content, even happy. Gran was such a soft touch and just so easy to work to her advantage. She was pleased she'd kept her grandparents' address when she'd stalked so many years ago.

Recently, she'd turned up on their doorstep just to see what they were like. After her visit, she'd felt ecstatic: she'd liked the house and particularly liked the idea of staying there; she'd just see how things played out. They were both old, which was a good thing. *This house is going to be my current address.*

This thought came very quickly to her mind. She renewed her driver's license using the oldies address and put her name on the electoral roll using Glenelg as her first place of residence. *This is my entitlement. My new home,* she decided. She moved into the spare room very unobtrusively, a covert operation that Ernie and Pat hardly knew about. By the time they did, Sheila was well and truly settled into the Glenelg Homestead. She now just had to wait a few years to get rid of the occupants.

The more she thought about this, the more excited she became. It was easy enough to make tea for vulnerable old people, who soon became emotionally indebted and co-dependent.

After work, Sheila drove to Luke's place on the outskirts of the city, past Salisbury, and was reminded again how rich people live close to the city while poor people live on the outskirts. Luke was outside the dilapidated shed, working on a piece of machinery. He was easy enough to get along with and when they'd been on the mine site, she had done deals with him for drugs, carefully though as one of the bosses closely watched workers' behaviours.

After many years of dealing methamphetamines with thugs at the nightclubs and workplaces, under the pretence of being a chemical auditor, Sheila had learnt a few tricks, particularly about evidence. And she was always open to learning new methods. Cops had to have firm evidence that would stack up in court, and Sheila had learnt how to avoid that happening. She was also currently preparing to sell her black ute, which, just as Metho Mike had told her years ago, attracted the attention of the cops. She now had her eye on a little old white car which she could flit around in quite unobtrusively, the kind of car driven by old ladies. Every second car on the road seemed to be a small white car, some old, some new. She remembered how much she'd enjoyed her stalking games – any games really where she could extract a dollar or two – it was still hard work spending time with old gits who were stingy with their dough. This deal with Luke was only transitory; she needed to be careful as, each time they had a drink together, she wasn't really sure which side of the law he was on. One thing was for sure: she didn't want to end up in the clink, so she trusted no one. Time would tell, but for now, she climbed out of the ute to have a conversation.

Surprisingly, Luke wanted to buy her ute, as well as sell her some Meth, so this turned out to be an excellent day for Sheila.

*****

Back at the Glenelg Homestead, Ernie helped Pat with the morning tea; his job was to put out the cups and saucers on the benchtop to receive tea as it was poured.

'Let's not talk business today, Ernie. I know it's tempting but let's just enjoy the moment and allow Bonnie to share some more of her adventure stories. I love listening to what she has to say,' Pat said.

This pleased Ernie as business stuff was becoming a nuisance these days, and he was glad he and Ian had made succession plans years ago. Now the dairy was in Ian's name, and he dealt with all the tax business; Ian had a real head for business. Ernie's idea of business nowadays was to check his bank statements for share dividend payments and to give Pat some cash for her passbook savings account.

'This scone needs more jam, Pat. They look beautiful and I'm pretty hungry. Let's hope they hurry up so we can start on them soon.'

Almost instantly the doorbell rang and Bonnie burst into the room. 'Does anyone live in this gorgeous house?' Bonnie called out in her normal boisterous way.

Ernie and Pat grinned widely, loving the way she came into their home after all this time. 'You don't need to ring the doorbell. Just come straight in. This is your home, remember. Oh, well it will be one day. But hey, let's hear all about your adventures. Let me look at you. My, you look well.'

Ernie thought Bonnie looked tired, but he wasn't going to disagree with Pat. It was never easy to see one's own children ageing as the clock marched on in its relentless way. He hated thinking about it, but for now, his daughter was here, and so was Ken.

Ernie needed to ask Ken something, but he'd forgotten what it was as he focused on Ken's hug instead of his normal handshake. Ernie was a bit surprised at the intimacy a hug implied, but later Ken told him about his arthritis and subsequent pain in his hands. It all made sense. He was such a sensible chap, Ernie thought, and his trust radar sent him positive vibes. He would share this secret joke with Pat later and felt sure she would refer to it as rubbish, but all his life his trust radar had served him well.

'Ken, I've forgotten how you like your tea.' Ernie remembered his job of pouring while Pat served the jam, cream and scones.

'Black,' replied Ken, who felt the calmness of a loving family penetrate his body. It made him feel like he'd been injected with endorphins. Considerable time had passed since Ken had enjoyed the hospitality of a generation who valued the qualities of a good cup of tea. When he'd been at work, others had made tea for him and he'd become accustomed to drinking it however it came. To actually hear someone ask him how he liked his tea was a treat.

Having lost his own parents long ago, Ken felt himself being swallowed up by warmth, kindness and generosity. They loved their daughter and now he was lucky enough to be loved, by default, as a pseudo-son. If Ken had any say in it, this pseudo-son business would be strengthened soon, but for now, each person in the room wanted an easy conversation that focused on cream, scones and tea.

Soon enough, Ernie remembered he was going to ask Ken about his line of work in the hospital and he held it in his mind until there was a gap in the conversation. When Bonnie's conversation stopped, he asked the question and Ken began his story. Bonnie listened with intrigue as Ken's work, past and present, was explained. She was impressed that he still undertook consultancy work and used his skills in assisting the training of the next generation of doctors. In teaching, while in Zimbabwe, she'd heard teachers refer to sharpening their pencils ready for classroom action, and she imagined surgeons sharpening their knives for theatre action. She reasoned that every profession had inside jokes and jargon that they shared with their peers.

'Gosh, Mum. It's nearly lunchtime!'

'I have some quiche in the fridge. Would you like some? I can always make up a quick salad to go with it.'

Ken made the decision easy. 'Pat, that would be lovely!'

Ernie laughed out loud. He had an easy laugh and a way of putting people at ease. 'Ken, you know the way to a woman's heart.' They both did.

Ernie quickly moved the conversation on as he was astute enough to know he was veering close to forbidden territory. He wasn't going to refer to affairs of the heart. 'Let me show you around the garden, Ken. I want to show you my new rose bushes.' So, the pathway to lunch was reached smoothly, and quiche and salad were enjoyed by all. In the mid-afternoon, Bonnie and Ken made a move for home.

'We've got a few things to get for the house. If we go now, we can beat the traffic,' Bonnie said as she and Ken moved towards the doorway. 'We're planning to go to the farm and see Ian and Sarah within the next few weeks so if you need us to take up anything you can keep it in mind.'

As Ken and Bonnie left and headed north in the Prado, a small old white car rounded the corner. It slowly trundled up the road before turning into the grassy patch near the fence of the Glenelg home. The driver was not presumptuous enough to claim a right of passage and park in the driveway. She had time on her side as she wondered about the identity of the occupants in the departing car. *It looks like the daughter's back*, she figured, so she would need to be extremely careful from now on.

She slowly turned the front door key she'd recently been given by her grandmother. She hoped she didn't see anyone and was relieved to hear the oldies sitting out the back jabbering away as she crept down the passage. Quietly, she shut her bedroom door to seal herself away for the night, hoping she wouldn't be called for dinner. She thought about telling Gran she was going out but couldn't be bothered, just as she didn't want to tell them both about her day and have to interact with them. They were probably starved for conversation but she wasn't going to exert herself by being social. She simply couldn't be bothered doing anything, so she lay on the bed and promptly went to sleep.

Ernie and Pat had another cup of tea after Bonnie's and Ken's departure and revelled in their happiness.

'Who would believe that our middle-aged daughter would be living happily with a man who was retired … or semi-retired? Seems like he still does a bit of work at the hospital.'

'Well, she always said she was going to marry a doctor, and now it looks like her dream has come true. He seems a very nice man and I think it's good to know now, as we approach old age, he can help us when we reach our decrepit state.'

'Pat, I think with us in our seventies and eighties, we have reached the decrepit stage.'

Both were terrified of losing their intellectual capacity, as they'd seen many of their friends fall victim to, and each denied that limited intellect capacity would make its mark on them. 'I've still got my marbles,' Pat would frequently say.

Ernie let his mind wander to his daughter's future. His son was settled with his family, who adored him, and of this he was grateful. Now his daughter looked set to overcome that adventure nonsense of living and working in Africa. She'd had a few years now to recover from it all. At long last, she'd outgrown the romantic notion of helping others. Sometimes Bonnie was just too trusting and he wondered if he should instruct her on her trust radar. He made a mental note to look for the opportunity now she was back in town and settled. He knew he would see her every few days or so, and for now, he felt at peace with his children.

He was going to articulate his thoughts to Pat when she returned from the sink, and tried to do so, but he became frustrated because she was only interested in putting away the uneaten scones. Regularly now, she was too intent on the banal. She seemed to live from one meal preparation to the next with nothing in between. It was as if complex thoughts no longer existed in Pat's reality. He felt annoyed that it was becoming increasingly difficult to connect with her on any cerebral level, and told himself not to bother too much with this and tried hard to push it far away in his thinking. For now, he reminded himself, he was happy his daughter was contented and that she and Ken were planning a visit to Trevilly.

Chapter Thirteen

Back to Trevilly

2005

'Gosh, your parents were pleased to see you, Bonnie. I love that quality about them; they make me feel so welcome,' Ken said as he loaded his Prado with their suitcases, ready for the road trip to Trevilly via Carson.

'Well, if they knew the other half of my adventures, they'd be *really* pleased to see me.' A broad smile spread across Bonnie's face as she opened the car door.

'You did well to keep the conversation light and breezy. I guess it's fair to say you could share your experiences with Ian and Sarah. We'll have plenty of time too, so it makes a difference. It's not the kind of thing which you can refer to and then skip over.'

Bonnie noticed Ken loading the car with precision. *Yes, he is a keeper,* she remembered her brother saying many years ago. She reflected on the counselling Ken had organised for her, and the psychologist's diagnosis of Post Traumatic Stress Disorder. PTSD. She had thought this condition only applied to soldiers at war but her psychologist had explained how any life and death situation can leave victims with trauma symptoms, especially individuals who had feared for their lives. Yes, she hadn't been sure she would survive when escaping from the house and fleeing Zimbabwe. She had gradually accepted that the fight or flight response had served her well but it had left her traumatised. Gradually, she had learnt to relax and stop looking over her shoulder. She also thought less often about Thelma and Craig these days even though she followed the News regarding the political unrest in Zimbabwe and the abolition, eradication or eviction of the white farmers from their lands. They were refugees and she was thankful Thelma had family in Britain. Their money, or lack of it, was another story but at least her friend was in a democratic country where law and justice were valued.

'Have you locked the front door?' Ken inquired.

Soon they were on their road trip to Carson, the kilometres steadily decreasing with the time. They were keen to not rush, allowing quality time to enjoy each other's company in the countryside. Ken noted Bonnie hadn't discussed work yet and was pleased their partnership was progressing really well. He cooked dinner and took her out. He listened attentively and gave her the space he believed she needed after her traumatic escape from, what could have been, an international drug ring. He realised he was probably being overly dramatic, but no one ever knew what to think when considering rogue governments and how they operated. He noticed she'd become more relaxed and could see the youthful vibrancy appearing in her face. She was becoming the Bonnie of old, the girl he knew when he was young, or at least youngish. Sometimes the years just blurred together. He nearly bought her flowers one day but resisted the urge to push this friendship beyond where Bonnie felt comfortable. Clearly, he was hopeful for some bedroom action but so far Bonnie had remained in her own room all night so his quest continued. He was a betting man and figured Bonnie would have made their separate room arrangements with her brother and Sarah very clear when she'd spoken on the phone. He would also put money on hearing a patter of female feet in the middle of the night one day and bingo, she would come to his bed!

He liked daydreaming about how this move in the relationship was going to play out and, as time crept on, he became more confident they would end up as a couple. In time, they would be just like any other folk in a long-term relationship. Well, that was his plan!

Bonnie's question jerked Ken out of his daydream. 'Shall we stop for morning tea soon?' *A thermos!* Really, this was old age and therefore a comfortable relationship in the making, so he resisted the urge to tease Bonnie about this symbol of 'oldies road trips'. She had even made tomato sandwiches so he played a role and endorsed the whole notion with mock enthusiasm and silliness.

Bonnie loved Ken when he pretended to enjoy this country tradition of having a thermos and all its attachments. She knew he was trying, albeit making fun, of her home-spun personality and played along. *Ken knows how to play his cards right*, Bonnie thought. Even the acknowledgement of this country lifestyle made her realise she was actually falling in love with this goofy bloke who was such a different man from the surgeon she'd worked alongside so many years ago. Retirement was good for them both.

All too soon, they arrived at the gates of Trevilly and saw Ian walking from the shed as they drove towards the house.

'Still waiting for some rain. We're preparing machinery for seeding the oat crop for our hay. Bit early yet, but as you know, one needs to be ready.'

Ian moved towards Ken, his hand outstretched. Then he moved towards his sister for a big hug. Ian was a true farmer and Bonnie could readily see the resemblance to their father on many different levels. They were easy-going and carefree. Soon he'd be telling her how to live her life, just as Ernie was prone to do, but she embraced the notion regardless.

'Come on in. Sarah's prepared lunch and then you can unpack your bags.'

Friendly dogs complimented the farm scene and readily joined the welcome party for the city dwellers, their tails wagging as if it was an Olympic competition.

Soon the traditional drive around the dairy farm took place. The farm was dry and parched looking, apart from the irrigated paddocks, and not inviting at all but Ken and Bonnie were mindful of autumn being the worst time of the year for a delightful vista. When Ken first visited the farm, he wondered why dead trees weren't attended to, but he soon realised time was money in a farming business. Even old buildings were just left, not cleaned up or buried, or dealt with to somehow make them magically disappear. He assumed farming inhabitants became used to their surroundings and merely focused on the moment and what was important. He regularly marvelled at how individuals adapted to their environment and all the sensory organs gradually became desensitised to allow this adaptation. He dreamily assumed that he would adapt too if he was suddenly thrust into a foreign environment, just as Bonnie had to in Africa.

As if to read Ken's thoughts, Ian said, 'I've become accustomed to the shortage of rain but if we just had twenty mils the landscape would drastically change overnight. Make sure you come here again in July so you can see the before and after effect.'

Ken knew they would be here again in July. For now, he was very content in the comfort provided by Bonnie's family on the Trevilly farm. The feeling was like a warm blanket surrounding them on a cool night and, as long as the blanket was bereft of holes, then all unwanted coldness could not penetrate.

'So how was Mum when you saw her?' Ian asked as they took up chairs for a sunset drink later in the day. Sarah had made a plate of savouries and relished the company of visitors to the house. They made a comfortable couple, Ian and Sarah, and complimented each other, almost completing each other's sentences as people in long-term relationships tended to do.

'Same old Mum. She was good. I hadn't seen her for a while of course but she was still fussing over the food.'

'Did she tell you about her surgery?' Ian asked.

'No, she never mentioned anything like that. So, what was her surgery?'

'Mum told me the doctor wanted to remove a lump from her pancreas but that doesn't sound right to me. Last week when I rang, I asked her if the lump was benign or malignant. She didn't quite know what I meant but she told me a light dose of chemo would be necessary for a while. She totally underplayed the situation.'

'Now that you mention it, Ian, she was a bit vague. I noticed she wasn't really interested in my time in Africa which, when I think about it, was a bit strange. Dad was fine but not so sure about Mum.'

Ken intervened: 'If she's mentioned chemo, she's got cancer. Chemo treatment has become the norm nowadays to lengthen the patient's life, but I'd be checking her out a bit more closely when we get home, Bonnie.'

The house and its surroundings were mostly unchanged from when Ernie and Pat had lived there. It had been stylish in its early days, but, like all houses, it had aged over the last few decades. The brick and tiles had survived many storms and the house lived to be the centre of many tales around the kitchen table. It was a living testament to history and the passage of time. The expanse of garden had been toned down a touch for ease of upkeep as Sarah worked in Carson as a part-time teacher. From what Bonnie had seen in Africa, teachers everywhere worked overtime and Bonnie had developed a new respect for this occupation previously unknown to her. She had only ever known farming and the medical world. For the moment, Bonnie wasn't going to think too much about her mother; she was going to enjoy the serenity and calmness of the evening.

Looking at the stars reminded her of their transitory time on Earth and now with the news of her mother, she deliberately focused on the huge steaks Ian was cooking on the barbeque. Her psychologist had advised her to enjoy the moment and 'mindfulness' was a new term in current thinking for mental health, to appreciate the here and now. Bonnie liked the idea and went into the kitchen to help Sarah with the salads. She was impressed to see how the idea of salad had morphed from a tin of beetroot with iceberg lettuce and half-ripe tomatoes, into a Greek salad and a potato bake.

'I guess you've been busy lately with school starting and kids travelling in the heat,' Bonnie said as she opened the door for her sister-in-law to pass through into the barbeque area.

'Flat out,' replied Sarah. 'In a few years, I will retire and travel the world, just like you, Bonnie. I'm going to leave work behind me and become a full-time tourist. You must tell us all about Africa. I'm dying to hear about your adventures.'

Sarah's eyebrow rose as a glimpse of reluctance momentarily passed over Bonnie's face. But Bonnie had given the subject some thought and had decided to tell them the whole truth, including her unfortunate departure, and the look quickly passed.

'Ok when you all have your steak and salad on your plate, I'll start. Ken's heard all this before so he can keep the drinks up for us.'

Ken suppressed a yawn. He wasn't bored, just tired. It had been quite a long drive and he quietly acknowledged that trying to be interested in the farm had been hard work. His knowledge was limited, but he'd enjoyed listening to Ian's account of selling the milk both locally and interstate and grain and hay to local horse trainers. How things had changed in such a short time. He planted his oat crop with modern machinery using GPS navigation. He continued to be really astounded at the technology involved in modern farming. Ken was also impressed at the intelligence of his soon-to-be brother-in-law — well, he hoped to be his brother-in-law.

While the night crept on and the darkness enveloped them all, the isolation comforted Ken. He knew Bonnie would feel safe here in the remote farming area of South Australia, with two trusted souls — three, counting himself — who she depended on more than anyone else in the world.

'You've gone through hell, Bonnie. How dreadful. I'm just so pleased you escaped,' Sarah exclaimed with awe.

'I hope you won't be using your passport any time soon,' Ian said, looking serious. Then he realised he needed to reassure his sister of her safety. 'If you're considered a druggy, I'm sure druggies are just so commonplace today. Anyway, you're here in Australia. You're home, so no country can touch you. I'm glad you told us, so there is always a spare bed here if you ever end up on the run.' He was only half-joking and hoped all would be well for her and Ken. *Honestly*, he thought, *I'm sure she's safe.*

'Actually, talking of beds, I have made up two rooms and you two can sort out your own sleeping arrangement while I make the coffee,' Sarah called as she carried plates inside. The kitchen was the same as Bonnie remembered as a child: orange benchtops and huge Aga stove ready to churn out country food when prompted. Sarah held onto the benchtop as she bent down to stack the dishwasher. 'I'm a bit tired tonight,' she said as she turned around to gather and load more dishes.

She looked like she could do with a decent night's sleep and had aged considerably since Bonnie had last seen her. She was pleased her brother had found the perfect companion this time: Sarah exuded kindness and was pleasing to the eye, so she could see why there'd been an attraction.

'Leave them for me. I'll do them in the morning. I think we're all ready for bed,' Bonnie said as she turned to go into the passage that led to the bedroom. She smiled. Ken was quietly snoring already. *Well, that solved the bedroom dilemma adequately*, she thought happily and prepared for a good sleep. She smiled inwardly as she realised how easy Ken could be. *Low maintenance really*, and she mentally made a note to be more amorous when they returned to Adelaide. Her smiled widened as she settled down to sleep with the gentle snoring being a soothing sound in the next bedroom. But she couldn't sleep. And her feet were cold, she thought sometime later. She decided to warm herself next to Ken, so she crept out of bed and tip-toed into the next bedroom. As she climbed into Ken's bed in the dark, she felt a big arm surround her and he pulled her towards him.

'I thought you were asleep,' she whispered to him.

'Yes, I am asleep,' was whispered back to her and Bonnie snuggled in closer, smiling at Ken's sense of humour. She'd found herself smiling inwardly quite a lot in recent times and figured it was called Happiness.

The following morning Bonnie and Ken walked around the farm. As they passed the cows in the milking shed, Ken stopped. 'I believe this is an appropriate place for me to ask something.' He cleared his throat. 'Bonnie ... will you marry me? You love this place, so now we can remember our special moment. I know this is quick, but we've wasted enough time, don't you think? Let's not count the decades.'

'Ken ... yes! Absolutely! I'd *LOVE* to marry you!' Bonnie squealed and hugged him as hard as she could. 'Let's hurry back home so we can share our news with Mum and Dad. They'll be as thrilled as I am.'

Chapter Fourteen

Sheila's First Lawyer Visit

2005

As the old white car rounded the corner approaching the Glenelg home, Sheila saw the Prado in the driveway. *Again! What's Bonnie doing here?* So caught off guard, Sheila became cautious, like a wild animal emerging from winter hibernation. She decided to drive on to the park around the corner where she could contemplate her next move. She ran a hand through her hair, frustrated: her whole day had been a challenge.

Her friend, Rex, had provided her with the phone number of a trusted friend – more a colleague or acquaintance really – who was a lawyer, and Sheila had attended his office for business. The cramped room looked cheap and cluttered, with an elderly woman as the receptionist. The woman had looked at Sheila laconically through watery eyes. Sheila had thought they could attract more business by getting rid of wrinklies who should be home watching daytime television. She realised she didn't like old people with frizzy grey hair; they all seemed to have a habit of telling her what to do.

'Look, I'm going to be frank with you. I need some legal advice,' Sheila had blurted out as soon as she reached the next room. At this stage, she hadn't been asked to sit down, but, ignoring convention, she sat upright in the shabby client chair as soon as the door closed. 'Actually, not advice so much as information I can rely on. I've looked on the internet and information has been conflicting.'

'So how can I help you?' David asked as he mentally tried to sum up his new client. Sheila was dressed in her smart work clothes, which meant she could pay, so at least it was a start. She had an angry countenance and David thought she needed a lesson in good manners. He could smell her perfume which reminded him of snake's venom or some animal excrement he'd smelt somewhere in the bush.

Sheila's eyes were bloodshot, and she hated the feel of sore eyes, but she took a deep breath and asked her question. 'How long do I have to live in a house before I can claim it as my own? I live there and the oldies, my grandparents, live there too.'

She'd read about squatters' rights but wasn't sure which state of Australia acknowledged that section of the law. At this stage, she wasn't going to reveal too much to this geeky-looking bloke with the short hair and thick glasses.

Eventually, geeky David adjusted his glasses and stood. Pushing his chair back, he moved to the bookshelf at the back of the office, where he took out one of his books from the shelf and flicked through the pages. The dreadful smell of old books permeated the room, making Sheila nauseous. It took an eternity for David to resume his position at his desk as the oracle of the office. He sat there with his few wispy bits of black hair spoiling the perfect part on his head. With a great sigh and his eyes glued to the book, he looked like he was going to make a statement.

Sheila reasoned those great orators must assume this kind of pretence just to intimidate whoever was listening, but she wasn't going to put up with too much pomp and ceremony from this bloke. She wanted a number and a number only. *How many years? Perhaps he's taking his time so the old tart in the reception area can give me a hefty account,* Sheila thought.

She felt twitchy and had to concentrate hard on keeping still in the chair, which was difficult. Her legs just wanted to keep moving and so did her arms. She'd had some meth a short time ago and was conscious her supply at home was running low. *Yes,* she thought, *the Glenelg Homestead is my home now*, even though she stayed in her room most of the time. She didn't want to interact with old people and listen to their stories; she'd leave that kind of maternal nonsense to their daughter, or their son … her father, Ian. She had a life to live, which consisted of working as little as possible and getting as high as possible … without topping herself. She knew how much she could take without addiction setting in – or at least she thought she did. She knew where to get a stash. Her local supplier was either Rodney, Luke or Metho Mike, who she often met near the beach, which was lucky really, as she could tell the oldies she was going to the beach, and they believed her.

At long last, David blurted out some words. 'I've checked, and it says if you stay there and call it your home, then under the Family Law Act, it will be considered your home. It doesn't actually state a length of time, but how long have you lived there now?'

'Not long really, perhaps a few years, but recently I've used it as my address on my driver's license. I intend enrolling for the elections and using that address. Previously I haven't bothered about voting. Seems like a waste of time to me but it's not what we're worried about right now. I know your time costs me dough, so let's hurry things up.'

'Do you look after your grandparents?' David asked. 'If you do, then it would certainly strengthen your position in the eyes of the law. If you are currently employed and you give up your job, you would be entitled to a social security payment from Centrelink. That would also strengthen your position with the law.'

'I need all those words in writing before I go,' Sheila said. She could feel herself getting excited as she considered all sorts of possibilities. 'And I want it on your legal letterhead.'

Crikey, David thought as he moved towards the office stationery cupboard. *This woman's a bit of a nut case*, he thought, noticing her fidgeting. He checked his law source closely and copied it out verbatim. He could see this woman was serious and he didn't really want to deal with her in the future. She had a wild look in those bloodshot eyes.

David had not been a lawyer long. He was in his first year after graduating as a mature age student; he certainly didn't want any client misquoting or second-guessing situations. He therefore asked his secretary to come in, so if any witnesses were needed in the future, Mrs Harper could be counted on to verify statements. It was the first time he'd ever had to do this, but his instinct assured him of its importance.

'Mrs Harper, I'm going to read this to you and then I need you to type it out for our client here, Ms Finch.'

The woman entered the room carrying a stool, which she promptly placed beside David's desk. As she looked over her horn-rimmed glasses like an old school teacher, David began to dictate. In his head, David took a mental note to later tell Mrs Harper not to accept any more appointments with this client. His gut instinct had served him well all his life and he'd heard awful stories about the Family Law Court. Quietly, he suspected Sheila was a drug user by the way she kept flinging around, and he had the feeling something sinister was afoot. He simply didn't like the look or tone of this sturdy young woman, who lived with her grandparents and appeared to be formulating plans.

'Mrs Harper, please type this on an official letterhead as the client has requested. Include words that allude to the fact that the client has requested it in writing. Then the three of us will sign and date it.'

Mrs Harper was slow but thorough – she'd been a legal secretary all her long, working life. She sensed the tension in the office but said nothing.

After what seemed a long time, Sheila heard the scratching noise of Mrs Harper's stockings as she moved past her and then a waft of old lady smell lingered in the air as Mrs Harper silently left the room. Sheila wished she'd left the door open; at least that way the smell could escape but she felt compelled by social etiquette to sit still. She thought she'd better pay attention until the old bloke behind the desk dismissed her. *Thank goodness he didn't want to shake hands!*

David subsequently put a red star on the notes about his client. Someone else in the legal field could have the pleasure of dealing with her next time. And he knew there would be a next time. But it wasn't going to be with him!

When David heard his client striding down the steps to exit the building, he called to Mrs Harper: 'Can you please bring me a cup of tea?' Despite the early afternoon hour, he thought he'd go home after his tea. He didn't have any more appointments and needed to do a few things around the house. He suddenly felt tired and old. He wasn't like some lawyers who fitted in as many clients as possible and took on all sorts of lowlifes with all their lies and manipulations of facts in an attempt to win their case in court. He reasoned some lawyers had a moral compass while others were merely interested in words on a page, which constituted the law at that time and place. Then learned lawyers, as judges, make judgements, he thought.

David rose and looked out the window, through which traffic noise drifted, creating pain in his head. After his cup of tea, he heard Mrs Harper packing up her belongings for the day so he did likewise and locked the door on his way out of the office.

****

Meanwhile, at the park, Sheila sat in her car thinking. Subsequently, she placed her document in the glove box. It was late in the afternoon and, after an exceptionally long day, she sure as hell wasn't going into the house while the white Prado was in the driveway. *Or is it silver?* She didn't know and didn't care. Sweat ran down her back and between her breasts as she wound the window down and luckily caught a slight breeze past, which cooled her down. The noise of traffic passing by, the kids playing in the park, annoyed her, and she thought about going to the beach and waiting for Metho Mike. He always seemed to have the cheapest stuff –

white powder in little plastic bags – just waiting for someone to pay up and begin snorting. She was short of cash due to the lawyer's fee, but thought Mike might take a late payment so, with that thought in her head, she started the car and pointed it in the direction of the beach. She fumed slightly, sure the lawyer had deliberately taken his time to add as many minutes as possible to his bill. *No wonder some folk say lawyers have a license to print money!* Then she thought about what she had to do to get money. She dismissed the thought as quickly as it came.

Her eyes had cleared slightly but she still hoped the police would not stop her on the way. She slipped her sunglasses on and pressed her foot on the accelerator; soon she was speeding along the freeway toward the beach. She found a parking space close to where Metho Mike hung out, but she was a little early, so she opened the glove box, where she kept important documents and took out the folded letter from her father.

She'd been surprised when her boss had handed her the letter and had instantly recognised the handwriting. Her jaw dropped as she realised her father knew where she worked and assumed somehow he'd spied on her, just like she spied on him. Her first impulse was to tear the letter to pieces right there and then she remembered where she was and politely thanked Bert and shoved it in her pocket for later reading.

'Is it okay if I go to the bathroom, Bert?' she'd asked, more than keen to see what the loser, her father, had to say.

'Sure, Sheila. You want me to come with you?' Bert always thought he was being funny, and Sheila had to appease him by laughing at his pathetic joke. *One day I'll not be working for you, Bert.* In fact, her dream was to not work for anyone. She wanted a lot of money to indulge her drug habit, and she'd seriously considered becoming a full-time dealer. But, not wanting to be at the mercy of criminals nor following what they dictated, she'd remained a deliverer, just a deliverer, even if the demarcation of roles was quite blurry, she decided.

For now, Sheila was ready to read her letter from her father.

Dear Sheila

It's been a long time since we have seen each other. Are you interested in visiting the farm for Christmas and seeing your cousins and the rest of the family? I know we have had our differences, but time has passed and I do not hold grudges. Let's just put the past behind us. We have much to discuss and if you're interested, I will wait for you in a fortnight at the Dome, just near the tramline, on May the 4th. It's the weekend so I will be there at 10 o'clock waiting for you. I look forward to seeing you then.

Love from Dad

Sheila felt like tearing it up, putting it in the toilet and flushing it away but she controlled herself as she folded it and slipped it back into her pocket. *What a loser,* she thought. *He has that same patronising tone where he thinks he's the boss.* She could feel her rage rising and felt her neck go red as the blood accumulated just under the skin. She physically had to unclench her fists. *I just want to smash him!*

No, she wasn't going to visit and put up with all those losers. She wasn't going to be nice to the new wife when it should have been her mother. And as for holding a grudge, she was furious! Even if her father didn't hold a grudge, she sure as hell did. She wasn't going to visit *A* farm, let alone *THE* farm.

And yes, she was going to get even with her father for his abandonment. She wasn't sure how this would happen yet, but somehow, she would have her revenge and obtain atonement.

Suddenly there was a bang on the car window. *Who the hell is that?* Sheila thought, startled. She looked around to see Metho Mike waving a little bag in front of her.

'Oh no! What are you doing? Put that away,' she hissed as she wound down her window; she snatched the bag away from him.

'What's up your cloaca?' asked Mike, looking totally puzzled.

'Never you mind. Sorry old fella. Out of line. Just had a rotten day, that's all. Will fix you up next time I see you.' And Sheila quickly drove off before he could say anything more. Mike wasn't happy about that.

Chapter Fifteen

Pat's Plight

2005

Bang! The front door slammed loudly, and Pat jumped. She shouldn't have been surprised because every morning it was how the pattern of behaviour began. She physically relaxed after a few minutes and poured herself a second cup of tea.

'I wish Sheila would find herself somewhere else to live. The way she slams doors and storms around really annoys me.'

Ernie looked up as he spoke and saw his wife of many years taking her time to sit down. Gone were the quick movements of years ago, but he knew he also took his time to move around these days. They both shuffled through the house from room to room as the days unfolded and blended into each other. It was like a never-ending rainbow with a pot of gold at the end, but for them, the end was not quite a pot of gold! It was death and each day they had to banish demonic thoughts about how their final days on Earth would play out.

'I wish she would too,' said Pat, almost to herself, but Ernie had his hearing aids in, and heard her. 'On the other hand, she's had a difficult life and feels abandoned by her father. I know what it feels like. I remember Dad coming home from the war, ordering us all around, shouting and banging doors. When he left, we were all so relieved. I remember Mum saying as much. Poor Sheila ...'

'Poor Sheila, my foot. I'm sure Ian has tried over the years to repair his relationship with her. He's told us, don't you remember?'

Pat remembered now Ernie had mentioned it, but recently she

realised she was having trouble remembering lots of things. She found herself writing notes and using a diary for the first time in her life. It was because she was busy, she reasoned with herself. She prided herself on her memory of her childhood, and she wasn't too bad in the present. But she couldn't remember events from yesterday, last week and last year very clearly. Somehow a kind of fog had invaded her mind and she'd become agitated when she tried to clear it away, when she tried to focus on whatever had demanded her attention. It was all very tiring.

'That's right. We were talking about Sheila. We *have* tried to move her on, remember? But she told us she was going to leave and then she didn't. Ernie, do you think we should ask her again as it doesn't appear to be a concern for her?'

Pat left the question hanging so it could consume the void that crept in every time Sheila's name was mentioned. 'My job is to prepare dinner and not rock the boat. I have tried to encourage her to see a doctor and obtain a referral for an anger management program. Remember all the trouble we had then?' Pat observed the curtain blowing in the morning breeze and shuffled to the door to open it and let in some fresh cool air, wishing it would blow away the problem. She didn't care about letting in the dust. She felt too hot and flustered.

Ernie, indeed, remembered. Sheila had the gall to accuse them of trying to control her and had lost her temper. Once again, the doors were slamming. The striding down the passage became more hostile and her appearances in the kitchen diminished. He recognised how good she was at turning situations around when it suited her and throwing blame onto others. He was not surprised the relationship between Ian and Sheila was irreparable, or so it seemed. In fact, it was the same relationship Sheila had with her mother. As her grandparents, Pat and Ernie were prepared to try hard and give her the time and attention she thought she lacked as a child. But she didn't want to spend time with them! Instead, her hostile, belligerent manner underpinned the household and its functioning in their home. This was all behind closed doors, of course. To strangers, Sheila could be quite charming and then Ernie and Pat were left doubting themselves.

'Perhaps we have made life too easy for Sheila with the ensuite facilities, air-conditioning, television and all the home comforts. She has a kettle and fridge. She's just taken over our house,' Pat said, exasperated by it all. She was on the verge of tears.

'All right,' Ernie sighed. 'How does this sound? I'll ask her to move out. If I can see she appears conciliatory … if you stop making her lunch. And last night I noticed you put a tray outside her room for her dinner! Really, Pat, she's not some teenager. Waiting on her has to stop.'

Ernie's voice was stern. He didn't like seeing his wife used up like a servant, and he didn't like using a stern voice with Pat. This wasn't at all how they usually interacted with each other.

'Yes. You're right. What a good plan.' Pat left the table and soon the rattle of dishes began. Domesticity gave her the feeling of peace but Ernie continued to sit at the table pondering his next move with Sheila. *What a nuisance*, he thought. He would much rather be walking to the Post Office to pick up his mail and continue his daily walk. It was a bit far to reach the Glenelg beach these days so often he bought himself a coffee at the local café where all the staff knew him and talked to him.

Soon he made a move to find his walking shoes. He loved being outside; it reminded him of his younger days at Trevilly when farming was uncomplicated. He made a mental note to prepare some time soon to go to Trevilly and perhaps Ian might have some ideas about how to move Sheila out. *Yes*, he decided. *We'll go to Trevilly in the winter, after seeding and before hay cutting starts, and speak to Ian. He will know what to do.*

Ernie realised that, as the years progressed, his ability to solve problems was becoming more of a challenge. He wasn't sure if it was his age or perhaps the problems themselves were becoming harder to solve.

Despite being in his eighties, he felt fit and agile and attributed this to his daily walks. He'd read somewhere that hydration was important for good health, so he always took a water bottle on his walks, and he'd embraced this idea, not only because of his reading, but he'd seen others carrying water bottles and decided it was a good look. Sure, he was on blood pressure and cholesterol medication but he figured lots of people over eighty were on this kind of medication so it assumed normality. He was probably on other medication too but, for now, he didn't want to think about it, just like he didn't want to think about Pat's memory and vagueness.

'Pat, do you want anything at the shops? Remember Bonnie and Ken are coming for tea tonight. You haven't forgotten, have you? Are we having roast beef? Do you have all the vegetables?'

Ernie knew he was bombarding her with questions, and she wasn't very coherent when the questions were fired away relentlessly like a tidal wave moving towards the shore. He allowed her to take her time.

'I will make a list and drive down later,' Pat replied so Ernie made his way towards the door for his walk.

Usually, when they had visitors, Sheila made a point of being out somewhere, which suited everyone. Sheila's day consisted of going to work, coming home late afternoon, and then going out somewhere until eight o'clock or so. Sheila only interacted with her grandparents when she deemed it essential. Mostly when she came home, she went to her room and shut the door for the night.

Sometime later, the doorbell rang and in bounced Bonnie with Ken in tow behind her. 'Hi there, Pat,' Ken greeted. 'Unfortunately, I can't stay for dinner as I have been called into the hospital for an emergency op so only Bonnie can stay for now. I'll be back later to pick her up.'

'Would you like me to put your dinner in the oven?' Pat asked.

'Yes, please! Ahhh, Pat, you're amazing. You always know just what to do. And Bonnie, don't tell your parents our news until I return.' Ken, indeed, had a spring in his step as he hugged Bonnie and kissed Pat on his way out.

Ever observant, Ernie needed no prodding! He waited patiently until Ken had left before he made his move. 'Wow! What was that all about?'

'Dad, you heard him. I can't tell you our news until he comes back!'

Bonnie promptly sat down and pretended to read the paper. She was so excited, but only engaged her father with trivialities about the garden and the weather, and the content of the newspaper. Soon the front door opened, and Bonnie waited in surprise to see who would enter her parent's home. Who else had their own front door key? By this time, Ernie was watching television and Pat was attending to the cooking. Bonnie sat dumbfounded by her parent's acceptance of this odd situation – someone was living in their house. Had they heard the front door open and the heavy footsteps thumping along the passage?

'Mum, who is that in your house? Did I hear the opening of the front door? What's happening?' Bonnie's eyes and mouth were wide open.

Pat kept her head over the stove, knowing her daughter was going to ask some difficult questions. Just then Sheila's huge frame appeared in the doorway, and she looked at Bonnie with an air of confidence. She hadn't seen a car in the driveway, so she too was caught off guard. The two women sized each other up, both realising they had a role to play. Sheila was not perturbed. She was good at playing roles, so she took a deep breath.

'Hello there. You must be Bonnie. I'm Sheila.'

Taking a step forward, Sheila leaned in and gave Bonnie a hug, much to Bonnie's amazement. The huge frame stayed in the embrace just a moment too long and squeezed just a fraction too hard. 'I'm staying here, just for a while, until I can get some accommodation sorted out. I didn't see a car outside, so I'm as surprised as you are. I've been at work in the city but Gran and Grandpa were kind enough to offer me a place to stay.'

Gran and Grandpa! Who calls my parents by those names, Bonnie thought, her eyebrows still raised. Even in Pat's ears, the names gave her an uncomfortable jolt. Pat was rational enough to know Sheila was her granddaughter, and now Sheila had turned on her charm. She felt confused. She didn't want to be confused and she blamed Sheila for her unsettled state, which she knew was totally irrational, but she didn't tell Ernie this.

'Gran, what are we having for dinner? It smells delicious.'

Sheila knew the way to win over her grandmother was to compliment her on her cooking. She plonked down into the seat where Bonnie normally sat but Bonnie was too polite to say anything. In fact, Bonnie was too stunned to move so she just observed what was happening. Her father was intent on watching television while her mother remained intent on stirring the pot on the stove. So Bonnie's role, it seemed, was to engage with the newcomer.

'So, you've just come from the city, Sheila?' Bonnie's excitement with her news and the bounce in her step fell flat.

'Yes. I work at a chemical distribution warehouse, in auditing, and oversee the office and a handful of totally incompetent women,' Sheila said, laying claim to her position of importance.

Bonnie could see by the way Sheila dressed, she could have been management material.

As Pat listened to this conversation, she was taken back to her time at Trevilly, where Sheila pocketed whatever items she wanted. She wondered if she still did this. As she turned from the stove, she saw the back of Sheila's frame sitting where her daughter normally sat. It was totally unreasonable, Pat thought, but she could feel the hair on the back of her neck tingling, and attempted to calm herself. The atmosphere morphed from jovial to frosty as Sheila prattled away, spurred on by answers that were monosyllabic.

Bonnie was astute enough to see the game-playing Sheila was engaged in but wondered if it was apparent to her mother. Gradually, both parents lapsed into non-committal responses when required as their eyes glazed over. Pat could see Ernie watching the television and Bonnie was tempted to join him, but she was polite enough to give her niece the attention she so clearly expected. *What an entitled, self-centred young lady*, Bonnie thought. *And what are my parents thinking?*

Bonnie had been looking forward to spending time with her parents but the show was now being hijacked by a stranger, albeit a relative. She sensed her mother's unease and went into the kitchen at the first break in the conversation, hoping Sheila would leave the room. But Sheila was too clever to be fobbed off so easily.

Much relief was felt when the front doorbell rang and Ken entered. He looked tired but pleased to see Bonnie and her parents. He squeezed in next to Bonnie at the table, gave her a peck on the cheek as he reached for his can of beer, his excitement noticeable – this was the big day for breaking good news.

'Hello. Who's this? I see we have a visitor.'

Sheila looked directly at Ken and then dropped her eyelids coyly, silently flirting. 'I live here. Well, I guess I will rephrase that statement. This is my family home. My grandparents allow me to stay here.'

'Whoa! That changes things.' Ken proceeded to make polite conversation until Pat brought his dinner to the table: his favourite, roast beef and vegetables, cooked to perfection. The smell of home cooking made his mouth water. He quickly turned his attention from Sheila and Bonnie to the food on his plate. Sheila watched, practically drooling with each mouthful he took. He knew he was under close inspection but oblivious about why, but Bonnie had a sixth sense about this newcomer. *How dare she refer to my parent's home as* her *family home! How presumptuous she is.* Bonnie saw her for the overconfident young lady she was; someone who had weaselled her way into the lives of her loved ones.

'Mum, Ken and I will visit you again in the morning as we clearly can't talk now,' Bonnie whispered to her mother. She remained in the kitchen washing dishes, taking refuge from having to interact with Sheila. The wise Pat understood and soon Ken and Bonnie left and made their way to their car, waiting for Ernie to join them.

'We can talk tomorrow,' Bonnie said, feeling like she'd thrown her parents to the wolves by passively allowing the self-opinionated Sheila to remain in the room unchallenged. More was unsaid than said.

Chapter Sixteen

Ken's Idea

2005

'Well, our 'tell-all' visit didn't go as we expected! Fancy Sheila turning up, and what a presumptuous little cow. Did your parents say anything, or did she just talk all night? I'm still in shock and I'll bet you are too. Honestly, how the hell did it happen?'

Ken could hardly focus on the road ahead. He'd had a rough night at the hospital. Things were not going as expected, and they'd almost lost the patient on the operating table. Only the anaesthetist's quick thinking at the last minute prompted the woman's breathing to start again. Two shocks in the same night didn't sit well.

He knew he had to keep his wits about him when he was driving home, and turned the car heating up onto high as a chill went right through him. His belt was tight around his waist and he made a mental note to not eat much for the next few days. *Pat's cooking was sensational though.* Soon the headlights shone into their street. *It's lucky we live relatively close.*

As Ken turned into the gravel driveway, Bonnie spoke. 'I'm still stunned. I can't get over the fact that we go there to tell my parents about our engagement, and we come home without divulging the most important thing that's happened to us. I simply can't believe it!'

'With all the foibles of Sheila's upbringing, I guess it's no wonder she's strange. I cannot believe she has such an important job. Doubtless she'd be throwing her weight around – excuse the pun – but she certainly seems very self-assured. Perhaps in time, she'll take over the Glenelg household too. Just kidding!' He shook his head. 'Nah, I think Pat and Ernie are too smart for that and Ernie, for sure, wouldn't allow himself to be usurped, dare I say it, by a woman.'

'You're right, Ken. Dad comes from a world where women were, and still are, domestic beings. Hence Mum's size. She samples all her cooking and does a lot of sitting!'

Upon entering the house, Bonnie filled the kettle and flicked it on. Domesticity had crept quietly into their relationship, making decisions easier on their way forward. Ken's romantic proposal was a testament to their commitment and love for each other. He'd even had a ring in his pocket! Bonnie's glance at Ken reminded her of his attractiveness and he took pride in his health and appearance. It would have to be a good start, she thought and caught herself smiling. She picked up two mugs of tea and moved to the lounge chairs, still smiling as she looked at him.

The moment of happiness didn't go unnoticed. 'I like it when you act like a domestic goddess,' Ken almost whispered. 'And I like that top you're wearing. In fact, I like it whether you wear it or not.'

He sized her up and down, like a cat meowing. Shifting quickly in the chair as if a sudden thought had just entered his head, he said, 'Did you notice the way Sheila eyed me up and down?'

'I certainly did,' Bonnie replied. 'What a piece of work!'

As she sprawled out on the couch with her cup of tea, she decided Sheila wasn't going to spoil what remained of the evening. Here, in Ken's beautiful home, with the man who was about to become her husband, she thought her life was complete.

The next morning, as they drove to the Finch household, Ken broke Bonnie's reverie. 'Carpe diem,' he said. 'Seize the day! Let's not mention Sheila's behaviour last night. And after we tell them our news, we must discuss your Mum's illness with her. I hope it's not too bad. Perhaps we can talk to Ernie on his own too. That might be more insightful.'

Soon the Finch home came into view. Ernie was outside, dressed in his old tennis hat, red checked shirt and baggy brown trousers: his gardening uniform. He stood up slowly, stopped removing weeds from among the rose bushes and put the garden fork down; he moved the wheelbarrow away from the path as the silver Prado pulled into the driveway. It was a beautiful sunny day, the weather serving as a good omen. After car doors slammed and greetings were exchanged, the three of them went inside to the lounge room where Pat joined them.

'Now, Mum, before we have any interruptions, Ken has a question to ask!'

'Do I? Oh yes. Just kidding, Bonnie. I think we all ought to sit down. Let's not worry about any distractions because, Ernie and Pat, I would like to ask your daughter to marry me. Actually, I have asked her and she accepted and now we want to tell you. In fact, we've been dying to tell you but, lately, other things seemed to be in the way.'

The words spilled from Ken's mouth in such a tumbled, nonchalant way, it even surprised him. He'd been thinking about the moment for so many years and now, it seemed the most natural occurrence one could imagine.

'That's the best bloody news I've heard for years,' Ernie shouted, springing out of his chair. 'Did you hear what Ken said, Pat? At long last, our daughter is getting married! How old are you, Bonnie?'

'Stop it, Ernie! How wonderful, Bon! Don't take any notice of him. And, of course, he knows how old you are, and it doesn't matter. He's just talking for the sake of talking. Actually, we both are. That's wonderful and it makes me so happy! Ken, we love you like our son. Have you told Ian yet?'

Both Bonnie and Ken seized the moment; they would tell Ian later. 'No, Mum. You and Dad are the first to know. We would have told Ken's parents too if they'd been alive. But now we are middle-aged, lots of our friends have lost their parents.'

A shadow flickered across Pat's face and she grimaced as she tried to get out of her chair. 'Mum, I'll make the tea. You sit and talk to your soon-to-be son-in-law. Do you like the sound of that? Hasn't it got a lovely ring to it? Better get used to it, folks. Oh yes, while we're talking about rings, I'll show you something special.'

Bonnie held out her left hand and her parents stared in delight for what seemed an eternity. 'Now, Mum, what about your health?'

The mood quickly changed as Pat's cancer story unravelled and the tension set in. The family matriarch spoke slowly and quietly as she told them about the trips to the doctor, the scans and blood tests, which had all led to the appointment with the oncologist and the diagnosis of pancreatic cancer.

Pat believed the chemo treatment would be the ultimate remedy, mistakenly thinking that, by remaining positive, life would continue as it always had done. Ken frowned. He'd heard this kind of talk throughout his working life, where patients were encouraged to cling desperately to life rather than come to terms with the reality of a terminal illness, which everyone had to face at some stage. He cringed, feeling her desperation as she talked of a cure and the miracle of modern medicine these days. He'd been in many hospital meetings where this kind of talk had been an item on the agenda. Illusion versus reality, particularly in the early stages, was often discussed and palliative care was one of Ken's career interests. He listened attentively as Pat told her tale.

When she finished talking, they each sat quietly, reflecting on the diagnosis. Then Ernie broke the silence as he moved in his chair and gave a tiny shake of his head. The grandfather clock ticked loudly and, outside, chirping birdsong became suddenly intrusive as they each painfully mulled over the situation.

In true stoic style, Pat stretched out and moved closer to her daughter to examine the ring. 'Bon, it's beautiful. Ken, well-chosen and welcome to our family. Actually, talking about family, it seems Sheila has taken a real shine to you, Ken. If I didn't know any better, I'd say she tried flirting with you. Bad form, and clearly she needs to learn a few lessons.'

'She needs to learn a few lessons all right, on many levels,' Ernie responded, keen to change the subject away from Pat's illness. 'Anyway, I'm going to talk about her with Ian soon as we don't want her staying here anymore. We helped her out when she was going through a difficult time in her life but now … …'

'Good idea, Dad. Let Ian handle her. And who knows, they may be able to resurrect their relationship. Anyway, folks, I think it's time Ken and I left to do a few chores before the day ends. You can get back to your gardening now, Dad. What are you going to do today, Mum?'

Still seated in her chair, Pat looked vaguely around the kitchen as the others dallied their way to the front door. 'I'll see them off, Pat, then come inside for the broom,' Ernie called out as he moved onto the verandah. He followed them down the front step, staying behind Bonnie.

'Dad, we'll talk more when we've had time to digest this awful news about Mum. Take care.'

'I'm concerned your mother is becoming increasingly vague, and it worries me. But never mind … when we get rid of Sheila, it will be one less thing to worry about. Not that she's a worry, really, as she often eats out after work. It's not for long, and she only uses her room for sleeping, so all she does is occupy space.'

'Dad, I'll ring you and see you soon. We will keep in touch each day.' Bonnie felt tears welling up in her eyes as she hugged her dad. She opened the car door and climbed into the passenger's seat, trying hard to not let the tears spill.

Ken let the car slowly roll back down the driveway. He didn't look at Bonnie as he, too, was lost in his thoughts. So Pat was dying – he knew the prognosis for this type of cancer. It wasn't good. Twelve months, perhaps a few years – but clearly it was going to be difficult for the Finch household from now on. The good times were about to fade away.

'I was surprised Mum had noticed Sheila's attraction to you,'

Bonnie suddenly said. 'Perhaps Sheila has a fetish for older men … you know, like a father figure. Though it wasn't really a father figure kind of look! It was a real 'come on' kind of look. Every woman recognises it, and so do men! She couldn't keep her eyes off you, and the way she looked you up and down was obscene.'

'Well, I could pretend I'm flattered but I have a better idea. Apart from her not being my type, and young enough to be my daughter, I'm going to suggest something which will really test the morals of that disgusting young, or not so young, woman. Listen to this, Bonnie. Why don't I pretend to respond to her and see what her reaction is? Soon all will be revealed and her lack of moral compass will expose her to all the family. What do you think?'

Bonnie pulled a face, so Ken knew she was mulling it over. Then she said, 'The thought is shameful … but … it could well work. I'd just like to sleep on it … after I sleep with my almost-husband.' Her thoughts ran rampant for the rest of the drive home – as horrible as it sounded, if it worked, Sheila would be exposed as the tart who targeted her husband-to-be. Being in his mid-sixties, Ken could handle himself, but the thought repulsed Bonnie just the same.

Ken enjoyed this kind of playfulness that Bonnie dished out to him and, in due course, they both laughed as each imagined the new game that Ken was about to embark on.

'Righto. We'll see how it plays out right up until our wedding and then when she attempts to seduce me, we'll know her game is up. Let's set a date and plan a wedding. It's much more exciting than thinking about Shelia.' He put his hand on her knee. 'But don't worry, my love. I'll see what she's up to and expose her.'

A few moments passed.

'Actually, talking about daughters, I suppose we'll need to tell them about our marriage. Now I won't be looking forward to having *that* conversation with them, but needs must, I guess. I'll call them tomorrow. But for now, let's walk down to the tram and have a meal at the foreshore. I just feel like some scallops. We haven't had seafood for ages. Who can we ask to join us?'

'Let's ask Christine and Andy. They'll be at home doing nothing. I'll call them.'

Christine and Andy lived just to the east of Glenelg so it would be easy for them to catch the tram and join them for a meal. They were extremely excited to hear the news of the wedding and handshakes and hugs were extended all round, after Christine's squeals of delight. Of course, an engagement party had to be planned and a guest list discussed. This led to a conversation of gossip about who was on the party list and who wasn't.

'Bonnie, come back to work! It just isn't the same since you left. Well … work has become busier of course, and people are much more demanding. And patients still expect miracles. Honestly, I could tell you some stories, but you know how they all go. Don't work in Casualty Department though. Just get a Ward job – perhaps a few hours at night when everyone is asleep. What do you think, Ken? The hospital is always looking for casual night staff and Ken could easily arrange a few shifts for you.'

'Great idea, Chris. What do you think, Bon?' Ken replied. 'It'll keep you out of the kitchen for a while – I don't want you to end up the size of your Mum. You have to fit into your bridal dress.'

Instantly, he regretted his flippancy and was thankful Bonnie took it in her usual good form. *She's such a good sport*, he thought. Indeed, very little seemed to bother her and he loved her pragmatic, down-to-earth nature.

'Mmmm. I've been thinking about it, but now, with Mum and her cancer diagnosis, I'm not so sure. But I guess a few nights would be good. Certainly, the house is quiet enough during the day to let me catnap for a few hours. I know! Ken, you can tell your daughters I'm sleeping and it would be my excuse for not visiting when you tell them. We'll invite them to the engagement party where they can mix with others and not be so likely to ask impertinent questions. And that's not a good reason for working, but I do feel I want to be more productive. And I need an income.

I know I'm prattling, but we are just so excited about the wedding.'

'Consider it done. I'm at work on Tuesday so I'll contact Sonia from H.R. She'll be thrilled.'

Bonnie smiled. Ken was such a man of action, and he always had her best interests at heart. That's why she loved him.

She felt his foot slide alongside her ankle and up her calf, and moved her leg to further enable the foot stroking! Life seemed so comfortable, and she remembered how easily friendships were formed at hospitals where like-minded people worked alongside each other. Soon their meals arrived and the flow of easy conversation continued. Ken had been right about the taste of seafood, too, as he was about many things; it melted in her mouth before it slid down her throat. She almost purred with contentment.

Chapter Seventeen

Sheila settles into the Homestead

2006

In room 515, at the old hotel in central Adelaide, Sheila and Rodney did business, money passing between them during the deal. Small plastic bags of Meth with first names written on them were laid out on the bed as the exchange took place and the deal reconciled.

'Metho Mike isn't happy with you, and I think you know why,' Rodney said. 'I would hate my favourite dealer to disappear … like others we know.'

'Hmm. Yeah, I owe him money. He's got a long memory, but I'll square up with him soon.' Sheila placed the packages into her large handbag.

'Why are you planning to see Metho Mike? I thought you weren't using these days.'

'These days, my dear Rodney, I live in Glenelg, in my oldies house, and am just waiting out time. I was going to suggest you rent a place nearby, in Brighton maybe, as I intend to move my patch into the rich area of town.'

Rodney frowned. 'But you've got good regulars where you are.'

Sheila half smiled at her own logic. 'Yeah, rich folk often take recreational drugs but don't overdo it. Who wants to deal with a potential corpse and have the cops on their back?' She continued to position the bags into crevices in the handbag. 'I guess you would need a big place to make the stuff, but if you lived closer, it'd be easier.'

Rodney shrugged. 'You gotta realise, I need plenty of room to make the stuff, and I don't want nosey neighbours. In Elizabeth, I reckon every second house has their own lab. Meeting here each month still works for me. We can continue to do pick ups and drop offs just like we do now. And good luck getting new clients.'

He started to pack up. 'Make sure you don't step on someone else's patch, and be aware Metho Mike is extending his area up the beach.' With all his stash packed away, he prepared to leave. 'Just don't lose your phone,' he told Sheila.

That reminded Sheila about her clients and she cast her eyes over the phone screen for a few messages for drop-offs. Metho Mick often wanted packages delivered around the place and she decided to contact him and settle her outstanding debt. She didn't want to fall out of favour with him. But, there was nothing new on her phone so she cast her eyes back to Rodney. He could be a nuisance and get angry at times and she currently didn't feel like an argument with him or anyone else. Right now, she felt rather hungry as she'd rushed to make it to the tram and now had a headache coming. She took some Panadol from her bag.

Looking up, she saw Rodney looking suggestively at the bed. She ignored it – she didn't want to perform for money or anything these days. 'I do my runs in the evenings but if business picks up, I may be able to chuck my day job. Honestly, what a mob of tossers! They count every cent these days and I have to be so careful.'

Over the past few weeks, her line manager had started paying greater attention to the petty cash and it wasn't quite so easy to slip a tenner into her pocket or put in a fake receipt. She lay awake at night, wondering how she could create fake invoices, but financial auditors were very astute. She used to audit the company's books back in the day, but outside auditors were now used and of course a few fake entries on the odd occasion had become far more dangerous.

'Rodney, I'm not going to end up in the clink,' Sheila said with conviction. 'Soon I'm going to end up with a decent house in

Glenelg. You just wait and see.'

'Dream on! How so? They'll kick you out.'

'Nahhhh. I've got the law on my side.'

'That would make a change!'

'I've seen a lawyer dude and got it in writing; keep it in a safe spot. I always shut my bedroom door. *My* door – take note! It's a joke really. I must be a good girl and play my cards right. It's amazingly easy to see how old people tick.'

Recently, her grandmother had been going to doctor appointments more regularly, and she'd made a mental note to investigate what was going on. Hopefully, the downward slope was starting to landslide! Things could be about to change for her.

'You want to grab a bite to eat? There's an awesome Japanese restaurant just around the corner,' she suggested to Rodney, but he was keen to leave and make his way home.

Sheila decided to leave as well. Perhaps if she went home, she thought, she would ask Gran about her many doctor appointments. It was a tough decision – hang out at her favourite Glenelg café in case some of her regulars came in, or go home? The word 'home' had a great ring to it, which made up her mind.

She made her way along the hotel passage towards the rickety lift, waited a while, and was soon walking through the foyer, avoiding eye contact with anyone. She reached the noisy street with its bright sunshine and was soon on the tram to Glenelg, and thinking about her next move. The tram's smooth rocking movement lulled Sheila's mind; she had her supplies now so she was happy; she could now supply those druggies and make a handsome profit. The headache diminished as she walked from the tram stop to the homestead, and before long, she was grateful she had worn her comfortable sneakers with her jeans.

She stopped. The freshly polished Prado was back in the driveway! She swore under her breath as she slowly, silently, unlocked the front door. Bonnie was sitting outside on the back verandah with her parents chatting away, so Sheila decided to stay in the passage near the kitchen and eavesdrop. She stepped onto the plush carpet to further cushion her footsteps and listened to Bonnie talking to the oldies. The way they all adored each other made her squirm – she was clearly the outsider.

'When Thelma and I returned from our holiday, I found Gaz had made an appalling mess of things at the medical post. A patient I had tended just before we left died from a reaction to a drug I'd administered. I had no qualifications for treating a condition as serious as his, but he refused to go to hospital. Mum, it was horrible. Then there were folks receiving little or no attention and, to make matters worse, he had totally stuffed up the records of the supplies. Unfortunately, I had to use Gaz as there was no one else with the slightest hint of medical knowledge.

'Anyway, when I did the paperwork for the medical inventory, there were drugs missing. Narcotics! I suspected Gaz of theft but, Mum, what could I do? I couldn't accuse him of stealing as he'd just totally deny everything, and all those Africans would side with him. On top of that, he said the authorities wanted to talk to me about the farmworker's death and I didn't dare do or say anything that would make him turn against me.

'I decided to try to let it go undetected but when I told Craig, all hell broke loose. He told me the authorities would be looking for me and accusations of drug dealing would be made. He told Thelma and me to make a run for it and get out of town before we were arrested. We were not safe in the current political circumstances. The black government over there wants white farmers off the land and is making life very difficult for anyone who is white. A few years ago, they were even talking about deporting anyone who wasn't a black African. Craig and Thelma had considered leaving Zimbabwe then and had expected this was how it was going to happen.

'Thelma and I fled under cover of darkness! Mum, it was so scary! I was petrified.'

Sheila stood stunned! She didn't need to hear anything else yet remained where she was, deciphering what she'd just heard. This meant Bonnie was a suspect drug dealer and a killer! *Surely not!* She grinned widely. *Oh, this is hilarious!*

'But, Bonnie, if you had explained to the authorities … surely they could see the error. But you fled in the night?' Ernie frowned, concerned his daughter's way of covering a situation was a bit underhanded.

Sheila gulped back a laugh before it escaped. They were such babes in the woods, and just ripe for the picking!

'Dad, Zimbabwe isn't a democratic country with a just legal system like here. If I hadn't escaped, I'd be rotting in an African jail right now, or worse. I'm only safe now because I'm here in Australia.

'Mum, don't worry. Our country wouldn't send me back to a country like Zimbabwe, not with its political furore against whites. But it's lucky we have a lawyer in the family.' She smiled with slight reassurance.

'So what happened to Thelma?' Pat asked.

Sheila didn't need to hear any more. In a state of total disbelief, she slowly slid along the passage to her room and quietly opened and shut the door. She fell backwards onto the bed, still in shock at hearing this family conversation. *Bonnie is a drug dealer*, and she wasn't interested in hearing any further details! This was an outstanding piece of information – an absolute gem! Here she was with a handbag full of dope, and there was innocent little Bonnie, the foreign drug dealer spilling all her guff into the genteel Glenelg air.

Little did the family know how important Shelia's eavesdropping had been. She couldn't believe her luck! She took a long time revelling in her newfound knowledge before opening the handbag full of little plastic bags. She put them in a safe place in the bottom of the wardrobe, gently replacing the extra blanket on her bundle of goodies and wealth. She wondered which of the two was worth more, her dope or her information, which she was certainly going to use.

Sheila turned on the television but couldn't focus with so many thoughts running through her head. She decided to wait until Bonnie left and then she'd go to the kitchen to play Miss Nice Lady; perhaps learn more to help form her revenge on this family who excluded her. They were rich and she was going to have some of that wealth.

What Sheila had overheard put her in a powerful position to execute her most savage revenge. Bonnie had made Sheila's task really easy. She wasn't quite sure how things would unfold yet but time was on her side. She could certainly afford to play the gracious granddaughter to her benefit.

As her confidence grew, so too did her ability to role-play the part. Sheila felt exhilarated. She was on fire!

As her grandmother cooked dinner, Sheila listened to her grandfather's stories about the early days when he milked cows and repaired machinery. The food smelt delicious and she wished Gran would hurry up as she was starving. She regularly stifled a yawn as he droned on, yet she prodded him to keep talking.

'Grandpa, tell me about the war.'

And so, he talked and talked. Thankfully, Gran arrived with dinner, after what seemed an eternity. Sheila felt famished and, while her headache had gone, her leg had gone to sleep as she hadn't moved for at least an hour, just sat listening as attentively as she could. Frequently, she wanted to get out of her seat and leave the table but she knew she had to play a part. As her eyes glazed over, she reflected on her day.

No, Rodney won't leave his place on the outskirts of Adelaide. It suits him. He liked living in a mess with old things all around him and junk everywhere. He also had a flea-ridden dog which was too lazy to move, *just like Rodney really.* His place was far enough out of town where all the outsiders lived, and each respected the others' privacy. They were all bits of slobs and Rodney was amongst the worst.

She heard Gran ask if she wanted any sweets and, of course, she had a great helping. She loved apple pie with custard and cream, and Gran appreciated good eaters. Ernie didn't eat very much and told Sheila he was looking after his health these days. Sheila breathed easy as her grandmother heaved her way across the kitchen carrying the loaded plates. She shuffled along, her weight preventing her from moving any quicker. Sheila thought she should offer to do the dishes to immerse herself deeper into the role of a good granddaughter and decided that she had completed an excellent day. She watched television with them until she could see they were both sleeping in their chairs. They snored softly as Sheila locked the house and began her pre-nocturnal routine. Her scheme could come together very easily. The old girl would be a pushover, but the old boy might be more of a challenge.

Later, as she snuggled in between the sheets, she couldn't settle and lay considering her next moves. This had been her lucky day.

Chapter Eighteen

Ernie Visits his Son

2006

Ernie began his preparations for travelling to Trevilly quite early in the morning and was soon on his way to Carson and the green paddocks in the southern part of South Australia. He enjoyed driving, particularly on his own, without anyone talking. It gave him time to think. His main aim on this visit was to ask Ian to come and speak with his daughter about vacating the Glenelg home. He rehearsed his lines carefully to avoid offence as the last thing he wanted to do was to upset his son, but he worried too that Sheila had continued to infiltrate his space in his home with Pat, and he didn't want Pat relying on Sheila. As a husband, his role was to look after his wife, first and foremost. He felt that a stranger had snuck into his territory in that regard, and debated whether he should use this kind of language with Ian.

Thinking so hard about these issues, he nearly ran into a passing car at one stage. This jerked him back to reality and, at the age of eighty-odd – he didn't like to think how old he was, and eighty-something suited his thoughts – he needed to concentrate hard on tasks at hand. He'd recently had a cataract operation, so his eyes were sensitive to light. To combat the glare, he always made sure he had his sunglasses and hat on, and regularly caught himself wearing them inside the house too, but Pat didn't seem to notice.

After a couple of slow sections with roadworks, Carson came into sight. Everything was so familiar to Ernie and, as he drove through town, he scanned the street to see if there was anyone he knew. Reason told him his friends had retired, just like he had, and many had moved to Victor Harbour. He and Pat had thought seriously about retiring there too but had decided on Adelaide. Glenelg suited them fine and now, with Bonnie home, life was ideal.

He had a fair idea Ian would be in the shed when he arrived and liked the idea of having his son to himself. Sarah would be at school until the late afternoon, which would give them a chance to talk over a few things. He allowed his Toyota Hilux to glide to a smooth halt near the silos and the auger, narrowly missing the dog that had come out to greet him. All farms had dogs and Ernie instantly felt at ease.

As he walked toward the dairy, he could smell the cow manure and hear a machine whirring in the distance. The sun was still high in the sky after his long drive and he looked forward to a cup of tea which he knew would soon be offered. Then Ian appeared and they shook hands heartily, one man to another.

'Come on, Dad. Let's have a brew. I guess you stopped for one on the way, did you?' They fell into step as they walked towards the house, two dogs accompanying them to the verandah beyond the gate. Soon the kettle was boiling and two large mugs were taken from the cupboard, one chipped, which Ian claimed for himself. Both men liked their tea strong so several teabags accompanied each cup.

'Well, Dad, what brings you to Trevilly, apart from Mum wanting some fresh milk?'

How like Ian to include some reference to milk. Such a champion. 'Son, I've got a favour to ask you and I'm not sure how you'll feel about it, so I'll get straight to the point. I don't suppose you know Sheila is staying with us? I have asked her to find a place of her own and she says yes but then does nothing about it. Remember how I used to talk about my trust antennae? Well, I hate to say it, but I feel something's not quite right.'

Ian put his cup down quietly and paused. Nothing was said and the ticking clock groaned in the ears of both men. Ian reflected on the letter he'd sent Sheila and the sleepless nights he'd had wondering how things would be when they met. He soon realised his sleeplessness had been wasted when Sheila didn't turn up at the Dome on the appointed day. He'd rung Sheila's boss to check if she'd received the letter, his heart missing a beat when he realized the rejection by his only child. He felt flat and sad. His daughter was a grown woman now; she made her own choices, and now Ian felt his old pain returning after all those years. It had taken Ian some time to come to terms with this disappointment; now his father had dropped this bombshell on him. He felt stunned.

After some time, Ian's audible sigh echoed through the room as he recounted his failed efforts to reconnect with Sheila. 'Dad, she's making a choice. How did she know where you lived? Has she stalked you or Mum?' He then told his father about Sheila's visit to the farm so many years ago, and how he'd hid in the shed to avoid her. He now felt shame at that lack of courage in confronting her to find out her true motives for the visit. All he could think about was the antennae radar for trust.

He told his father: 'I wondered what she was going to steal. I wondered why she didn't go to the house. I wondered for years why I didn't trust the situation and leave my hiding spot. The simple truth Dad is, I didn't trust her then and, now, with you telling me this, my trust antennae, which you taught me, is ringing loud and clear.' He shook his head. 'Sorry, Dad, but I don't trust her. Why is she staying with you and why won't she leave?'

'Look, she's quite kind to Pat, and to me at times. She's been staying for some time now but I simply find her a bit of a nuisance. Perhaps I'm being petulant, but she's upset the pecking order in our house. With your mother's illness, I simply want to be the one to look after her and I feel it's time for Sheila to leave.'

Ian smirked at his father's last comment as he lifted his head. 'Bloody women, Dad! You can't trust any of them. Just ask me! But seriously, Dad, I'm at a loss to know what to say, except my radar, like yours, is going off too. Let's sleep on it for now. Let's take a drive around and we might even visit Aunty Enid and the crew. What do you think?'

'Bugger Aunty Enid. She's hard work. She was a bit of a tyrant when she married George and she's probably got worse. Nah, son, let's not visit her. Let's give all women a miss for a bit until the lovely Sarah comes home. Guess if we're going to sleep on things, I'd better ask for a bed.'

'Of course, Dad. You're always welcome and the bed's probably made up from last time. Just take your things in, have a rest and when you're ready, come over to the shed. We'll take a drive around and you can check out the cows. And don't forget your hat and sunglasses! Nice time of the year now so that'll cheer us up! We'll go when the milking starts in a few hours.'

Ian helped Ernie carry in his overnight bags and put them into the spare room. 'You might want to have a bit of a sleep after your long drive, so I'll leave you to it for a bit.'

As Ernie lowered his head onto the pillow, he felt the massive wave of reassurance that always followed conversations with his son. *What a great relief! Ian's going to deal with this bloody woman dilemma. God, they're a nuisance and certainly Ian knows all about this.* He realised his thoughts were a bit harsh as, really, the other two women in Ernie's life were his reason for living. He adored his wife and daughter. As for others, including Enid, they could all get lost. He didn't even want to consider Ian's first wife!

In an instant, Ernie was asleep.

*****

Ian used his time in the shed to distract himself from this enormous problem. Of course, he knew why Sheila had moved into the Glenelg Homestead and he was mortified. He didn't want to remind his aging father of his mortality, nor suggest how 'inheritance impatience' was part of society these days. As soon as he heard the situation, he suspected Sheila was manipulating and positioning herself for the inheritance of the Glenelg Homestead! He'd heard of several situations of fathers and sons being in conflict over farming issues and breathed a sigh of relief when he thought about when Ernie had given the farm to him. Ernie had driven up to the farm to tell him and discuss details on how this was to happen, stating that Ian could run his own show. It had evolved into a tradition, where both men attended the annual bank meeting at Goolwa when the farm budget was discussed, and where Ernie liked to sit back and let Ian do all the talking. Ian had been grateful ever since. And now Sheila looked like she was making a move on his vulnerable parents. He'd discuss this again with his father in the morning after Sarah left for work. This was serious business and he didn't want to burden his father unnecessarily.

After a few hours, he knew he'd have to wake Ernie to show him the new solar panels on the pumps, and outline his plans for buying a new tractor. It seemed to be always about paying tax or bank interest on a farm, or so his father had taught him, and now this conversation had to take place. The dairy business was the easy conversation. The other one would require some overnight thought.

'Wake up, young fella. Time for a farm inspection.'

Ernie woke up with a start. He'd been sound asleep and was pleasantly surprised to find himself in his old house. He jumped up quickly, forgetting about his sore knee, which became increasingly painful the more he walked. Of course, Ian wanted to drive him around the farm to show him what he missed. This ritual filled Ernie with delight as he walked quickly with Ian to the shed, listening to the squawk of the galahs in the trees along the path. God, they were noisy! Flies too were friendly and they intensified as the dairy came closer. Ernie felt sorry for cows as the flies crawled all over their eyes and faces and their only defence was to shake their heads to provide temporary relief.

*****

Sarah was pleased when she saw Ernie's ute near the driveway and remembered she'd left some prime steaks out of the freezer, ideal for a special guest's dinner. She prepared the meal, completed the chores for the day and then sat outside to wait for Ian and Ernie. Fairly soon, she heard the vehicle humming as it approached and looked up to see familiar faces through the windscreen. Inwardly, she smiled. She liked her father-in-law and knew that, despite his sometimes-gruff manner, he approved of her. She knew the whole family warmly embraced her. Then amusingly, she thought it was just as well as she dropped another delicious steak into the pan. No doubt this was Ernie's favourite meal!

The following morning the serious conversations commenced when Ian suggested Ernie stay for a few days. They could go to Goolwa, do the budget with the bank manager, Stan, and then drive to Victor Harbour for lunch at the pub. Ernie's job was to ring Stan and make an appointment and then arrange a visit to his annoying sister-in-law who just talked too much.

In the afternoon, he drove his Hilux to the adjacent farm, through the oat paddock and up to the colonial-style, rather shabby-looking house. He slowly slid out of his vehicle and he remembered painfully the night George died after a night out in the pub. Enid and her family had recovered well after George's death, he thought as he made an effort to listen politely. For some reason, he didn't mention Sheila, instead, happily talked about the upcoming engagement party Ken and Bonnie were planning.

Ernie couldn't miss that Enid's place needed maintenance so he decided to stay an extra few days with Ian and help out Enid and his nephew, Ron. In the interim, Ian and Ernie planned their trip to Goolwa.

Soon it was time to attend the meeting at the bank, so Ian took all his costings for the upgrade of the dairy equipment and the new tractor, and they headed off for the day. Whilst at the bank, Ernie marvelled at internet banking and quietly revelled at his son's intellect.

'How incredible that we can see these bank statements at a click of a button.' Ernie had always been intrigued with the workings of technology, and was disappointed time had marched ahead of him and that he was left in the dust trying to work out which buttons did what. For some time, he'd been forced to acknowledge computers were too advanced for him.

'Why don't you insert your bankcard, Dad, then you can see all your transactions in an instant.' The three men waited until all Ernie's transactions were there on the screen. 'Gosh, Dad, it looks like you've had a few cash withdrawals at the local ATM.'

'But I don't use an ATM. When I want cash, I ask at the local Coles.' Ernie's jaw dropped open. *But bank statements don't lie.*

In silence, the three men examined the computer screen again, not quite sure what they were hoping to see. Ian eventually spoke. 'Dad, do you know what this means? Someone has withdrawn cash from your account using *your* card. And they would need to know your PIN. That's your personal identification number. Dad, do you keep you card in your wallet … with your number written down … also in your wallet?'

Ernie felt his legs go weak. His stomach churned. He was in trouble and it was his fault. Ian had told him not to write down his number but Ernie was afraid he'd forget it. Of course, he kept it in his wallet. Straight away, Ian and Ernie knew someone in the house had taken the card and the number to use for their own means. It wasn't Pat as she didn't know how to use a card. It was Sheila! And neither Ernie nor Ian needed to verbalise this.

Stan, sensitive enough to know when to keep quiet, offered them coffee, which Ian gratefully accepted. It gave him time to have a chat with his father, whose face had now turned ashen.

'Dad, all we have to do now is change your PIN. Stan can do it here. Someone's taken quite a bit of cash out already, but with a new PIN, it won't be happening again. Why don't we make your new number the same as your postcode and then you can remember it without writing it down. Just leave your wallet the way it's always been but you, and you alone, will know what your PIN is and don't tell a soul. Even the bank won't ask you.'

'Yes, son. That sounds like a sensible idea. Thank you. I feel such a fool.' Ernie hung his head. *You had been told.*

After some time, Stan returned with the coffee and they drank in strained silence. 'Dad, would you like me to be able to monitor your transactions?'

'Great idea, Ian,' said Stan. 'We can easily arrange for Ian, or someone else in the family, to have access to your statements online. Ernie, this means Ian can turn on his computer and see your accounts. How do you feel about that?'

Ernie closed his jaw, and fought off his shame. But he was still in a state of disbelief. 'I would absolutely love it. Thank you. I trust my son but there is someone else I don't trust and she's infiltrated my home.'

As they left town after the bank visit, Ian turned to Ernie. 'Dad, at least we know where we stand now. Always trust the radar. She's a shark, Dad, and she needs to be dealt with.'

'I cannot believe it. I'm still in shock. Now, however, I'm starting to feel anger. She must take me for a fool.'

'Don't be too hard on yourself. It's just a good thing we discovered what she's up to. I'll come to your place soon and sort her out. Try not to worry too much. When you return home, just carry on as normal, and I will ring you to let you know when I can come up. Whatever you do, don't say anything to her. I'll deal with the wretch.'

Once again, Ernie rested easily, safe in the hands of his trusted son. He planned his return to Glenelg after doing the maintenance at Enid's and wondered how he could avoid interacting with Sheila.

Chapter Nineteen

Ken Receives an Offer

2007

Ken dropped bread into the toaster as Bonnie walked through the door. She looked exhausted, the night shift proving stressful

'Oh well, at least it allows me to do things during the day,' she said, flopping down onto a chair. 'Not sure if today is a chemo day for Mum but I'll ring her soon.' She spread out the newspaper, relishing the noise of the humming kettle, and Ken whistling softly as he watched the toaster.

'Today I'll go to the Brighton house and ask my family to attend our engagement party. I hope Rhonda doesn't come, but my girls are delighted so I'm sure they will. The joys of an ex-wife!' Ken said, turning from the kitchen bench. 'But today is the day I'm going to do it. Oh, did I tell you … Chris and Andy are keen to organise the party? I reminded them they are our bridal attendants and the party itself will be in November sometime so we can have a January wedding. So, we have a fair bit of time until the party to arrange a guest list and food. Would you like me to liaise with Chris and Andy, now you've started work? Actually, there are lots of bits and pieces I've been putting off until I had more time, so I'll need to attend to paperwork at some stage.'

Ken realised, with his approaching marriage, he'd also need to change his Will. This would mean setting up a meeting with Bonnie's cousin Mal. 'Anyway, shall I go ahead and organise the party?'

Bonnie nodded and smiled. She found working, even only a few nights, was very tiring, and she had to undertake a plethora of professional development as, during her time in Africa, she'd missed out on a lot of changes in the medical world. Now with a sick mother and medical appointments, not to mention an engagement, it was all quite overwhelming. Luckily, Ken's house was in a quiet street so she could sleep during the day. She realised Ken was certainly a 'keeper', as her brother had alluded to, as he was prepared to take on family responsibilities. She felt relieved and was incredibly happy to place the responsibility of family into his capable hands. She remembered the toast in the toaster and alerted him, then put the paper away and tried to look interested in what he had to say, albeit while stifling a yawn.

'Oh yes!' A supercilious grin crossed Ken's face. 'Sheila visited here last night. She made noises about a passport application and papers that need signing. Then she suggested a glass of wine too. She's a hussy, that one, and I'm going to catch her at her game. You just wait and see.'

Ken stacked the toast and brought it, with butter and marmalade, to the table. 'So, what did you say?'

Bonnie's eyebrow rose: this was a new role for the normally conservative Ken.

'I told her I was expecting you home fairly soon and more time was needed for me to examine the documents, or witness a signature, or whatever it was she wanted. I suggested she come over when I had more time in the evening and then we could both have a glass or two of wine. I told her in a few weeks you would be working extra nights, so perhaps it would be a good idea if we met then. I sort of made it clear she needed to be here when you were working. I'm sure she got the drift of it all.'

Bonnie looked at him closely. 'Are you going to record it all to show Mum and Dad? They need to know what they're dealing with. I could imagine her turning up here in her black, tight gear! To put it crudely, she would have been out for a bonk last night, don't you think?'

'She's a tart all right, but she didn't really get much of a foot in the door. But she was very agreeable to my plan. In other words, let's meet later without distractions.'

'So, did she actually come into the house?' Bonnie asked.

'No, we spoke on the doorstep but I was surprised she knew where we lived. She wanted to come in, I could sense that. She eyed me up and down and I did likewise to her! She was on heat.'

'I wouldn't underestimate her, Ken. We can't be caught with our pants down.' Bonnie laughed at her own joke and Ken smiled. 'That's what I love about you, clever kid. Now get to bed before I chase you there.' He collected the dishes and meticulously ensured the sink water was piping hot to kill all the germs. Soon he'd be doing the washing or cleaning something. He loved order and cleanliness, a legacy from his past hospital days.

Bonnie settled into bed, pulled up the blankets and felt ready to sleep. She liked the idea of working the night shift and then coming home for a long leisurely breakfast. The idea of a second cup of coffee was bliss. As she snuggled down, she checked she could see her clock and ensured a glass of water was on her bedside table. She could hear crows outside noisily scavenging scraps just to stay alive and listened till the drowsiness overtook her and she drifted off to sleep.

She awoke to Ken's phone ringing. At long last, he answered it and Bonnie listened to ascertain the caller's identity. In the lounge, Ken had likely fallen asleep while watching football, and this was probably a call from the hospital requesting him to attend. Quite often he accepted work and this complimented times when Bonnie clocked on too. However, as she lay in bed, she quickly realised it wasn't the hospital. In fact, the caller was quite upset if Ken's responses were anything to go by. As Bonnie looked at the clock, she thought she'd dress ready for work. She would have an evening meal and then catch the tram into town for another shift at the hospital.

As she left the bedroom, she caught the tone of Ken's

conversation – agitated. She stopped and listened. *He's talking to Dad!*

Bonnie became more alert. Her father never phoned Ken, and a chill washed over her. *Is everything all right at home? Mum?*

'Your father's coming here,' Ken told her. 'He's on his way. Not quite sure what's up, but he sounds furious. I think it's something to do with your mother.'

Bonnie quickly placed last night's curry in the microwave in case her father stayed for dinner. Even if he didn't stay, she'd need to eat before going to work. She tried not to worry, *but what on earth is wrong?* She knew he'd been staying with Ian and Sarah for the last week. *Surely nothing's wrong there?*

Soon Ernie was banging at the front door, and calling out to them. 'Ernie, come on in and sit down.' *Thank goodness for Ken*, she thought and left it to Ken to manage, but her brow furrowed as she sat down next to her father. He was clearly distressed and dishevelled as he slunk into the chair, repeating, 'How could this happen?'

'How could what happen, Dad?'

'I'm so mad, just so mad!' Ernie screamed repeatedly. 'That bloody Sheila. She's infiltrated our household. I'm frigging furious, Ken. Furious! And she's stealing money from my bank account, but Ian dealt with that issue at the bank.'

'Take your time, Ernie. We're here. It's all right. Just take it easy and we'll talk about one thing at a time. What's happened?'

'Well, I got home from Trevilly and you wouldn't believe what I found!'

Bonnie had never seen her father so upset and distressed.

'Pat has made Sheila our legal carer! It's just not right. I don't know how it happened. When I asked Pat, she blamed me and said that I was away and Sheila was there to take care of her and Sheila would take care of me too. Bloody hell. That's not going to happen but Ken, it has. Sheila had forms from the hospital that she took to Centrelink and Pat signed, for both of us. Sheila's turned your mother against me. I went to kick her out, but Pat wouldn't have it.'

From their medical experience, Ken and Bonnie knew when to let a person rant, and poor Ernie was ranting now. He was beside himself, waving his arms in the air and gulping down breaths as he told his tale. At one point, he leapt out of his chair, paced the room and then sat down again. He kept repeating himself, and still Bonnie and Ken kept quiet, allowing him to unburden himself.

'Ernie, just take your time. I'll get us both a beer,' Ken said.

'Bon, Sheila's a nightmare! She's manipulated your poor mother and now Mum doesn't know what to think. Ken … Bonnie, what shall I do?'

'Okay, Ernie. What did Sheila do exactly?' Ken said, coming back to the room.

Ernie started to drink his beer and then let it out again in more detail. 'Apparently, Sheila told Pat that she'd lost her job. Then she told your mother she wanted to look after her and played the loving grandchild.'

'Uh-oh. Looks like Sheila groomed Pat while you were away at Ian's. She's taken advantage of your absence to target and manipulate a vulnerable person. We noticed poor Pat's vulnerability and absent-mindedness creeping in. Ernie, Sheila's not a very nice person.'

But Ernie hadn't finished his story. '… and I go to kick her out and Pat won't let me! Pat's gone mad. She was furious when I told Sheila to 'get out'. I've never seen your mother like this so it's not just Sheila, but Pat too. Bloody hell.'

Ken and Bonnie glanced at each other while Ernie held his head in his hands. Bonnie moved closer to her father and put her arm around him. Then Ken, the doctor, stepped in. 'Ernie, have you noticed any aggressive behaviour in Pat over the last few months? Just little things?'

'I sure have,' Ernie blurted out. 'She's just become unreasonable and seems angry all the time. She started off vague and unreachable but now she's just off the planet. I sure as hell can't talk or reason with her.'

'Ernie, sometimes people can have a series of mini-strokes which damage the frontal lobe – the front of the brain. This is the part of the brain where decisions are made. It's all about inhibitions and our personality. Sometimes individuals become aggressive. All this chemo, too, won't be helping. The chemicals used can ultimately poison people in the long term. Poor Pat. She's not in a good place.'

'So, not only has she lost her marbles but she's making bad decisions. I can't deal with all this. Bon, Ken, what are we going to do?' Ernie's head dropped back into his hands.

'How about a visit to her local doctor, Ernie. Do you think she'd go? She needs to be assessed by professionals.'

'She wouldn't go. She won't do anything I suggest.'

'Righto, Dad. Let's eat dinner, then I'll go to work and Ken will help you. You can trust him and he knows what he's talking about.'

When food was put on the table, normality reigned, each of them looking at the meal in front of them, deep in their own thoughts. Ernie just sat, refusing another drink and staying silent.

'Dad, has Mum lost her appetite in recent months? I know it's some time now since the chemo started, and it's certainly managing to keep the cancer in check, but perhaps the cancer path has changed. Ken, what do you think?'

'I can see Pat's lost a bit of weight, which is expected in cancer patients, but this change in behaviour suggests something else is going on. Perhaps the cancer has metastasised and spread.'

Bonnie shuddered inwardly. 'Recently Mum told me that all food tastes metallic. I thought it was strange, but, Ken, is it significant?'

'It is indeed significant. It indicates a stroke. That's consistent with frontal lobe damage in the brain. She probably wasn't even aware of anything different and even if she was, patients often are too sick to really observe a difference. It's certainly consistent with her change in behaviour and aggression. The only way one could be certain would be with tests, but I imagine Pat won't want this done, not in her current mindset.'

Ken cleared the dishes, put the coffee percolator on and Bonnie left for work. She was distressed but confident Ken would handle the situation.

'Ken, what am I going to do?' she heard her father moan as she headed out the door. 'I don't want Sheila to be anyone's legal carer. Not mine, nor Pat's. She says she felt sorry for Sheila having no job.'

'Ernie, tomorrow, we'll go to Centrelink and get this legal carer business sorted out. Don't worry. It is easily repaired. I will go with you and do all the talking. You don't need or qualify for a carer so someone has been telling a few lies. Now I suggest you go home. Don't say anything to anyone, and I will pick you up first thing in the morning. How does that sound?'

'Thanks, Ken.' Ernie had another cup of coffee. Being in no state to drive for some time, he watched some mindless television with Ken and thanked his lucky stars Bonnie's man was such a great person. He told Ken how much he looked forward to having him as a son-in-law.

Soon Ernie felt the return of comfort enveloping his being. His eyes kept shutting and his head kept dropping forward. At one stage, he started to nod off and jumped out of the chair in a bid to wake himself up and regain alertness. Steadying himself on the arm of the lounge chair, he bid Ken good night and thanked him for being such a good listener. Ernie fell asleep easily these days, so he took himself off home, confident Ken could solve his problems the next day. Then life could resume its normalcy. He was hopeful, too, that Ian would visit soon to evict Sheila.

Chapter Twenty

Sheila Weaves her Web

2007

Ernie awoke the next morning realising he'd have to interact with the devious Sheila, so he decided to stay in bed until he heard the front door slam. But he didn't hear any slamming or shutting of doors. *Perhaps she's cleared out and left.* But he knew he wouldn't be so lucky; she'd probably left early for work. He sincerely hoped nothing else had been done in the Glenelg Homestead while he was away; he certainly didn't want any more surprises.

Slowly he made his way down the passage and into the kitchen. There was no sign of anyone, and he breathed with relief. He remembered the conversations from the previous day and hoped Ken would soon arrive to undo the unpleasant events that had happened while he'd been away at the farm.

At Sheila's work, all her possessions were gathered and put in her bag. She grabbed her lunch from the fridge and left without a word to anyone and was grateful she didn't meet anyone in the lift where she'd have to make small talk and exchange the time of day. Her line manager had pointed out discrepancies in her accounting, suggesting some funds had been transferred into an account that was not one of their nominated payment accounts. She felt irritated this discrepancy had been noticed, and her boss had suggested she resign before an investigation began. Misappropriation of funds had been referred to by her line manager. Sheila knew what this meant! She realised that she'd better leave soon before the police were called and was grateful, in a way, for the chance to move on without any fuss.

She reflected on the events of the past week or so as her old car purred along the main road towards Glenelg, Sheila preparing herself for her next move. Long ago, she'd changed her address on her driver's licence, bank accounts and electoral roll to reflect her main place of residence at her grandparent's house. Now she luxuriated in this knowledge. She had already told her grandmother she was out of work and, as she arrived, she saw Grandpa's Hilux wasn't in its usual place. He was still at Trevilly, so it was just the old girl at home.

Sheila had braced herself and realised this could be her opportunity to have a quiet word in the ear of this hopeless old woman who wouldn't know what time of day it was. Her mood suddenly improved as she cut the engine and prepared to eat her lunch in her car. She felt like a meth hit but she'd recently stopped using, knowing it was expensive. She also sensed she needed more of it to give herself a greater high. That was not a good sign, so several weeks ago, she'd just quit. *No more meth for me*, she thought. *I'm a dealer, not a user*. She thought about her deliveries for that night as she ate her lunch and realised the three drop-offs would be quite lucrative. However, what she planned with the old girl was going to be even better, if things went her way.

Eventually, she went inside and made a cup of tea for herself and her grandmother. A few tears didn't go astray too in the telling of the tale, which, of course, varied greatly from the line manager's version.

'Gran, why don't I become a carer for you and Grandpa? Then I can take you to all your appointments, given that he isn't here. Where is he? I can't believe he left you when you need him so much. You poor thing, Gran.'

Sheila worked her magic. Soon she was on the inner sanctum and poor old Ernie, who was with Ian, was on the outer – which was just what Sheila wanted!

'I've got a good idea, Gran! Why don't we make this all legal so the government pays me to be your carer and it can be my new job?'

Pat thought this was a great idea so Sheila set up her computer and printer in her room. 'There's a slight problem. Gran, are you able to sign on Grandpa's behalf?'

'Of course. I have power of attorney for him and he's not here. Let's just get on with this.'

Soon the pens were found and forms were signed so both parties were happy. She would make an appointment at Centrelink to verify everything, taking Pat, who would verify she was a carer to both.

'Thanks, Gran, for giving me my new job. Now I can make us a cup of tea and have some of the lovely chocolate cake you made yesterday. Or was it the day before?'

Sheila made a mental note while the kettle boiled that she could easily increase her grandmother's dependency on her by creating confusion around her appointment times; just like her grandmother couldn't remember when she'd made the chocolate cake. Now all she had to do was to wait for those government payments to come into her bank account each fortnight. Having free rent, it was enough to survive on until she inherited the house. She laughed inwardly: she knew she'd been sacked for a reason! She knew deep down, if she told herself a story often enough, then even she would come to believe it. And it was easy enough to convince others!

In the late afternoon, Sheila heard the Hilux pulling into the driveway. This was her cue to escape and let Gran inform Grandpa of the new rules in the house. She went to her room, shut the door and lay on the bed so she could listen to the fallout. And she was right in her anticipation of fallout! Grandpa was furious and what followed was a huge argument between the two oldies. Old Gran was laying down the rules, blaming Grandpa for not taking her to hospital appointments, accusing him of not caring and anything else that came out of her mouth, which was usually so lovable.

They were both furious and the argument so heated Sheila thought either of them could suffer a heart attack and die. Then Grandpa made a phone call, the front door slammed and the Hilux roared down the street.

Though painfully aware she had deliveries to do around sunset, Sheila stayed in her room for a while. It had been a big day and she was indeed quite tired. She lay on the bed and pondered the merits of her plan, almost drooling over how it was evolving. She felt like making a checklist, just like criminals record their trophies with photos of victims, but realised this was being childish. Besides, she was firmly settled in the house with one of the key players on her side. She would work on the other next and slowly win him over with her angelic nature. She nearly laughed out loud then realised nothing was stopping her from laughing. As for dumb Ken, he was easy pickings and her plan for him included Rohypnol – roofies – liquid ecstasy. She would ask Rodney to source some at their next meeting. Or she might have to contact Luke, who had a smorgasbord of narcotics, whereas Rodney made his own meth. Then she would instigate her plan – spike lover boy's drink so he'd pass out and then inject him with enough meth, or some morphine, to take him into the next world. The fool had almost set a date!

She lay on the bed thinking of other plans too but it was early days. Her grandmother had been ill for years but unfortunately looked like she wasn't going anywhere soon. As for her grandfather, he was a force to be reckoned with. She might have to do exactly what she'd signed up for – look after them until they both dropped off the perch.

She almost dozed off but looked at the clock in time to see she would need to keep moving. She opened her bedroom door and went to find Gran, flicking on the kettle as she went past. She didn't really like tea. It was an old person's drink, but she would drink it just to be social with the old girl. And there she was, head bowed, asleep in her chair, with the television blaring. It seemed all old people were deaf so Sheila coughed loudly to wake her, asking if she wanted any tea. She had to repeat it and Sheila found this really tried her patience. She'd only been a carer for a day but already she felt like she needed respite. Thankfully, no tea was required so Sheila went and showered.

She let the hot water run over her as she washed her hair, standing in the shower for ages. She thought she'd take her work clothes – black skirt, neat blouse and jacket, black stockings and high heels – with her in the car and make a little fire on the beach and burn them. *What a ritual that will be.* She'd always been intrigued by fires and this was now the end of an era for her! This was the end of her life as a middle-management worker. She liked the idea, knowing when she returned home she could buy some takeaway somewhere so she could go straight to her room. Hopefully, the oldies would be asleep.

She turned off the water and towelled herself dry, making a mental note of the delivery places and soon she was in the car ready for the first café. The little plastic bags with their contents of white powder assuming their rightful place in her handbag were worth a lot of money.

Her 'clients' had a routine to follow to minimise disruption or the chances of suspicion, and Sheila explained this to them. Firstly, they had to do the exchange at a café, then a pub and finally at the beach. Then a month later, this routine changed again, the aim to not be predictable. Clients could name the café, pub and beach but mainly it was kept local so the deliveries were not too far from Glenelg. New contacts were welcome. But it was strictly cash on delivery. Phone numbers were provided but no one was to text and changes in arrangements were not welcome.

The evenings were still quite cold so Sheila put her coat on and rubbed her hands together to keep them warm. Her jeans, sneakers and black t-shirt formed her evening uniform and her beanie was for outdoors. She even made a point of parking in different places to avoid a predictable routine. Eventually, all deliveries were done; talking was kept to a minimum and exchanges were made unobtrusively.

Now she could make a firepit in a quiet part of the sand dunes and burn her work clothes. Driving slowly along the road, looking for a dark, lonely place to do this, she turned off the radio. She really didn't like listening to music, and talk-back radio was outright ridiculous. She couldn't fathom why anyone would want to ring a radio station to talk about rubbish. *But then, there are a lot of crazy people out there who get enjoyment from anything.*

Before long, she found a lonely part of the sand dunes and stopped the car. Looking around, she saw no one, so bundled up her clothes from the back seat and set off across the footpath towards the beach. She felt for the matches and the little shovel in her jacket as she ran and felt relieved they were in the right place. A slight breeze blew, bringing hip-hop music in the distance to her ears. She retrieved her shovel from her pocket and dug a hole in the dunes, scooping out carefully and ensuring the sides were high enough to hold her clothes. Finally, she put some firelighters in amongst the fabric and inhaled the kerosene smell. It was intoxicating and she sat back for a few moments to relish what she was about to do.

The night was sufficiently dark that she had trouble seeing what she was doing but soon she struck a match and the flame created enough light for her to ignite the firelighters. It caught alight quickly and she smiled as her clothes turned black and crinkled amongst the smoke. Soon the flames took hold and this was the part Sheila liked the best. She imagined herself in some old-fashioned ritual, where she was a witch with all the power. Then she laughed loudly, realising she was gaining power in just the right direction! She was never going to take orders from anyone in Accounts Department again, and there would be no line managers in her future. No more high heels, no more meetings, no more deadlines. *I am in heaven!*

The flames leapt higher with no one in sight to annoy her.

Sheila watched the flames until there was nothing left to burn.

The coolness of the ocean spread through the pristine air, over the beach and up into the dunes. Waves crashed onto the sand, and the hip-hop music had stopped. She listened, as others had listened over the centuries, to feel the magic and intrigue. Time had no place then. She almost fell asleep on the sand but realised she had a car to drive and a roadway to navigate. She'd heard someone once say that driving a car was like driving a lethal weapon, and she thought about this as she slowly stood up. She was beholden to no one and was pleased about this. But now it was time to go home. Perhaps she'd come here again if life became difficult.

So self-satisfied, Sheila had travelled a short distance before remembering to switch on the headlights. She had enjoyed the last hour or so at the beach and now would have to endure the old people. She hoped they were in bed, and, as luck had it, the Glenelg Homestead was in darkness. Sheila turned the key in the front door and then realised she'd forgotten to have dinner. The fridge provided leftovers and there was always ice cream in the freezer, so she didn't go to bed on an empty stomach. She munched away on what she could scavenge up in the kitchen, put her dishes in the sink noisily and went to her bedroom, oblivious to the loud bang of her door.

Chapter Twenty-One

Engagement Party Preparations

2007

Ken was pleased he'd helped Ernie and thought about the caring family which was soon to be his own as he drove from the Glenelg Homestead towards his house. Ernie had been waiting for him, keen to ensure Sheila was not his carer. He wanted to prevent this as soon as possible and had even made a joke about dying in his sleep or becoming incapacitated overnight. The whole procedure had been quite smooth as Ernie advised the Centrelink staff member, thus Sheila's payment for Ernie was cancelled. Ken and Ernie chuckled when they realised Sheila would not be receiving the income she'd anticipated. What would she do about it? They guessed she wouldn't be approaching Ernie!

'I need to call Ian and let him know what's happened. Actually, we need to discuss a few things and sly Sheila's just brought it to a head. I'll do this as soon as I can and I don't want to be distracted.'

Ken turned to him as he pulled up in Ernie's driveway. 'I'll call you later in the day … hope you survive a Sheila onslaught!'

But Ernie knew Sheila would avoid him. She was smart, and he would be on his guard. Reluctantly, he opened the car door and took deliberate moves to extract himself from the seat. He had his sunglasses and hat on to keep the sun away, and his red checked shirt was crumpled, just like his skin.

As he alighted from the car, Ken watched him move slowly up the driveway and felt his elderly friend's pain, this man who would soon be his father-in-law. He felt reluctant to leave but eventually turned the key in the ignition as Ernie entered his front door.

All too soon, the Prado pulled into its own driveway and, a few minutes later, Ken made his way through the garage and in through the front door. He went into the kitchen, thinking about the phone calls he'd need to make to organise the engagement party. Andy and Chris were coming soon so the guest list preparation would begin. So, too, would the catering ideas. Ken perused the internet for party equipment suppliers to assist in their planning, surprised by how many local companies offered this service, so he assumed it would be quite easy. Looking at all the delicious food made Ken's mouth water and his tummy rumble. He rose from his seat, thinking it was well and truly time for his morning coffee and he would liked to have had morning tea with his future in-laws but the thought of interacting with Sheila made him feel uneasy. When he thought about it, he realised he felt uneasy about Sheila for many different reasons.

He was saved from giving it further thought as the coffee percolator began boiling, and the doorbell rang.

Chris and Andy were full of excitement and Ken found this contagious as he made coffee for three instead of coffee for one. Still clouded in thought, Ken put the internet pages he'd printed onto the table as they sat ready to embark on planning for this life-changing event.

'Shall we start with the catering or the guest list?'

'Let's think about who we can ask and then we can think about food.' Andy hunted for a pen and paper from his backpack so he could start writing names. 'This is going to be a reunion for all those medicos you've known for years. How far back do you think we should go?' Andy groaned and shifted in his chair as he stretched his legs. 'Do we just start with the obvious and then work our way down until we've got a full house? You're a numbers man, Ken. How many people do you need to fill this house?'

'It's November we're planning for so why not have it outside and we can hire one of those gas heaters if it's still cool.' Ken felt a chill run through his body and hoped he wasn't coming down with a cold. He thought about taking a Panadol but chose to wait until Andy and Chris went home, hoping they wouldn't stay too long. He'd raked up the leaves in the backyard yesterday and perhaps he'd overdone it as his knee was also sore. The backyard was large and Ken thought it'd be a good idea if he and Bonnie considered living somewhere smaller after they were married. For now, though, the house was close to the hospital and tram line, and also close to Bonnie's parents, who needed them at this critical time.

Just as his mind was starting to wander further, Andy asked him about renting a heater for the party which jerked Ken's thinking back to the present.

'Yes, I'll organise the gas heater. Let's work on about fifty for the engagement party and then we'll look at the same crowd for the wedding, which we thought we'd have some time after Christmas. The Adelaide Hills look beautiful anytime so that's our plan at the moment.'

'What a pity Bonnie's not here. But then, I guess she's settling into work, Ken, is she?' Andy said at the same time as composing the guest list. Chris scrutinised the pamphlets from nearby catering businesses.

'Bon started on nights but lately, she accepted a few day shifts too. She's happy doing work on the wards and it all fits in with parent visits and domestic stuff. It allows me to do house business, plus a bit of contract work during the day. No nights for me! Anyway, I've got a party to organise and a wedding to think about! How good is that? Then I cook for us in the evenings or whatever shifts fit Bonnie's roster. Lucky, we live reasonably close to the hospital. It makes life easy really. However, I must make an appointment with the accountant, but I think I'll leave it until after the party. I hate doing office work. Good old Stephen can sort me out, but I must remember to do it before too long.'

Chris looked up from the mass of pamphlets on the coffee table and moved towards Ken so they could see the brochures she had selected, so the food organisation commenced. There were photos showing food and prices which all looked impressive. Ken felt dizzy and his headache intensified. 'Chris, I just need to take a Panadol. I've developed a headache and I'm really not feeling well. Can you just do the ordering for me? Let's do a supper for fifty people. Thanks, and I'll leave it to you. Just let me know the costs.'

'Ken, we might shoot off home now. Why don't I organise the heater too? I'll make out a guest list of twenty or so from our old workmates, bring it around tomorrow and then you can do the family guest list after Bonnie gets home tonight. We can start writing out the invitations tomorrow or we can wait until the weekend when Bon is home. Oh yes, and Chris can organise the food after you set a date for this party!'

Andy could see Ken looked really tired so it was clearly time to go.

After they left, Ken decided to lay down until he heard the front door opening, signalling the end of Bonnie's day at work. She wouldn't undertake a double shift, so he looked forward to dinner together. There was a lot they needed to discuss but he tried to put thoughts out of his mind and let the Panadol ease his headache. But he couldn't go to sleep or relax: he kept thinking about how he and Bonnie were going to expose Sheila as the tart and charlatan she was. When a party date had been set, he would seek out Sheila and let her know she could come over the night after the party. Then she could get her passport, or whatever paperwork it was, signed and Ken would organise a recording of the night to oust her. They needed to catch her at her shenanigans and a voice recording device of some sort would accomplish this mission. Bonnie would consult her roster for the party date and ensure she was working the following night. Perhaps she would even change her roster for night duty. With Sheila recorded trying to seduce him, Pat would be disgusted with Sheila and her promiscuous behaviour. This would constitute the proof needed, but it had to remain confidential for the moment. Sheila was smart and Ken had to be careful in exposing her. He wondered how she managed to hold down such a demanding and responsible job but wasn't going to lose sleep over it as he pondered the intelligence of many successful, sneaky people. He'd seen it in his own work as a surgeon with responsible people prescribing drugs for so-called friends, who would sell the products outside the hospital to drug dealers. He also suspected particular doctors were falsifying their records for their own use or the use of others. In large organisations, smart people worked the system to meet their own needs, and hospitals were prime targets, from employees at all levels. He'd seen much corruption over his many years as a doctor, yet it always surprised him. He'd seen many colleagues lose their good reputations by the slightest hint of inappropriateness. Regularly he'd thought situations were unfair, but reputations could easily be dented and they all had to guard against any slurs. Just as he was thinking of a case in his early years as a doctor, he heard the key turning in the front door.

'Bonnie, is that you?'

'Of course it is! Who did you think it could be?'

Ken quickly left the bed and went to embrace her. He was totally in love and realised he'd loved her for many years. Now, becoming part of her wonderful family was such a privilege, but he felt upset poor Ernie was unhappy. He remembered he had to phone him, as he'd promised earlier in the morning. His day had been a challenge and just thinking about Sheila made his day even worse.

'Let's light up the barbeque and cook those beautiful steaks we bought yesterday. I'll do it so we can eat early and have a night on the couch. What do you think?'

'Excellent idea,' Bonnie replied as she headed to the bathroom for a shower. She let the warm water pour over her and felt rejuvenated. *Let the night begin and thank goodness I'm home for this one,* she thought. She heard Ken calling but figured he'd work out something. He always did and he didn't need her help, she mused.

She felt thankful for her great life and the way it was unfolding was delightful. But they needed to expose Sheila and get rid of her.

Ken used this time to call Ernie and braced himself. Ernie was still upset, but thankful Ian was visiting on the weekend to deal with sly Sheila. Ken promised to ring after the weekend visit and went outside to light the barbeque and the mosquito coils. He tried not to think of the carnage that would be unfolding in his in-law's house in the next few days as Sheila achieved her goal of sabotaging the relationship between her grandparents. There were three people clearly established in the Glenelg Homestead, and a demarcation had been drawn between the opposing sides. Ernie's words rang in Ken's ears, and he decided not to inflict this pain on Bonnie by telling her tonight. Perhaps, after Ian's visit, Bonnie might have to drop in to pick up the fragments of her parents' relationship. Ken hoped it wasn't too bad, but he felt pessimistic as he struck a match and watched the gas ignite. Flames were burning on several fronts and it was dependent on the outcome of Ian's weekend visit.

But Ian's visit only served to inflame the situation further. Sheila refused to move out, and Pat took her side against Ernie, so Bonnie took time off work after the weekend to visit her parents. She thought she'd call Ian to ascertain his version of events, plus she liked to keep in touch. The news from Ian wasn't good – he'd made an appointment with Mal to see what the legal situation entailed, and he'd be taking his father with him.

The ever-calm Ken added his opinion. 'Bonnie, it's easy to overreact to these emotive issues; let's talk about this before you say anything to your parents. From a medical perspective, Pat's chemo days will be ending shortly. She's been given extra time but I hate to say that this will soon come to an end. I don't think she has many weeks or months to live. Clearly, her brain is deteriorating; whether it's the chemo or the illness doesn't matter. When you see her, you need to be objective about her cognitive impairment and we've both seen patients with frontal lobe damage.

Their behaviour can be atrocious.

'From what Ernie's said, she's confused and uncooperative. We both know what that looks like in the end-of-life stage. Also, remember our plan to expose Sheila the night after our engagement party. I'm going to buy some recording equipment, small enough to wear under my shirt so that we can act after we have evidence of her bad form, which your mum will hate. Sure, it might not be legal, but seducing me … well, who does that?'

'Yes,' said Bonnie quietly. She didn't want to upset either of her parents but she didn't want them to be manipulated like they were, particularly her mother. But she didn't want them at odds with each other because of Sheila. She couldn't bear the thought of her mother dying and her father holding this grudge against his wife. She knew her dad was tough, but she'd never seen her parents in this particular predicament. Ernie was paternalistic, to the point of being outright bossy, even controlling, and this was a position never challenged by anyone, so she could well imagine Ernie would want Ian to seek legal advice from Mal. Bonnie shook her head, unsure what to do.

'Ken, perhaps I'll see Mum and Dad and then find out what day Mal calls in. I think he still comes each week or so with the pretence of doing the roses but he always stays for one of Mum's famous afternoon teas. I'll just ask questions and will not breathe a word to anyone about our plan to expose Sheila when she makes a move on you. Perhaps we should set a definite date for the engagement party. We don't want Mum and Dad agitated by this awful person inhabiting their home for any longer than necessary.'

'I agree. The party can happen whenever we choose, Bon. I can have those invitations in the mail by the end of the week. So, what date, my love, suits you?'

They set the party date for the first Saturday night in November.

Chapter Twenty-Two

Mal's Advice

2007

Mal's old Volvo pulled into its bay marked 'Director' in the carpark off a quiet street in Brighton. He liked this car, and it had seen many trips to where he worked as a lawyer and Carson to visit the family farm and see his mother and brother, Ron. Each time he visited, he was reminded of his father's death on that fateful Sunday night so many years ago, when Uncle Ernie delivered the dreadful news to his mother. He pushed this thought away as he quickly ran a comb through his hair.

The day began like any other with Mal thinking about his workday ahead. He didn't have many appointments or meetings. He didn't have to be in court either so he could have a leisurely coffee to start the day. This also meant he could leave early and visit his Uncle Ernie and Aunt Pat on his way home. He shut the car door and made his way across the carpark to the building marked 'FINCH LAWYERS' where he opened the double glass doors and entered the building. Several women were already at work and he liked the idea of his secretary at her desk taking early morning phone calls. She handed him his mail as he passed the reception desk.

There was an invitation to Bonnie and Ken's engagement party, which he put to the side as he slotted the event into his calendar. He thought it a bit strange that it was mailed to his work address and not his home address, but then quickly dismissed the thought as the phone rang. It was an internal call, put through by

Reception. Much to his surprise, it was Uncle Ernie.

'Ernie, my friend. What's up?'

'Mal, it's awful. I have Ian here with me and I think we might need to talk to you about some serious business. I know you often pop in on Mondays, but this stuff needs to have no extra ears, if you know what I mean. Do you have some time in your day?'

'Ernie, I always have time for you, and yes today is a good day — even better if I can see Ian. How about I meet you for lunch at the little café downstairs? My shout. I need to make up for all those afternoon teas at your place.'

Mal deliberately met 'family' at an outside venue so his secretary didn't bill them for an appointment. As director, Mal didn't really have a lot of clients because running a large law firm was a full-time job and recent compliance laws had added to everyone's workload, particularly his. This made him reluctant to take on new clients and he often referred them to other lawyers working for him. However, he missed the human contact and would have preferred not to do compliancy work, but it came as a total necessity, not to mention the dreadful happenings if his employees didn't comply with updates to legislation.

Lunchtime came around soon enough and people began moving around the office. Ian and Ernie were already in the café when Mal entered. He sat down, looked at Ernie and immediately saw he was upset. 'Shall I order for us before we start talking?'

Ian nodded and Mal went to the counter. He knew the staff in this café but even they had the discretion to know when to act in a solemn way and read the state of play. This was not a day to be jovial and frivolous. Soon the food was delivered to the table and the men began eating.

Ian started: 'Mal, I'm sure you remember my estranged daughter, Sheila.' Ian didn't wait for a reply. He had a message to deliver, so didn't care if Mal remembered or not. 'Well, she's moved into the Glenelg Homestead and refuses to move out. That's really the essence of the issue. That's why we've come to see you.'

Mal chewed on his ham sandwich and swallowed a mouthful of tea. 'I assume you have both asked her to move out?'

Ernie and Ian answered together and Mal frowned as he realised this was serious, both personally and legally. Clearly, they were angry and upset by the looks on their faces. Silence reigned for a minute or so while they ate their lunch and Mal contemplated the enormity of their statements. 'And where does Aunty Pat sit with all this?'

'She wants Sheila to stay as she feels sorry for her. You can imagine all the talk that's gone on.' Then Ernie's voice lifted in pitch. 'Sheila didn't have a father when she was growing up so now she can join the family,' he mimicked Pat in falsetto, throwing his hands up as he spoke. 'Pat's lost her marbles is all I can say. She won't listen to me and she refuses to see reason.'

'What do you mean she won't see reason?' Mal frowned. He knew his uncle could be a bit of a controller, but he was keen to hear what this phrase meant in this uncle's words. He knew he was using lawyer techniques to ascertain a degree of clarity, but he needed to hear what Ernie had to say.

Ian started to speak. 'When Dad and I went to the bank a week or so ago, we discovered that money had regularly been withdrawn from Dad's account. The PIN was in Dad's wallet so someone took the PIN and the card to withdraw money at the local automatic teller machine. Dad hadn't given anyone permission to touch his wallet but he did confess to leaving it around the house. Perhaps he left it on the bench or the table.'

'A bloke's got a right to leave his wallet in his house without someone thieving from it,' Ernie shouted as he banged his fist on the table. 'Well, someone's stolen it and used it.'

'It's all right, Dad. We're just telling Mal. It's not your fault at all.'

'Anyway, that's one thing, and of course, Mum didn't believe us when we told her. In fact, she's got no idea now how banking works, so it was all beyond her. She's that far gone.' Ian shook his head.

'That's terrible for poor Aunty Pat. What does the doctor say?'

'Pat won't discuss this with anyone and refuses to think there's an issue. And I use the word 'issue' really as a euphemism. She's happy to have chemo but that's as far as anything medical goes.'

Ernie calmed down again and resumed eating his sandwich. Mal watched him wolf down his food and wondered if Aunty Pat still cooked beautiful scones for morning tea. He felt like asking but didn't think this context was appropriate.

'Denial, eh? It's not unusual, guys, but it does make Aunty Pat vulnerable to charlatans or anyone who is prepared to listen to her. I'm assuming this Sheila is saying and doing all the right things, according to Pat?'

'Look, Mal, Sheila's in and I'm out. It's as simple as that.' Ernie heaved a deep breath, but the quaver in his voice was palpable.

Ian put down his sandwich and breathed in deeply. 'Some time ago, I wrote to Sheila requesting a reconciliation, but she turned me down. I even rang her workplace to ensure she'd received my letter. All I could assume was she was angry. She didn't want to hear from me. She'd made it quite clear. And now she's in the house all over Mum, and Dad's on the outer. Somehow, she knows how to divide families. I can only wonder why and wonder where this is all going to end up.'

The three men continued to eat their lunch and were surrounded by café noises and people going about their daily business. The waitress brought out fresh teas and left without saying a word.

'My gut reaction is: get her out of there but I can see it's not easy. Apart from that, Uncle Ernie, how is Aunty Pat's health? She seems to have been having chemo for so long. I know we're veering away from the topic but it could be relevant in the big picture. I'm so sorry for you both but let's look at this in a rational manner. Have you spoken with Ken about Aunty's medical condition?'

Ernie scratched his head, thinking, then he said, 'Yes, I have. He was a bit vague too. He basically said that she was living quite well, despite her cancer, which appears to be contained by the chemo. At this stage it hasn't spread but no one could be sure of when her downward spiral will begin. Even oncologists can't be certain about her time left. He explained that once her cancer spread, then her end would be near.'

'Righto, Uncle Ernie. I know this sounds heartless but from a legal perspective, Aunty owns half the house and so do you. I know Scott deals with all your legal business, including your Wills, and you have clearly bequeathed the house to Bonnie, but while you own the house, you're all right. I don't know how to say this, but once Aunty dies, then you own the whole house, so you can ask Sheila to leave with legal authority. I suggest you do it when I'm there. If she refuses, we call the police. I can do that for you.'

'Good, Mal. It sounds like a plan.' Ernie looked pleased. 'Pat and I checked our Wills only a year or so ago with Scott and it was simple. Yes, we bequeathed the house, and any money left over to Bonnie. We gave the dairy to Ian some time ago so Ian is happy, and we will bequeath some small personal effects to him. Ian, you're okay with it, aren't you?'

'Absolutely, Dad. It's all set in place so it must give you some comfort.' Ian remembered he had other things to do before he left for Carson and those tasks would take the rest of the day. He didn't really want to drive home late at night as he suddenly felt tired.

'Mal, would it be okay if we went out for a meal tonight and then I camp at your place for the night? We could spend some time together and have a few drinks while we're at it. Sorry, Dad, but I can't stay with you while Sheila's there. It's dreadful. She's my daughter and I should love her but I know she's up to no good and I always remember our conversations about trust. I hate to say it, but I don't trust her. And that brings me great pain.'

'Look, son, you go about your business today and then spend the night with Mal. I'll go on home now.'

'Ernie, one thing to remember before we go. Be nice to both those ladies and remember that our plan will work. Like you, I don't want bad blood to exist between you and Aunty Pat. Who knows how much longer she has to live? But when poor Aunty has passed, we will act. Not before, Ernie.'

'Ladies! They're not ladies! I feel like killing one of them. That could solve the problem.' Ernie laughed at his joke.

'Yeah, Ernie, then you'd really need me!' They all laughed and made a move to leave the table, just as the waitress came to clear away their plates.

'Son, have a good night with Mal. I'll probably come to Trevilly at some stage to escape. I'll see you later.'

The three men parted and walked towards their cars, each with entirely different thoughts in their heads. Mal called to Ernie. 'I'll come around later in the week for one of Aunty Pat's afternoon teas after we do some gardening.'

Mal realised his uncle had indeed come to play an important role in his life now. They'd grown close and Mal was always grateful for the help Ernie and all the family had provided after his father's death. He felt sad that a real rift had evolved between his aunt and uncle, because of Sheila, not to mention Ian's pain as well. This was a family in grief and, at this stage, no one had died but the conflict was rumbling around like thunder in a storm, perched ready to erupt at any given moment.

Mal was pleased Ian initiated dinner and a sleep-over as it would give him a chance to talk more about the legalities of this delicate situation. As he strode towards his car, Mal realised he didn't need to go there; he needed to head back to his office. As he walked past the receptionist in the main area, his secretary told him his cousin Ken had left a message for him. He wondered what Ken would want so rang him straight away before he looked at anything else on his messy desk.

Half an hour later, Mal prepared himself for one of his meetings. He'd rung Ken who wanted to come in and make a new Will after the engagement party, so he'd exchanged pleasantries with him before explaining how he'd need to refer him to Scott, who did all the family legal work to avoid conflicts of interest. He felt happy for Bonnie who, at long last, had found her soulmate in Ken. Soon they were to make it formal and begin their life together; he found himself smiling as he straightened his shirt and jacket on his way down the corridor to the meeting room. It wouldn't be long now before he would be spending time with Ian. Delivering the information he needed to impart wouldn't be easy or pleasant, but it had to be done.

Mal decided to have a beer with Ian at home before they went for dinner at a restaurant down at Glenelg beach. He considered that all the family living quite close to each other made maintaining relationships easy. Proximity was the key, he decided as he flicked open a can for each of them as they sat in his plush chairs.

'I'm glad Ernie went home happy today. We gave him a plan and now he feels content. He's such a grand man who needs to know what life has in store for him.'

Both men nodded with fondness as they thought of Ernie. 'Ian, we need to make sure that Ernie doesn't die before your mother. I know it's just so unlikely, but you know how we lawyers always need to consider worse case scenarios.'

Mal poured his drink deliberately into his glass and watched it intently. 'We need to have this conversation before we go out. If Ernie passes away and both those women are in the house, well, we have a real problem, and Sheila is legally entitled to what Pat wants. At this stage, Sheila could inherit the house if Ernie passes away. And the bad news is, she would inherit. She's bloody well entitled to it according to the law, and this is regardless of your parent's Will. She'll claim it as her home. We could go to court, but we'd most likely lose.'

'Bloody hell!' Ian exclaimed. 'How is that fair? We'd better not let the old man die.'

'Of course not,' Mal replied. 'Don't you worry. I'll look after him.'

The cousins quickly finished their drinks and made their way towards the tram, thinking a brisk walk before the restaurant meal would be good for them.

Chapter Twenty-Three

Party Night

2007

Towards evening, Andy and Chris arrived and set up the sound system in Ken's house. Several speakers were placed on the back patio and one was put in the shrubbery. They assured Bonnie and Ken their favourite songs would provide soft background music for the party and excitedly set about their task with extension cords and double adaptors. Soon Bee Gees music drifted around, and Bonnie and Ken were assured many great songs, including Beethoven's 'Ninth Symphony', would be played on a loop. The music would only finish when the night ended or when they wanted some quiet.

'Well, there won't be any speeches, so I don't anticipate the music will stop. I don't want it to ever stop. Let's keep the music playing for eternity,' said Ken as he danced around the kitchen and finished arranging special glasses on the benchtop. Andy wasn't so sure about the absence of speeches, but nothing was mentioned as party preparations continued and fairy lights twinkled.

Soon the caterers arrived, which was their cue to leave the kitchen and move to the back patio where Ken lit the gas heater. It wasn't really needed as the November evening was warm and balmy, which was rather rare for Glenelg in November. Ken put his arm around Bonnie and cuddled her as he admired the lighting in the backyard. Little, soft, twinkling lights lit up the area and added an ambience of serenity for the party. 'We're going to have a great life, Bon; you just wait and see. I've been longing for this night and here we are ready to publicly acknowledge our love for each other.'

Soon the doorbell rang and guests started to arrive. Mal was first to congratulate the engaged couple and he introduced his date, Anne. Bonnie recognised her as a lawyer who had worked at Mal's law firm for many years. With her short blonde hair, she was extremely attractive and was clearly attracted to Mal. However, Bonnie knew Mal wouldn't give his heart away easily, and didn't really expect to see her at the family Christmas. The thought of Christmas made Bonnie feel happy and contented. They would all travel to Trevilly and spend some time with Ian and Sarah, and this made her smile.

Ian and Sarah were next to arrive, with flowers and hugs all round. 'Adam is probably coming later,' Ian said. But Bonnie and Ken were excited enough now to not really bother about missing guests at this stage. 'We're staying at a gorgeous little place just walking distance from here. But I reckon we'll all be at the Glenelg Homestead in the morning for one of Mum's morning teas. I hope she can still cook scones. Sarah, what can I get you to drink?'

'I'll look after Sarah,' said Bonnie as she led her outside to the party fridge and away from the kitchen, mindful of keeping out of the caterers' way. Bonnie had prepared cocktails and delighted in serving the array of colourful little glasses, decorated in various ways with tropical fruits and jelly crystals. They looked like cordial but were heavily laden with alcohol. Bonnie gave one to Sarah and held one for herself. 'Let's propose a toast to ourselves, Sarah. And drink to our future happiness. Yaaaaay,' Bonnie exclaimed as she took a huge mouthful.

Friends kept arriving, many of them medical people Ken and Bonnie had known for a long time. They realised one of the perks of a long relationship, like theirs, meant many friends were on the invitation list. Later, they would need to work out who was going to attend their wedding but for now, it was enough to consider the engagement party, where family politics would reign: Ken's daughters were due to arrive at any moment. They were pleasant enough and Bonnie would introduce them to friends and perhaps they would enjoy the company of like-minded people. But with Sheila now on the scene, Ken's family was the easy bit.

Then Sheila arrived with Bonnie's parents; they entered the kitchen after letting themselves in through the front door. Pat was in her wheelchair these days, so Ernie had spent time unloading it from the car. Sheila, of course, walked straight in like she was the main attraction. Bonnie was tempted to ignore her but she was sufficiently civil and focused more on her parents. Pat was able to recognise all the family at the party, but conversations remained simple and Sheila steered Pat to an isolated part of the garden where she could sit and play the caring granddaughter and keep an eye on Pat. Ernie, of course, made his way toward other guests and interacted with Bonnie's and Ken's friends. As Ken delivered drinks, he remembered part of his role was to entice Sheila to visit his home the next night, to expose her while Bonnie was at work. This entailed having a conversation with his future mother-in-law and her carer. Poor Pat, increasingly unaware of her situation, comprehended very little of anything these days.

'Who is the young man over there near the table, Sheila?'

Sheila told Pat she didn't know, and soon Ken approached them with drinks in hand. 'You will soon meet cousin Ron, Mal's brother,' Ken interjected as he overheard their conversation. Sheila pricked her ears up at the mention of Mal, the lawyer. Now she was going to hear all about his brother Ron, who had considered joining the forces until his father had died in the car accident and he had realised his mother would need him to run the dairy.

Ron was the eldest son, and without his father, he had assumed the role of farmer while Mal had gone to university. Ron had shelved his dream of the army, or air force, as he was needed by his grieving mother, and there was always a labour shortage on farms. Initially, he'd been disappointed, but his dream of life in the forces gradually, and surprisingly, morphed into an affinity with the land as the love of nature enveloped him. Many years later, he was content with his lot, working with his mother on the property adjoining Trevilly. The regular company of Ian and Ernie was a comfort for him. Now, as he approached middle age, he'd accepted the notion that a romantic companionship would never be a youthful and sex-charged fantasy. Ian and Sarah's marriage was a second chance relationship, and they were lucky.

Occasionally, Ron thought that a mature woman, with a child or two, could be a good idea and, as the years progressed, he decided he shouldn't be too fussy. But the special person in his life had never materialised. When Ken introduced Ron to Sheila, Ron decided to move on quickly and meet some of the medical people at the party. He sure as hell wasn't going to get stuck with Sheila, having heard about how his uncle's bank account had been compromised.

His Uncle Ernie had been so angry he'd told his story to almost anyone who'd listen, so now Ron looked at Pat's companion with disgust. He worked hard at keeping his feelings to himself as he took a sip from his drink and moved away.

As Ron mingled, he saw Ken talking to Sheila and wondered why he would waste his time. As he took a second look, he noticed the way Sheila eyed him up and down. *What an absolute tart*, he thought as his disgust increased. *She's making a play for Bonnie's fiancé … at their engagement party!*

Ken soon left Pat and Sheila and joined his friends in a different part of the garden. Ron's disgust increased as he told his mother, who was equally horrified. 'I believe Ernie's going to get rid of her soon. What a set-up! Poor old Pat's lost her marbles and is being manipulated by that horrible wretch.'

Mal heard his mother's comment to Ron as he approached. 'Awful situation for sure,' and Mal too looked at his aunt in the wheelchair. She had assumed the look of a frightened rabbit as her cognition increasingly failed and Mal felt pity for her. He realised she must be close to the end of her time, but Ken had told him often it was unclear how much time was left, even when the end was near. Sometimes they died quickly. Other times, they defied medical odds and took a long time to fade out.

Ron looked at Mal. 'What do you mean, Ernie's going to get rid of her? I thought he'd be full-on doing this after having his bank account raided and his money stolen.' There was no other word for it: theft!

'I'll leave you two to talk,' Enid said. 'I'll go and talk to poor Pat. Or at least I will try.' She moved away and as Ron watched her, he realised she too was getting old, and his heart contracted with the love he felt for her.

'How can he get rid of her, Mal?'

'I've convinced Ernie to lay low for a bit. Pretend all is well and when Aunty passes away, then he can kick her out. It will have to be with the help of the police, as she won't go easily, I suspect. I have had to work hard to convince Ernie to keep quiet and when the right time comes, then Ian and I will be there. If needs be, we'll ring the police. Perhaps we won't need to but that, dear Ron, is the plan so keep it under your hat. Unbelievable really, and I feel sorry for Ian, but the love he has for his father overrides other feelings.'

Ron glanced over his shoulder and saw Sheila still looking Ken's way. 'Unbelievable all right. Look at her, Mal. What a shameless bitch!' Ron took a sausage roll from the tray as it passed and bit into it hungrily. 'I should have eaten before I came but I ran out of time.' He finished his sausage roll and looked around for the waiter for another one, but he was gone. 'Mal, she's clearly in it for an inheritance, is she? You probably know about these things. How often does this sort of thing happen?'

'Unfortunately, it's more common than you think. We call them seagulls or leeches in the industry. They swoop in at the last minute claiming to be a carer and bang, they get a payout. They must be in the direct family line, like Sheila, and most times they've done their homework. They know what they're doing. They select a vulnerable family member and groom them. Have you heard of the term 'gaslighting'? Probably not, but it's all part of their game. Look it up when you get home.'

'But what about the Will? Actually, wait here until I find another few of those sausage rolls. Don't go away. We've got a bit of catching up to do.'

Ron soon returned with a small plate of sausage rolls and canopies and placed the plate nearby. He kept an eye on his plate as he ate a sausage roll but was eager to pursue his conversation with his brother.

Mal continued. 'Sometimes they persuade their victim to change their Will but they don't really need to. If they've done their homework and consulted a lawyer, they will know that being a carer makes them entitled. Not to mention living in the home. I suspect Sheila knows what she's doing. At this stage, we're onto Sheila and her game. I don't think she'd risk a Will change as she must suspect Ernie and Ian know her plan. Ernie's debit card has a new number so if she uses it, it's not going to work. She also knows Ernie changed the legal carer business, so she doesn't receive an allowance for two like she'd planned. She only receives government carer payment for Pat. She knows she's surrounded by sharks and legal eagles too. Nothing, of course, is said.'

Ron contemplated all Mal had explained. 'Okay. But what is she drooling over Ken for? What's that all about?'

'Who knows. She's just dreadful. That's all I can say.'

Mal and Ron finished the plate of nibbles, as they listened to the music and watched the crowd. 'Chris and Andy are such good friends for Bonnie and Ken. As for Bonnie, it's so good she's found love at last. It has been a long time coming, but good on her. Actually, speaking of dates, where's Anne?'

'Over with Bonnie and Sarah. Why don't you make an honest woman of her?' Ron asked.

'Bit of mystery, mate!' Mal laughed. 'Can't have her knowing all my faults now, can I? Nah, I like my life how it is.' They watched the women interact with each other and enjoy the party. Mal had been a lawyer long enough to quickly dismiss his conversation about Sheila and all her foibles. He knew her type, but preferred to think about Anne, hoping she would stay over at his place for the rest of the night. As he looked at her, he appreciated her beauty, the way she held her head, the way she listened so carefully to whoever was speaking to her. He was very aware of her intellect at the office, but now he was seeing her in a different context and felt his spirit lift. Gone was the talk of seagulls and leeches; he was now in the mood for romance. It must be something about the music, he decided, as he felt a stirring in his loins. He caught her eye and smiled as he wandered towards her.

Mal didn't leave Anne's side for the remainder of the evening, relishing her conversation and delighting in her company. Around midnight, the party drew to a close and gradually guests started leaving. It had been a fabulous evening for Bonnie and Ken, a time of friendship and fun. Bonnie was very much in love with her fiancé and her feelings were reciprocated. They bid their guests goodbye and turned off the music. Slowly, the caterers gathered their belongings as they cleaned the kitchen. Leftover food was put in the fridge and they stacked the dishwasher with the remainder of the glasses and plates. Andy and Chris were the last to leave after the gas heater was turned off and finally the front door was locked. Bonnie and Ken had their home back to themselves. The evening had been perfect, and they had a lifetime to enjoy their lives together, they thought, as they turned off all the lights and made their way to the bedroom. They didn't mention Sheila or their plan to expose her to Pat the following evening.

Chapter Twenty-Four

Sheila visits Ken

2007

Sheila dressed in her best underwear, her 'little black number', ready to seduce her target, Ken, and by default, upset the pretentious Bonnie. She thought of it as 'little' even though it was large enough to accommodate her rotund body. She had her drug kit in the car boot: the date drug Rohypnol, morphine, meth and other bits and pieces Luke had supplied. If things went wrong, she would give lover-boy some nice morphine to help him out. How much he received depended on how her seduction routine played out.

She was ready! No communication today by text; last night all the plans were outlined by Ken who was like a lap dog. The pickings were too easy, and she intended to inflict as much pain as possible on all those family members who deserved to be shoved off their pedestals.

She took a few deep breaths as she walked down the path towards Ken's house. Her handbag was full of narcotics and a syringe, which was ready to use when needed. Ken opened the door before she even rang the bell, so he'd been waiting for her. She felt like a cat that had found the cream as she smiled back at her target. *He's easy pickings all right.* The plan was to have a meth-fuelled bonk, which would leave him panting for more. She knew her part in the planned sexual routine. Ken poured two large gin and tonics and left them on the sparkling clean glass table. *He's expecting a guest! Bless his little heart, he even has the music on and the lighting dimmed.* She was going to savour this, after being with grizzling Gran all day. 'Ken, may I please have some ice and a slice of lemon for my drink?' Through her calculations, Ken was going to get the best sex ever with his meth, then Bonnie and her routine, whatever it was, would be reduced to the banalest of sexual activities one could imagine. Once this started, Ken would hanker for more meth, and soon tire of Bonnie. She aimed to wreck the marriage through drug addiction, without him even knowing, and leave him panting for more each time he saw her.

As Ken left the room for the lemon, Sheila nervously checked the contents of her bag. Luke had charged her a fortune and she wasn't happy about it, but, hopefully, this would be worth it. She looked at how much was in the ampule and almost shook her head at Luke's rip-off. Anyway, she tipped it into Ken's drink after taking a mouthful of his gin and tonic to make room for the few drops in the glass, then she put it back in her bag. She heard Ken's heavy footsteps as he returned with the ice and lemon. Sheila took a sip of her drink, smiling innocently. She leaned back in the comfortable chair and waited for the date drug to take effect, trying not to purr too loudly as she watched Ken closely.

Sheila was satisfied with the quality of Luke's narcotic, so her money had not been wasted. Slowly, Ken's eyes shut as his speech became slurred. Knowing that Bonnie wouldn't be home until well after midnight, Sheila allowed herself to enjoy her gin and tonic. She looked around the room at all the expensive household appliances and plush furnishings and waited longer, knowing the drug and its effects would last for hours. He'd be drowsy yet alert enough to appreciate her meth routine as she began her seduction.

'Ken, why don't you move to the couch where you can lie down?' she suggested.

Ken did as requested and staggered to the couch, where he flopped down and struggled to stay alert.

Sheila removed the glass from his hand and moved to stand next to him. She dropped a meth pill into his half-empty glass and replaced it in his hand. 'Drink up, lover-boy.'

Ken slowly complied, too drowsy to resist. Sheila smiled inwardly, realising he was about to get the show of his life. But before anything else happened, Sheila went to the bathroom and then checked out Ken's fridge. Making Ken wait wouldn't do any harm, and the longer she waited, the more time the meth had to work its magic in Ken's bloodstream.

More minutes ticked by. The fancy wall clock's rhythmical pattern marked time. The stainless-steel refrigerator in the kitchen purred, making all the noise of domesticity. She opened the fridge, noticed a custard tart, one of her favourite snacks, and was about to sink her teeth into it, but realised Bonnie may come looking for a snack when she came home. Her cautiousness crept in and she remembered her mission – eating could wait until after Ken had been dealt with.

She leant over his chest, not touching him yet, as she looked at his glazed eyes. He was awake and waiting for her, even though he was barely conscious. Sheila felt the power within and knew her actions would change life for the vulnerable Ken. She felt vindicated as the power became an aphrodisiac for her. Heaving with pleasure at the anticipation, she put her chubby hand on Ken's chest and then onto his crisp blue shirt, which screamed of conservatism.

But this wasn't the Ken Bonnie knew – this was the Ken Sheila created, and she was enjoying seeing the results of the administered Rohypnol. She stretched her hand across his chest and felt something hard under his shirt. *What's that?*

She moved her hand further, across his shoulders. The hardness continued so she unbuttoned his shirt, firstly one button and then the next.

What the hell is that? She could hardly believe it! Some kind of small metal and plastic object with thin wires coming out of it was strapped to Ken's shoulder. Sheila looked closer. Stared at his chest. *It's a recording device!* Then she noticed the small microphone!

He's recording our conversation! She still couldn't believe it. Now she had to change her whole way of dealing with the situation. *Why would he want to do this?*

Slowly, she figured it out. *He wants to catch me out! Well, I'll just beat him at his own game. I'll give him something to remember all right. Something permanent!*

She moved away, back towards her bag containing the narcotics. Riffling through it, she found the clear plastic syringe. She looked at it, her jaw clenching. *Morphine. Only to be used if something goes wrong.* And something had gone terribly wrong for Sheila. She'd been tricked!

Well, I'll get even with you lot. With the syringe in hand, she moved back to where Ken lay on the couch, his mouth wide open, one arm hanging over the edge like a corpse. *He's probably in a coma now and with this little sweetheart, he'll be in the coma of a lifetime.* He would never wake up from this dose of morphine. She ripped the recording device from Ken's chest and back and tossed it in her bag. She held the syringe upwards, like in the movies, and relished playing her part. She pulled Ken's sleeve up, exposing his bicep and quickly thrust the syringe into it as far as she could, all the while pushing down on the plunger. She kept pushing the plunger until all the fluid had gone. It was now 'goodbye, Ken'. She felt disgusted as she looked at his closed eyes, which would never open again. *There! Beaten at your own game.*

Then Sheila took her gloves from her bag, wiped down the syringe, then placed the syringe in Ken's hand, ensuring his fingers made contact with the cylinder. His prints would be all over it. Then she placed the syringe behind his body at the back of the couch, so it would be found when he was moved. She picked up the glasses and poured the contents down the sink, before putting them in her bag. Shivering, she scanned the rest of the room, wondering if she had left a trail.

As she looked at the refrigerator, she thought she'd have that custard tart and slowly opened the door, her mouth watering as she removed it from its alfoil container. She bit into it, the tasty delight dissolving in her saliva as she took pleasure in the taste and texture of it. She finished it and then looked at Ken, who lay so peacefully. She thought about making a hot chocolate but it really was time to go. When Bonnie returned home after midnight, the aftermath of his silly mistake would unfold. Ken hadn't played his part properly so now he was paying the price.

With her gloves still on, Sheila let herself out of the house and sat quietly in her car, slightly in shock that Ken's game had been to record her seducing him. *For what reason? Was he going to reveal me to Gran? She wouldn't approve of my actions with her prospective son-in-law? Does Bonnie know about this?* She felt gratified she'd had the sense to bring a full syringe of morphine, just in case it was needed. But she had to be careful now as she prepared for what could lie ahead.

She started the car and drove around the suburbs for a while trying to calm down from the shock, trying to keep her wits about her and assume an air of normality. Yet her fury bubbled as the car purred slowly along the road. On this night, which was so dark the streetlights seemed dull, she deliberated her payback on this family that had abandoned her so long ago.

Later, as she approached the Glenelg beach, she decided to create a fire pit and watch the flames. Often this soothed her. She gathered dried twigs and put them in a hole she'd made on the isolated beach. Old newspapers, matches and kerosene firelighters were permanent fixtures in her boot for occasions just like this. She threw the recording device fiercely into the fire and watched the plastic melt. With no one in sight, she sat and watched the flames until they'd burnt down to smouldering embers. Eventually, the fire went completely out so she kicked sand over the remnants to bury all its signs. She looked around but could see no one. In the distance though, she could hear people and was unsure if the noise had woken her or just brought her back to reality. She moved her legs around in a bid to stand and let the tension fade from her body. The noise in the distance grew louder and drowned out the sounds of the waves as she walked towards the car park. It was deserted, just as she liked it. She soon found her keys to unlock the car. Bright headlights slowly moved towards her as she opened her door and slipped into the seat, where she sat motionless until the car had passed. Conscious of the contents in her handbag, which was now in her boot, she worried about being stopped by police for being there so late, and started the engine and put the car in gear.

In no time, she was at the Glenelg Homestead where her grandparents would be snoring away inside, sound asleep in their separate beds. She had sensed the tension between them in recent times, and she knew she was the cause but didn't care. She liked the conflict between them: it caused them distress. And now, what she had done this night would cause even more distress – it was about to come crashing down around them. She quietly inserted the front door key; moved it sideways to unlock it and slunk inside. Soon she too would be snoring, just like the oldies. *Well, tonight they'll sleep soundly because from tomorrow their sleeps will never be the same again.* She felt a tad awful at the circumstances, but it was short-lived. *They deserve to be brought down, the whole lot of them*, she thought as she slid into slumber, still in her lacey black underwear, with her body occupying most of the bed.

Chapter Twenty-Five

The Discovery

2007

Bonnie turned her front door key as the sun rose and red clouds spilled across the sky. *Red sky in the morning, shepherds' warning – it might rain soon.* She saw Ken sprawled on the couch and called to him as she moved towards the kitchen: it was their ritual to make a cup of tea for each other when they entered the house. She called to him again but he still didn't answer. Despite the noise of the kettle boiling furiously, then whistling, it failed to wake him so she moved towards him and touched his arm. Then she shook his arm more vigorously and he flopped, almost onto the floor.

She screamed when he was unresponsive. Her eyes widened and her heart thumped furiously as she made a horrible realisation!

'Wake up, Ken, wake up,' she screamed. Then she dropped to her knees, shaking him, her nursing training kicking in. She raised his eyelids to check for vital signs: his pupils were fully dilated and unresponsive. She checked his pulse. *Nothing.* She leant into him and listened for breathing. *Nothing.* He was totally unresponsive. She rang for an ambulance and had one despatched to their home and then immediately commenced cardiac compressions to restart his heart. Then she remembered the recording device Ken had bought to tape to his body so he could record Sheila's advances, but it wasn't there, only the adhesive marks where it had been attached. Sheila had been here like they had planned, and now the device had been removed.

Then Bonnie saw the small puncture mark on his arm, the

surrounding skin still red. All this became part of what she recounted later as she furiously began resuscitation.

Then a banging sound came on the front door and she rushed to it and hurried the ambulance staff to the lounge to take over from where she had started life-saving compressions. But when she stepped back, she knew Ken was beyond help: he was cold and grey, and she began sobbing loudly. She flopped into a nearby lounge chair as the two ambulance officers checked vital signs and assessed the scene. They looked at Bonnie weeping in the chair.

'He's gone,' one said as the other walked outside with the two-way radio. She could hear the conversation outside, the sound carrying on the air. 'Tell me what happened,' the young woman beside Bonnie asked. 'I can see by your uniform you are familiar with procedures.'

Bonnie nodded and told them how she had come home and found Ken. She described how he'd been well when she left him and then described his medical history, all through blubbering tears. The police were called and everything was left in situ – any death of a well and fit person was considered suspicious until deemed otherwise. They moved into the kitchen and sat and waited until the police arrived. From that moment on, the mood became more formal and tense. The police asked questions; forensics took photos then the ambulance officers moved Ken to a gurney and a sheet was placed over him. The syringe now lay in full view. The two ambulance attendants looked at each other. No one moved.

'I told them I found an injection site on his arm,' Bonnie murmured.

'Are you aware your fiancé had a drug problem?' the police officer asked.

'No, he didn't!' Bonnie said indignantly. 'Someone did this to him!'

The syringe was placed in a paper bag, the collector being careful not to destroy evidence and fingerprints.

'Who would do this to him then?' the police officer asked. 'Do you suspect someone?'

'We planned to marry soon. He wouldn't do this to himself!' She watched, stunned, as Ken's body was wheeled out and loaded into the ambulance. The back doors were gently shut and Ken was driven away, never to be seen again. After countless questions, the police left, informing Bonnie that the coroner would be in touch. They expressed their condolences, which merely reinforced the finality of Ken, her lover.

Inconsolable, and in total shock and disbelief, Bonnie sat in the chair and the clock ticked endlessly on. She was unaware of how much time had passed as she had wondered what she should do. Eventually, she rose and rang Mal and, between sobs, told him there had been an incident, an emergency.

Soon Mal was knocking on the front door. 'What's happened, Bon?'

And Bonnie told him the details. Everything.

'So Sheila was meant to be coming over? And Ken was wearing a wire?' Mal confirmed, scowling. 'And the plan was for Ken to make a play for her and see how far she would take it? Oh god, Bonnie! That's a dangerous game! Now you think she killed him?'

'Mal, it's all that could have happened. Maybe Sheila discovered the wire and drugged him. How else could it have happened? Ken wouldn't hurt anyone! He was always so kind and gentle. This was the only way we could think of to expose Sheila as the tart she is, to show Mum what an opportunistic fraud she is. We wanted to expose her with the evidence.'

Mal's mind went into lawyer mode, a thousand questions racing around in his head, but he didn't verbalise any of this to Bonnie. For now, she just needed comfort, and a consoling cup of tea so he left her sitting in the lounge, immersed in her early grief and disbelief, while he made the tea for them both. Gradually, Bonnie revealed what had happened from the moment she entered the house that morning.

Mal listened and, after a while, excused himself, went outside and phoned Bonnie's parents. He knew they'd be shocked, but sometimes there was no easy way to impart information like this. He said he would bring Bonnie over later in the day so she could tell them everything. This was a family in crisis!

Bonnie forlornly entered the open front door of her parent's home and saw them sitting in the lounge room, grief-stricken. Mal had told Ernie about Bonnie and Ken's plan to expose Sheila so they were aware of the details surrounding Ken's death. They remained silent as Bonnie hugged her mother, then her father. They were all stunned. Then Sheila entered the room.

At the sight of her, Bonnie screamed: 'You killed him. You killed him. How dare you come into my home and seduce my fiancé! Why did you kill him like that?' she screeched. She'd waited all her life for a man like Ken to come along and now he'd been extinguished by this imposter who sat with her parents in their home. 'This defies belief, you're an absolute monster! And you have the gall to sit there with my parents and pose as their caring granddaughter. How dare you! How dare you!' Then she kept shouting at the top of her voice. 'You killed him, and you planned it all. You're nothing but … … a cold-blooded killer!!'

'What are you talking about? I've been here with your parents. I've got no idea what you're talking about. Have you gone crazy?'

Sheila lifted her ample body out of her chair and moved into Bonnie's personal space, pointing her finger within inches of Bonnie's face. 'Don't you come here abusing me when I'm helping you out by looking after your parents!' She maintained piercing eye contact with Bonnie, clearly adopting a fight response. She wasn't moving and Bonnie didn't move either.

Bonnie bit her bottom lip hard and clenched her fists by her side. Her breathing heightened and she felt like spitting into Sheila's face, knowing that if she did Sheila would strike her, but Bonnie didn't care. She was enraged and ready for anything Sheila threw at her.

Ernie struggled out of his chair, totally dismayed at what he was hearing, while Pat sat silent, also totally bewildered.

Seconds passed as Bonnie planned her moment to strike, but Mal stepped between them, seized her shoulders and moved her back. He turned her towards the kitchen, away from Sheila.

Bonnie continued sobbing and saying, 'I just can't believe this' over and over again.

Then Mal gripped her arm, gently led her away from Sheila and onto the front verandah. As they headed for the car, Sheila followed, and yanked Bonnie back just long enough to hiss, 'Don't fool with me, bitch. You tried to set me up but I know what you did in Africa and who is looking for you. You wouldn't want them to know where you are, would you!'

Backtracking, Mal gathered Bonnie up again and led her away to his car. He drove her to his home a few kilometres away where he made up the bed in the spare room and told her she was safe here and that she could not to return to Ken's home, which was now a crime scene.

After a long night of tossing and turning, Bonnie replaying what must have happened in Ken's house. Eventually, she dragged herself out of bed, made a cup of tea and sat on the lounge, still horrified, despaired, and now very lonely. Part of her knew she shouldn't have allowed Ken to take such as risk with Sheila, but she'd had no idea how dangerous Sheila could be.

Halfway through her cup of tea and still in her pyjamas, she answered the persistently ringing phone. *Who the hell is calling at this hour?*

'Guess who?'

Bonnie recognised the voice immediately, and her face flushed with rage. 'What do you want?' she snapped.

'You and Ken tried to set me up by using a wire, and you've seen what happened. The coroner's report will identify narcotics in Ken's blood and put it down to another drug-addicted doctor. We both know how that will roll out. So, you can protest as much as you like, scream at me as much as you like but you haven't any proof. There's no evidence. If you make any noises about me, I will tell the police about your escape from Zimbabwe on suspicion of murder and drug theft. Who can substantiate *that* story? Not your supposed friend Thelma since she seems to have disappeared. An extradition order will have you hauled back to Africa on charges. I'm not saying anymore, but that will give you something to think about when you come snivelling around *my* home and your parents. You set me up, you bitch, and you failed.'

The call disconnected and Bonnie plopped down into an armchair, stunned. Thwarted and heartbroken, she curled up like an animal in front of its predator and drifted between fear and logic.

Mal's hand landed on her shoulder. 'Is everything okay?'

Bonnie shook her head but said, 'Yes. I am just so worried about Mum and Dad in that house with Sheila.'

'Don't worry about them. I will keep a close eye out to ensure they are okay. You need to take some time out. You need time to get over this.'

Bonnie sat silent a moment, then said, 'I think I will drive down to Trevilly for a few days. I need to talk to Ian.' She hoped this would act as a circuit breaker and the long drive would do her good.

The next morning she rang work to take a few weeks' leave, saying nothing about Ken, knowing she would break down if she mentioned his name. All her years of nursing, those many years and times where she'd experienced patients dying, couldn't afford her comfort. But never before had she been responsible for someone's death – now she was – for her patient's death and Ken's. This was absolutely torturous.

The days limped by, Bonnie staggering with them. She never knew hours could be so long and her tiredness felt exhausting, all-consuming. People were kind and she soaked up the environment of the land, the cows and the quietness while taking long walks to pass the time. As she placed her head on the pillow each night, her eyelids shut but sleep evaded her. She felt Ken's presence and this comforted her but at the same time, it created the emptiness which permeated her being. And in her grief, exhaustion and disbelief reigned. She relived moments with Ken, juxtaposed with Sheila's conversation and threats. She wanted the horror to end but knew it wouldn't. *How can it?* The best she could hope for was for the melancholy to subside, but she knew from her nursing experience she was light years away from feeling mere despair and loss. And so, she gave in to her grief at Trevilly, and allowed the world to continue with her at the periphery.

Returning to Glenelg, Bonnie drove past Ken's house. Yellow crime scene tape still surrounded Ken's front yard and Bonnie's heart thudded with the memory of finding Ken. She now lived in total disbelief. She had lost her home, as this was now just Ken's home, and she had been considered the prime suspect in his death simply by being his partner and the last person to have seen him.

The house she had come to love as her own now looked ominous, a no-go zone, making her realise she was just as much a victim in this horrid murder as Ken. Indeed, she'd been questioned intensively about his death by the detectives, and the coroner and forensic team were still assessing the evidence to determine a cause of death. They had, she'd been told, deemed the direction of the injection in Ken's arm was not consistent with self-administration. Luckily for Bonnie, she had been at work all night, frequently interacting with staff and patients, so she had an alibi. The accusation of her guilt in this matter had astounded Bonnie – this was the man she was going to marry! How could they talk about 'a body' in front of her, and request her to provide an alibi! *How could things go so horribly wrong?*

Due to the party, there were many different sets of fingerprints at the crime scene; while police suspected foul play, it was hard to determine who was involved. Work colleagues were questioned, including about Ken's drug use, but no one confirmed that Ken had a drug problem. In fact, they expressed exactly the opposite, which pushed the case into a full-scale investigation. Bonnie knew she should have told the police about Sheila, as Mal had strongly advised her to do, but Sheila's threats about Africa worried Bonnie. All it would need was for her to plant the seed that Bonnie was responsible for someone's death and the case would turn back to her as being the prime suspect.

Sheila's sinister nature and her blackmail kept Bonnie awake at night and, when she did sleep, Sheila haunted her dreams. She remained silent, fearful, and Sheila retained all the power. But what scared Bonnie the most was Sheila's time with her parents! *There's a killer under their roof! A psychopath! A murderer!*

With Ken's death deemed a homicide, his track record with drugs protecting his reputation, the police were left puzzled by a whirl of contradictions. Though Bonnie's alibis protected her, she carried grief and guilt. Why had she and Ken ever embarked on such a childish game! They had seriously underestimated such a cunning and dangerous Sheila.

The weeks crept by, and Bonnie still suffered from Ken's loss, still feared for her parents, yet remained silent for long periods. Anne moved into the house at Mal's request to be company for Bonnie in her time of need. It was easy for Bonnie to let Mal lead the way through her nightmare. He always stepped up to be in charge and she was always indebted to him for the way he cared for her parents. She would eventually need to do something more permanent about her life, but in the interim, while she grieved, it was simpler to let others look after her.

During this time, she was delighted to see a romantic spark flickering between Anne and Mal, and to see Mal including the attractive Anne in his life. These lawyers were definitive in their private lives as well as their work-life! From conversations, she soon fathomed they'd been spending quality time together, away from the office.

One night when Mal cooked dinner and the two women sat on the sofa, Anne stopped what she'd been saying and looked steadily at Bonnie.

'You just have to take one day at a time,' she said. 'Just focus on the here and now ...'

'But how can I when Mum and Dad are so much at risk with Sheila living there! I can't concentrate knowing the danger they are in. I can't do anything to stop her. I can't sleep ... she has so much control. She can do so much to harm us ... all of us.'

Anne pushed her blonde hair back over her shoulder and took a sip of her drink. 'Bonnie, I know you're concerned ... ... but I want you to remember this: Sheila's *threatening* to blackmail you ... but she's bluffing ... purely to deflect her actions onto your grief and pain. And even if there was a case, it's all hearsay. They can't prove anything. Wow, Sheila is a manipulator, isn't she! If there were any doubts about her affinity for family, they're long gone. How difficult for Ian! But after this, I'm sure he's washed his hands of her. Did you have a chance to talk to him? I guess you did.'

The clanging in the kitchen continued as Mal prepared dinner and set the table. Anne went to help him and soon the meal was served, leaving Bonnie sitting. *If only they knew*, she thought. *Only Ken knows about the patient dying from my treatment. And Sheila. I do have to be afraid. Very afraid.*

'Bon, we'll stay here for a while, just until life unfolds slightly for you. Are you able to shop for the three of us tomorrow? Actually, make it a meal for five. I will ring your parents in the morning and pick them up after work,' continued Mal. He knew Bonnie would cherish some normality and the idea of preparing dinner the next night was like a visit from an angel from heaven. She thought Ken was looking after her and allowed herself to feel his presence as his spirit enveloped her and gave her peace, or at least some kind of comfort, despite its brevity. Bonnie clung to whatever she could and, as her world collapsed, she fought hard to prevent herself from collapsing with it.

Chapter Twenty-Six

May Ken Rest in Peace

2007

Ernie sat in total disbelief as he attempted to process the news of his prospective son-in-law's death, and kept repeating it to Mal when he phoned. 'Mal, I cannot believe this has happened. Poor Bonnie. This just isn't fair.'

'I know, Ernie. You're right. I'll pick you and Pat up around five o'clock and we'll have dinner with Bon. We can talk more then. So, you take care of yourself and Aunty.'

Ernie decided to take Pat for a walk in her wheelchair to get out of the house and away from Sheila. He couldn't get Bonnie's words about Sheila's part in Ken's death out of his mind. It was all too much for him. He wanted to hear the words from Bonnie's mouth again so, as he strapped Pat into the wheelchair and left the house, he kept thinking about her outburst only a short time ago. He really couldn't bear the sight of Sheila and wanted to talk to Mal about their plan to remove her after Pat passed away. He pushed the wheelchair in silence, communication with Pat now almost non-existent, and soon he reached their favourite café. He really didn't want to talk to anyone. When the coffee was served, the proprietor quickly read Ernie's body language and left him alone. So Ernie sat with Pat, both mourning Ken and in despair of their situation. Their only daughter was devastated, and so were they.

Ernie then decided to take a taxi to Mal's office to speak with his trusted nephew and hear the news about Ken's passing. He packed the wheelchair into the taxi and helped Pat into the back seat, all the time feeling furious. He should have been able to do this from home, but Sheila was there, watching and waiting. *Waiting for what?*

Mal and Ernie spoke at length.

'Bonnie said she had to organize the funeral now the police are releasing Ken's body …'

'She doesn't have to worry about that, Ern. I will have all that in hand. I've shifted all my cases to colleagues so I am totally available to the family at this time.'

'What if Sheila attends? After that screaming match they had, I don't think it would be a good idea.'

'It won't happen. She won't be invited. Close family and work colleagues only. As Bonnie's legal advisor, I will guide her through the process of winding up Ken's affairs, if his first family don't get involved …'

He knew how these situations unfolded. As for Sheila, well, she was full of bluff. Besides blackmail being a crime, despite its nebulous qualities, she was a femme fatale and dangerous. She was hungry for revenge, and who knows where she would stop. They would have to evict her from the Glenelg Homestead as soon as they could, but at this stage, it was difficult to lessen Pat's dependence on her without a major conflict. *Sheila's set for revenge and she's a ruthless, master manipulator*, he realised.

'Ernie, I'll take you both home now and will return and pick you up later. Perhaps you might like to think about cutting the hedge on the side of the house? It needs a trim. Load it into your ute and next week we'll take it to the tip.' Mal had a busy day ahead and knew Ernie needed something to keep him occupied. He felt agitated and tense as he noticed the pain of his family intruding into his headspace. He needed to ensure Anne would be by his side and his heart skipped a beat when he realised her role in this family tragedy. Perhaps she was a keeper? He was seriously becoming dependent on her, at work and at home. She was a brilliant lawyer and he realised he'd fallen in love with her, despite his best efforts of resistance to this notion of love. He conceded how totally consuming it was and chuckled inwardly. He was human, after all, and he needed her. He depended on her and knew he wanted her in all the ways that mattered. He felt his spirits lift, as he realised he was smitten, and he reached for the Panadol for his headache.

Several weeks later, the detectives had no further clues or evidence in the case and deemed it an Open Case homicide. Ken had died from a drug overdose, administered by parties unknown.

Bonnie returned to work. Working nights at the hospital was therapy for her. Her melancholy lifted with the thought of Ken's reputation not being tarnished by a lie. Ken had been murdered but Bonnie felt unable to change this status. Mal and Anne offered sensible and sympathetic counsel as she navigated through her trauma.

'Bonnie, if Sheila brings up this Zimbabwe nonsense and a police inquiry ensues, it will come to nothing,' Mal tried to comfort her.

She shook her head. 'While that's true, the threat of a police investigation will jeopardise my career. And you know as well as I do that being considered a suspect is just about guilty in the public's eye. It could impact on my prospects for future work. It may make me look like a criminal. I would have to declare I'm under investigation … for drug misappropriation!' *And murder.*

'Natural justice makes it illegal to state a person is guilty until the court dictates otherwise. It's just not going to happen, Bonnie. And no one can force you to leave the country. There won't be any investigation. There's simply not enough evidence.'

Bonnie sighed deeply. 'I guess you're right, Mal. Logically you're correct, but emotionally, I feel unsettled. I will just have to keep quiet, and meanwhile, poor Ken is left with a blemish on his medical reputation. That's so unfair! Where is the justice in that?'

'Our time will come, Bon, and Sheila will be legally ousted. I hate to say it, but your Mum won't last long. She's already surprised the medical fraternity by still being here, and she's weaker by the day. Poor Ernie, too. That household is a ticking timebomb.'

The funeral took place a month after the engagement party, so the same people, as well as many others, attended. It was a heartbreaking event for all. Mal enlisted Chris's and Andy's help as Bonnie sat quietly in her seat, feeling the despair of her loss. Pat, in the wheelchair, and Ernie sat nearby. Thankfully Sheila was absent, but Bonnie was beyond caring. She kept her gaze straight ahead as the words of condolence swam around her, barely penetrating. People placed flowers on his casket and Bonnie was coaxed to follow suit. Later a cup of tea was offered, and tiny sandwiches provided a focus for Bonnie as well-intentioned friends, Ken's colleagues and patients, offered kind words. Rhonda and Ken's daughters hugged her and it was clear they too were in shock. Time stood still for what seemed an eternity. Sarah and Anne stood with Bonnie as friends paid their respects and, at long last, it was time to go home. Ian and Sarah took Bonnie home. This time there was no joy, no words and no morning tea planned at the Glenelg Homestead. The little family – Bonnie, Mal and Anne – looked at the television for hours and eventually went to bed, exhausted.

Gradually life returned to as normal as it could be after a death, and work eased Bonnie's pain. No mention was ever made of Ken and a drug problem, at least Bonnie never heard any whispers. Bonnie continued to stay with Mal and Anne as turns were taken for dinner preparation and the pattern of communal living became the norm.

One evening as Mal prepared dinner, he asked Bonnie if she was still worried about the menace in Sheila. 'I've been thinking,' he said. 'If you are worried about the threats Sheila posed, why don't we put a tail on her? I have a friend who is a good private investigator and who's great at tailing people. He doesn't come cheap, but I guarantee he'll discover where Sheila goes and who she meets each evening when she leaves Ernie and Pat's house. It could well be she's up to mischief. I wonder where she sourced the drugs she used on Ken. For a fee, information could be quite powerful and I can see you are still unsettled. What do you think?'

'Mal, I love the idea!' Bonnie agreed, a smile spreading across her face. If she could get evidence against Sheila, she could use it if she ever needed to. She realised she and Ken should have done something similar instead of taking such a dangerous and disastrous position. The thought brought her to tears as she slowly accepted how she had endorsed the idea that had led to Ken's death. She left the room for a few moments and went to the bathroom to compose herself. But a wave of exhaustion swept over her as she tried hard to regain her composure before returning to the lounge room. Tearfully, she looked at Mal.

'Consider it done!' Mal exclaimed. He glanced up and saw Bonnie's face. 'Come here so I can give you a big hug.' Bonnie allowed herself to be enveloped in his big body once again, drawing comfort as he patted her on the back. Ultimately, she withdrew and sat down again.

'On another matter, Mal … today I received a letter from a real estate agent inquiring about the lease on Ken's house. I was shocked when I realised Ken was renting his home. Of course, he would have given the family home to Rhonda during the divorce settlement. Ken's Will is in the family home, and Rhonda has written to me saying Ken bequeathed his superannuation to his two daughters.'

'Holy Bejesus!' Mal exclaimed again. He was then silent as he contemplated the enormity of Bonnie's words. He remembered Ken had made an appointment to see him about his Will after the engagement party, and now it was too late. He didn't inform Bonnie of this as there was no point. He hesitated as thoughts went through his mind.

'Did you want to take over Ken's lease, Bon? Do you want to stay in the house?'

Bonnie sat silent a moment. Then she shook her head slowly. Every time she walked into that ill-fated lounge room, she would see Ken's body. She shook her head again, more determinedly. 'No. I couldn't … I … I …'

'Okay,' Mal replied, cutting her short from further discussion, 'so you will stay here. You will be good company for Anne.'

Bonnie slept soundly that night for the first time since Ken's death and began to look forward to her future. In a few weeks, it would be Christmas and they would all be at Trevilly. That included Andy and Chris. She was quietly chuffed, too, that Mal and Anne would spend Christmas with the family and looked to the heavens and felt thankful for the union of Mal and Anne as a consequence of Ken's passing. Since the funeral, they were inseparable, and the next few weeks would consist of making plans for Christmas. Thoughts of her childhood home brought a much-needed degree of serenity into her life, and she planned to attend a Christmas party organised by hospital staff just days before travelling to Trevilly. Also she recognised a slight regression of her despair and grief. As her mother's health slowly deteriorated, Bonnie acknowledged that soon she would not be here, but hoped she would last until Christmas. Time didn't stand still.

Chapter Twenty-Seven

A Visit to the Tip

2007

The number of visitors at the Glenelg Homestead had increased in recent weeks as folks prepared for Christmas. Ernie improved his roses in readiness and ensured the lawn looked immaculate. He moved with a spring in his step, albeit a small step now, and Sheila watched him and begrudged the extra days he was alive. She knew Ernie had changed his PIN and she was now unable to withdraw cash, which was rather an inconvenience for her. He had also changed the documentation at Centrelink, too, cancelling her government handout to care for him. The passive resistance existing in the household was silent but pervasive. Sheila ensured she was within listening distance when visitors were present. She even made cups of tea and served afternoon tea, like a servant girl, so the visitors would be impressed. But she knew Ernie still wasn't impressed. For that reason, Sheila believed he was obstructing her mission to call the Glenelg Homestead her home. But she would bide her time and not rush into anything brash and transparent.

Ian visited from time to time and took both his parents with him for a few hours, so Sheila didn't really need to interact with her father. In the time away from the house, Sheila took the opportunity to browse through Ernie's mail. In earlier days, he had left bank statements and other financial documents on his desk but in recent times, she noticed he locked both the filing cabinets. Sure, there was information on his desk, but now it was mostly nature magazines and newspapers. The interesting documents, the financial documents, had been put away out of sight, but there was another letter from Bonnie's friend, Thelma, with a London address on the back of the envelope. Clearly, Thelma was trying to communicate with Bonnie, but Sheila took the letter and put it, along with the other London letter, in her box of goodies in her room. Clandestine possessions or merchandise for her trading, as Sheila liked to think of them, were also kept in her room to ensure her car didn't contain narcotics if it was ever subjected to a police inspection.

As Sheila sat in the café, waiting for clients, she caught sight of a man she'd seen before. He was a discreet distance away, sitting at a table reading a paper, his face hidden, but she couldn't place where she'd seen him. After the drug and money handover with the client, she decided to make a fire pit as she strongly suspected the man was following her. If he was at the beach, she would have to swiftly inform clients that trading would cease for a week. She didn't want to have the police following her. Sure enough, the man followed her to the beach.

Sheila sat in her car and sent a coded text to all clients. 'Trading will cease for exactly one week.' Clients understood the meaning of the message. Rodney, too, was a recipient of the message so he would need to heighten his awareness of possible police interference. No calls were made to clients as it provided police with evidence.

Losing interest in the firepit, Sheila inserted the key in the car ignition, turned it and drove slowly along the road, hoping the suspected follower would leave her alone. She decided to stay home for a few days and ensured the house was pristine clean for visitors to admire and praise.

The week prior to Christmas, Sheila decided to help Ernie in the garden, much to Ernie's annoyance. But after some time, he thought she could be handy to do some of the bending and heavy lifting. Mal visited, as he normally did on Mondays, and helped with dumping tree cuttings and lawn clippings into the back of

Ernie's ute. Soon they had a load ready for the tip.

'Let's wait until after Christmas, Ernie, to go to the tip. It'll be too crowded this close to public holidays. Let's go inside and have afternoon tea with Aunty. I know it brings her pleasure and there's not much of it for her these days.'

Sheila realised she was always ignored in this household. Conversations went around her and never included her. She even noted that Mal and Ernie took their cups of tea outside and sat on the grass near Mal's car, so the exclusion was very pronounced.

'Gran, I think you and I will be here on our own at Christmas. Never mind, I will purchase Christmas food for the two of us to enjoy. Lucky we both enjoy our food, Gran. The others can all go to Trevilly … in fact, they can all go to Hell and rot, and we'll stay here.'

Pat had lost the power of coherent speech by this stage except for the occasional ramble about something that had happened when she was young. She would have an outburst and then remain silent for days, lost in her own world that she could no longer share with anyone. Even Ernie had given up, though he had tried hard from time to time; in recent days he was more in despair for the loss of the wife he once knew. Some days were fine but others were mainly silent. Her body existed, largely in the wheelchair, but her mind was lost. He quietly pondered at the amount of time she had left on the planet and discussed this, once again, with Mal.

'Ernie, we don't know how long each one of us will last, but I'll tell you something exciting which I think will make you smile and ease your misery.'

Ernie turned his head quickly towards Mal and his face lit up! Mal suppressed a chuckle but was delighted at the effect his words had on his uncle.

'I think I'm going to hook up seriously with Anne from the office. You know, the pretty one who talks a lot? You met her at the engagement party. She's been particularly kind to Bonnie, and I've seen such a loving side of her recently, so I think I'm going to ask her to marry me! There you are, Ern! How's that for news? In fact, I've asked her to come to Trevilly for Christmas so I can pop the big question then. On another matter, do you want us to take you to Trevilly? Or is Ian picking you up?'

'Yeah yeah … Mal, my boy! I'm ecstatic for you! Nothing could make me happier at this stage. What a fabulous Christmas present and even Bonnie will share your happiness. I know she will.'

Ernie slapped Mal on the back, beamed widely and shook Mal's hand vigorously. 'Let's go to the pub and have a beer. We won't tell anyone. Bugger them inside! Let's go in your car.'

They stayed at the pub, had a few drinks and then had dinner. When Ernie arrived home, he felt decidedly merry and entered the dark house singing his favourite song. Sheila was probably out somewhere again, and Pat was probably asleep, but he didn't care. It only made him sing louder as he staggered towards the bathroom and very soon, he was lying on his bed, fully dressed, snoring loudly.

But Sheila wasn't out. She was listening to his merriment from the comfort of her warm, soft bed, knowing Mal and Ernie had been to the pub and clearly the mood was one of celebration. Were they plotting to evict her after Christmas or whenever Gran died? She reasoned they would have to be. Mal was so secretive and was like a son to Ernie. They shared secrets. In fact, this whole family shared secrets so she was going to create a few secrets of her own. She lay in bed thinking for a long time before finally surrendering to sleep.

The next day Ernie felt sluggish and reluctantly admitted to having a hangover. He told Pat he had a headache but she didn't understand which increased his frustration. He made himself breakfast and a coffee, his cue for beginning his day. He sat for a long time at the table and it was only when Sheila spoke to him, did he decide to go into the garden. He sat in the wooden garden seat wanting to be alone, but Sheila had followed him from the kitchen.

'Granddad, let me help you finish putting the clippings into the back of the ute,' and without waiting for a response she began raking leaves and branches. She lifted them into the back of the ute and Ernie had to concede she could be quite useful as she was young and strong. He was too tired and a little hungover though to venture far from his chair but, after a while, he found his hat and sunglasses so he could think about doing some gardening. He told himself he was supervising and slowly made his way to tie the rubbish down in the ute and put tarps over the load to prevent it from blowing off.

'Come on, Granddad. Let's go to the tip. I can drive if you like and then we can put up some Christmas decorations to create some Christmas cheer for Gran.'

Sheila seemed in a good mood but Ernie felt grumpy. He begrudgingly admitted that his hangover was making him feel terrible so he didn't really have the strength to resist Sheila's idea. He opened the passenger side door and sat on the seat, feeling totally lethargic as he waited for Sheila to start the engine. The noise of the engine and traffic intensified Ernie's headache. He wished he'd taken some Panadol before he had to listen to Sheila's loud voice.

'Let's not go to the tip. It'll be too crowded. Why don't we save tip fees by driving quietly to the Adelaide Hills and dump the rubbish in the forest?'

'No, you don't! That's polluting the environment. You go to the tip, girl!'

'I'm driving so we will go where I say we go,' Sheila snarled back.

Ernie shot her a glance and the look on her face warned him to stay quiet. This was a side of Sheila he had seen before and didn't like. He closed his eyes and let the matter drop, for his own safety.

Sheila drove past the tip and the road to the city's outskirts. She turned the radio on so Ernie could listen to the News, but he wasn't interested so he turned it off and shut his eyes as the engine droned on and up along the road, which quickly became less congested. At Bridgewater, she woke Ernie up and told him to fuel up the ute while she ducked into the outside restroom. Ernie was chatting inside when she returned to the driver's seat.

Pulling out again, Sheila turned off the main road after some time and headed a distance down an isolated dusty track. The temperature was rising so she opened the window to let in a cool breeze, but it only let the dust in.

Ernie woke up and looked around, but nothing seemed familiar. 'Shut the window, girl. Keep the vehicle clean. Where is all this dust coming from?'

Soon the vehicle stopped and the little ticking noise could be heard as the engine cooled in the otherwise eery silence. Sheila shoved open the door and went around the ute to let her grandfather out the other side. Ernie sat trying to wake himself up. He removed his sunglasses and hat as he looked around.

'How about we both get on the back and push the rubbish out?' Sheila yelled as she untied the ropes of the tarps. Soon she was on the tray of the ute. Ernie decided he'd better help and climbed onto the back of the ute as best he could. His head still ached so he sat on the side of the vehicle while Sheila pushed the green waste off the back. He felt hot and consequently thought he should put his hat and sunglasses on when he stood, near the back, just a short distance from Sheila as she continued unloading rubbish. Without noticing Ernie had moved, Sheila turned quickly and bumped him. Ernie fell from the ute and landed awkwardly on his side and rolled onto his back. There was a loud crack. This was exactly what Sheila had hoped for! This was her moment to act and she instantly rallied herself around the old sage Ernie. He looked at Sheila, knowingly, worriedly.

'Can you get up, Granddad, and walk?'

Ernie tried to lift himself up but failed. Pain coursed through him, jolting his heart. It was unbearable. 'Help me up, Sheila!' he pleaded through gritted teeth, his anger and distress obvious. He groaned in agony as he realised his vulnerable situation. 'Bugger', he said under his breath as he realised with horror his sudden dependency on her.

'Granddad, I'll go and get help. You're badly hurt so stay there and don't move. I'll be back soon.'

With those words, Sheila opened the driver's door, started the engine and quickly drove away. Ernie lay furious, the sun blazing down on his head and blinding him to the point he struggled to see. He knew he should have his hat and sunglasses on but he'd left them in the vehicle thinking he was only going to shove a few arm-loads of rubbish out onto the ground but he was no match for the quick-acting Sheila. His folly had been to underestimate her and she'd caught him off-guard. He cursed as he tried to get to his feet but the pain in his leg and hip was debilitating and he realised he couldn't get off the ground or move into the shade. He'd been quite taken aback by Sheila callously leaving him, probably for dead.

Meanwhile, Sheila put the air conditioner on high and gulped a mouthful of water from her water bottle. She'd forgotten how hot it was in the Adelaide Hills. About half a kilometre down the track, she alighted from the ute and made a call to Rodney, who lived on a property nearby, getting him to drive her back to Glenelg. Then she walked to the road to meet him. Hopefully, by the time Ernie was found, it would be too late to revive him and those smug Finches would be sorry for the loss of the family patriarch.

They deserve what they get! They'd all be smooching around down there at Trevilly, eating and drinking, and excluding me.

By the time she returned to Glenelg, her plan was ready for action. And woebegone the Finch family. Before long, she had Pat bundled into her car, heading for the emergency department of the hospital. *What a fantastic alibi*, she grinned.

Fleetingly, she thought of Ernie, knowing he would be alone in the bush and, by this stage, he would be completely dehydrated, probably slipping in and out of consciousness before he finally perished. Christmas Eve was near, and time marched on, pausing for no one. Time was the enemy for the parched and desperate Ernie, alone in the isolated bush.

Chapter Twenty-Eight

Christmas

2007

Ian woke early on Christmas Eve and looked over at Sarah, who slept with her eyes shut and her mouth slightly open. He rolled over and switched on the light so he could see the time on the clock. They both had fun accusing the other of snoring, but this morning Ian was pleased to see Sarah sleeping soundly. Her work as a teacher was continuous, and she was a high achiever, but the end of the year thankfully created some respite. Whatever Sarah undertook, she was a winner and so today at Trevilly, the day would be fun-packed with an abundance of food, drinks and lively conversations. Ian sprang out of bed, wrapped his dressing gown around himself and quietly left the room.

Bonnie, Mal and Anne were soon awake and took their places at the kitchen table for breakfast. The Christmas tree was decorated and streamers hung all around the room. Only the balloons needed attention closer to Christmas night. Even the two dogs were excited with the visitors who left brightly wrapped presents under the twinkling lights on the Christmas tree. As Ian cooked bacon and eggs on the barbeque, Bonnie rose and joined him, picking up the tongs to turn the tomatoes.

'Bon, whatever happened to your friend Thelma? Have you heard from her since your days in Africa?'

'No, I haven't, which is very surprising. I knew she wouldn't have Ken's address, but I thought she would have sent something to the Glenelg Homestead but Mum and Dad haven't said anything. I have asked them occasionally, but they said there's been nothing. I did hear though that Vern went to live in Western Australia, so I guess we won't be seeing him for a while. I do hope he writes and keeps in touch. We should ring him later.'

'Yes. Ron and Aunty Enid are coming at three o'clock so we should call before they get here. Hello! Here come Chris and Andy.'

Through the large open windows that allowed the coolness of the morning to enter, two sleepy figures, both still in their tracksuits, ambled towards the house from the shed area.

'How was your night in your caravan?'

Andy smiled and yawned. 'Fine, until Adam and the five o'clock staff decided to milk the cows. We might move the caravan to the other side of the house where it will be quiet in the morning. I guess cows don't rest for Christmas Day. I don't know how you do it, Ian.'

The dogs jumped all over the visitors despite Ian's commands for them to stop. With the bacon sizzling and the eggs cooking in the bacon-flavoured fat, the breakfast looked and smelt delicious. Ian placed the food onto a tray and took it to the table.

'I'll go and wake up Sarah. Surely she can smell the toast and bacon. Dad must also be sleeping, though I didn't hear him come in last night. I'll wake them both up.'

Bonnie poured the tea and put more bread into the toaster while Ian left the room. The smell of bacon made everyone hungry and they all helped themselves to generous serves. 'Well, we'll have a big crowd here tonight as Ian has asked quite a few folks from Carson to join us. I do hope Sarah will play the piano so we can have a sing-along,' she said as she kept bread moving in and out of the toaster.

Sarah emerged on hearing her name and pulled a chair out next to Bonnie. 'It's been a while since I've practised but I'll sit down later and get out the music books. I'm going to have a fair bit of time soon as I've decided to finish teaching. I can't wait for the chance to sleep in permanently,' said Sarah as she raised her cup to her mouth. Everyone clapped! 'Yes, this is a new beginning. Roll on retirement and new adventures beyond the dairy.' She raised her cup as in a toast. 'Now I just need to entice Ian to slow down. I can feel a fabulous holiday coming up soon.'

Ian entered the room and closed the screen door behind him, muttering. His face was drawn and his brow was creased with concern. 'Dad's not here. Mal, did he say anything about coming to the farm? Perhaps he's going to drive here today … but he would have driven up yesterday, ready to embrace the events for today. Perhaps he stayed at Enid's last night but that's not very likely. I'll go and ring her.

'Maybe something's happened to Mum? I wonder what's going on. Dad would have been in touch if that was the case.' A tremor ran through him.

As Ian left, the others exchanged worried looks. 'I spoke with him recently, and we talked about Ian picking him up. But … wait a minute … when I think about it, he dismissed that conversation and talked about something else,' Mal said as he put down his toast and shifted uncomfortably. 'I'm worried, but let's wait until Ian rings.'

Mal's 'farm' shirt, as he called it, was rumpled from quick packing, but he liked it looking that way; same as the faded jeans he wore, both a stark contrast to the crisp, pressed suit he wore to the office each day. 'I'm sure Ern's on his way so let's all finish up here and prepare for our walk around the sheds and the farm paddocks. Ian has a new hayshed I'm keen to check out.'

A few moments later, Adam arrived ready for work after finishing the morning milking. He helped clear the breakfast dishes and mingled with the group as excitement mounted for the Christmas period. The day was warm with just the slightest breeze blowing, so each person dressed in shorts and t-shirts. Adam opened his mouth ready to say something, but realised others were waiting for Ian to return so he remained silent: it looked like it might not be the time for silly jokes or Christmas cheer.

'No one's answering at the Glenelg Homestead. I guess it could be expected.' Ian cleared his throat and then realised the need to be cheery. 'I'll try again later. If there's still no answer, I'll drive to Adelaide. Gosh, the roads will be busy. I do hope Dad hasn't come to grief.'

Try as he may, he found it difficult to dispel the belief that everything was all right. And the later it got, the more concerned he became about his father's continued absence. He tried to pull himself together.

'Come on over and see the new hay shed. And it's almost full of bales. We've got the small ones. They're a lot easier to handle than those big ones we sometimes use. That's our job after Christmas. Have we got any volunteers to cart hay?'

'Nahhh, it's far too itchy!'

The hours drew on as they all visited the new hay shed, walked around the dairy and then drove around the paddocks of freshly cut hay. Soon they forgot about the absent Ernie, and only Ian and Mal harboured the unsettling thought that something had happened to him. The huge eucalyptus provided shade as the sun shone and the galahs squawked in the branches overhead, signalling the signs of summer. The paddocks looked fertile and the farm had all the signs of prosperity. The cows looked contented as they spread across the green pasture which was only just starting to show signs of the summer dryness.

A few hours later, they sat with their backs against the tool shed, breathing in the fresh farm air. Mal fanned himself with a twig when he took charge. 'While we're all here at the best place in the world. Anne has some news to share with the best people in the world.'

Everyone turned their attention to Anne. 'Anyone would think Mal was about to embark on his opening address to the Court!' she said.

'No, this is much more important than any court proceedings,'

Mal interjected. He suppressed a chuckle and dropped his head to indicate his turn to talk was over. The grass started irritating the back of their legs, and a few annoying ants had started to crawl around. The firmness of the ground made its presence felt as small stones became uncomfortable to sit on.

'Righto, we're listening!' Andy announced before adjusting his walking boots and sun hat.

'Mal has asked me to marry him!' Anne rapidly blurted out. 'I had to say it quickly so I could get my words out!'

An outburst of good wishes erupted, and hugs of happiness circulated. Ultimately the group decided to return to the house for a champagne celebration; Mal had secretly placed bottles in the fridge before going to bed the previous night. The celebrations created a mood of merriment and Bonnie was thrilled for the pair, even though the loss of Ken had created a giant hole in her life. She did not wish to dwell on what could have been for her if Ken was still alive and cherished that work had given her new purpose – she would take one day at a time. She looked across at Anne and Mal as they all sat on the lawn in the dappled shade and hoped the moments would last an eternity. Surely this would mark the sign of something positive to happen in the family and she felt Ken's spirit looking down and smiling at her in the goofy way he liked to do. A lump rose in her throat but she stifled it quickly as tears welled up. The support she'd received after Ken's death had been overwhelming and, as she told and retold her story of Sheila's involvement in Ken's demise, it shocked all who heard it. Only a few knew of Sheila's threat of blackmail and Mal's legal interpretation, while Mal, Ian, Bonnie and Ernie were relying on the plan to oust Sheila when the time was right.

While the others sat on the grass, Ian made a quiet exit and made yet another phone call. And again, it went unanswered. Amidst the laughter and merriment outside, he felt the hairs on the back of his neck stand up. He wandered outside again, this time by the eastern exit so he could have a moment to himself. He looked at the garden that his mother had once tended, and the tank stand his father had built for the family. It was like time stood still, and he was a child again with his parents there on the dairy with the cows, the hay and the machines. He remembered clearly when one of the workmen had milked a cow, on the sly, for extra milk and cream, and his father had dismissed him. Trust was Ernie's catchcry, and everyone in his circle needed to be trusted. He wished his father would arrive now and see his trusted family enjoying Mal's new future. He smiled as he remembered all the years he'd joke with Mal about getting married! And now he was going to do it … at the age of fifty-something. *Well, wonders will never cease,* he thought as he walked around the corner of the house to join the group drinking champagne and proposing toasts to Anne and Mal. They were a noisy group as each person had their own toast to deliver to the happy couple, as they retold an exaggerated, funny story.

After a few moments, Ian moved towards Sarah and put his arm around her waist; he whispered in her ear: 'I'll have to go and look for the old man. Can you ensure Enid and Ron have some champagne when they arrive? And the others from town. Mal can take charge.' They both smiled over the idea of Mal taking charge! Of course, he would! He was good at that. 'Sarah, when things die down here, you can crank up the piano and start them all singing. I'll be in touch when I can. Not sure where I'll stay tonight, but I'll see you as soon as I can.'

Without any more fuss, he closed the car door and slowly left Trevilly. He made his way quietly towards Carson and then along the road to Adelaide. He passed through all the familiar towns, only stopping at Mt Barker to stretch his legs and take a break from driving. He walked around the service station, fuelling up and trying to empty his mind of thoughts about his father. His brow remained creased as he worried about his mother, who was totally bedridden and devoid of speech. He decided to traverse the countryside as quickly as he could, taking a few shortcuts and risking speeding fines, and was thankful he drove in the opposite direction to most of the traffic. He should arrive around sunset. It was Christmas Eve and most folks in Adelaide were escaping to the country or the beach.

Chapter Twenty-Nine

Sheila Reveals Herself

2007

As Ian pulled into his parents' driveway, he noticed all the shutters were drawn and immediately suspected something was wrong. His jaw clenched, and his heart raced, the thought of Sheila with his parents deepening his frown. He removed his sunglasses and slowly opened the car door.

The house was strangely quiet. Nevertheless, he banged loudly on the front door, to no avail. Several minutes passed, and Ian continued to rap his fist on the door. Still no response. So he sought out their front door key on his keyring. He turned the key in the front door and almost fell into the hallway, his anxiety at an all-time high.

Sheila was sitting in a lounge chair, nonchalantly reading the newspaper.

'Where's Mum, Sheila?' Ian shouted at her. 'And Dad? And why didn't you answer the door?'

'It's no good shouting at me,' Sheila replied with a little twisted smirk. 'Gran's in hospital, and as for Grandpa, I don't know where he is. I thought he was with you. Anyway, I'm not his carer. You made sure of that. Remember?'

Ian ignored her final comment. Instead, he went through to the kitchen, opened the fridge and pulled out a cold drink. He took a gulp and swallowed noisily, the cold liquid running down his throat as he stood deliberating his next move. Furious, he strode through the house, hoping his father was merely sleeping, but there was no one else at home. He called out to him in the yard, yet sensed it was pointless.

'When did you last see Dad, Sheila?'

'I haven't seen him for a couple of days. He often goes walking so I didn't worry. When he didn't come home, I thought he'd met you somewhere and you'd taken him to Trevilly. Aren't you all down there at your precious little farm … all your precious family there … leaving me and Gran here alone!'

Sheila rose, her voice loud and her finger pointing at Ian, showing her rising anger. She moved closer to him; stared him straight in the eyes, only inches away.

Ian met her steely stare, stood his ground and refused to move. Eventually, Sheila turned and sat down again, ripped the newspaper back into her lap and pretended to read. She rolled her eyes and sighed loudly in a gesture of defiance. He could hardly believe she was his daughter! At least his mother was safe, but he knew his father was in trouble. No one knew his whereabouts, let alone knew he was missing! The tension continued to build in the room, the hostile silence penetrating every crevice in the once cozy home. Ian eventually walked outside to use his phone. He rang the police and reported that his father was missing. The police on Christmas Eve were busy but the operator noted that Ernie regularly went walking to the café strip and beach at Glenelg. They told Ian they would let patrols know to keep an eye out for him and suggested Ian also drive around looking for him. If Ernie hadn't been found by morning, they would commence a thorough search. So Ian drove around for hours looking for his father but to no avail. Eventually, he rang Mal, who had been waiting for his call. He had already packed his car ready for the trip back to Adelaide. Anne and Bonnie were ready to leave with him, so the Christmas party at Trevilly was depleted and very subdued. Friends just sat sipping their drinks and waiting for the phone to ring or until it was time to go to bed.

Ian was already at Mal's home when Mal pulled up; he hurried to him blurting out information about what he'd been doing. 'I've made all the phone calls but nothing. They've listed Dad as a missing person and told me they would look for him in the morning if I rang again. Honestly! Talk about bad timing, Dad! Three hundred and fifty-odd days in the year and it has to be at Christmas time.' Ian knew he was ranting as Mal opened his front door, luggage in tow, and let them into his home.

'Let's sit down and I'll open up the house and let in some cool air. It's so hot. Then we'll talk about what happened and what we do now.' He trudged around the room and commented on the smell of dead flowers that permeated the air and silently hoped it wasn't an omen. Ian felt relieved his cousin was here to help him as this situation was developing into a nightmare.

'Ian, I've had a tail put on Sheila so we should know her movements as soon as I make a phone call. I wonder if she was involved with his movements or whether he did just wander off. I can't believe he merely went walking. Something doesn't feel right. Clearly, Sheila's not helpful from what you told me, so it makes it doubly difficult. At least Aunty is safe in hospital. Did you see her tonight, Ian?'

'No, I just assumed the hospital was a safe place. Talk about crazy! I've just been looking for the old man and driving around everywhere I thought he might be.'

They looked at each other, stony-faced, as words hung in the air. Mal's face looked drawn. 'Right … Bonnie, you need to be with your Mum. We'll drop you and Anne off, and then Ian and I'll keep cruising around and see what we come up with.' Mal stood straight as best he could, stretching his legs after the long drive, and then headed for the door.

'Good idea, Mal. Clearly, no one's going to get any sleep until we know Dad's all right,' Bonnie replied.

Mal rattled his keys in his heightened state of anxiety as they all headed out to the car. It was pitch black now so finding Ernie would be hard work.

As the car crawled down the street, Ian wound down the window and began calling: 'Ernie, Ernie Finch!' The streetlights were dull and, by this time, the party-goers had retired into their homes but there was would be no rest for the Finches any time soon. Hours dragged by and tiredness became exhaustion as they continued until the morning sun snuck over the horizon and signalled a new day.

'Let's do a final drive past the house and then we'll ring the police and the tail again. He's good so, hopefully, he's been watching the house like he's been paid to do.'

Mal drove towards the Glenelg Homestead and stopped a short distance from the house, away from full view. He paused. 'Stay here, Ian, and I'll do a quick walk to check out the place. Wouldn't it be great if we found him asleep in his car?'

Mal walked to the verge and looked, but couldn't find the ute. Mal stopped in his tracks; he could taste fear in the back of his throat and for the first time, his worst thoughts slowly aligned in his head. Something bad had happened to the man he thought of as his father. For some reason, Ernie had changed his mind about emptying the rubbish on the back of the ute. Had he been to the tip? With security cameras, authorities could check the number plates of everyone who entered. He must have been to the tip but something didn't add up. He called Terry the Tail now, even though dawn had hardly created a new day.

He sank onto the grass near where the ute had been as he hung up from Terry, who'd been keeping an incredibly good watch on the happenings with Sheila. Firstly, he had photographic evidence of an exchange that looked like a drug deal, but it could hardly qualify as evidence. It could have been anything, Mal thought and shrugged in disbelief. Neither did he take photos that day as he thought the drug exchange was all Mal wanted. He wasn't aware of any family issues so he finished his work.

Something was afoot, but Mal didn't know what.

He scanned the front lawn and up to the front door; noticed a piece of paper stuck to the flywire, and took a step forward before he registered fear. Sweat broke out on his forehead and began to form into drops, ready to run down his face. He wiped his forehead with the back of his hand and crept towards the door. He took the note and slowly unfolded it; a card dropped out. Mal's hand trembled as he read the note, which told him no visitors were wanted. If contact was needed, then read the card. It was a lawyer's contact details.

In the dim morning light, Mal read enough to infer what would come next; he suspected Sheila's plan was playing out as she'd anticipated. There were no more words but Mal didn't like what he thought would come next. *But where's Ernie?*

It was pointless banging on the door as he suspected Sheila wouldn't answer it. He also suspected the locks would be changed within days, or maybe Sheila would be smart enough to wait just a little longer. In the meantime, they would have to find Ernie, hopefully alive, as soon as they could. Pulling himself together, he crept back to his car, where Ian impatiently waited for news of his father.

'At least we can give the police some details to act on now,' Mal said, by way of consolation. He mulled it over for a few minutes and finally took his phone and rang the police, alerting them that Ernie's ute wasn't at home and that Sheila, his granddaughter was the last one to have seen him.

'The search for Ern will begin now,' he told Ian. 'He must be heading for Carson, but never made it.'

'His first stop is always Bridgewater,' Ian said as he ended his phone call with the police.

After a few minutes, Mal put the key in the ignition and started the engine but let several more minutes pass before he felt able to drive away from the family home. There was so much happening, including Aunty Pat being hospitalised but, for the time being, at least she was safe, and Bonnie was with her!

*****

The hours crept on and as Ernie was still missing, more police were put on the case. Alerts went out to police patrols. Ernie's photograph flashed across Adelaide News Bulletins. When a call came in from the service station at Bridgewater that Ernie had been there recently, road patrols were tasked to search the roads while volunteers searched bush tracks in the area.

Soon a full-scale emergency was declared.

But time was the enemy for Ernie.

*****

Hours later, when not a breath of air moved as another hot day continued its relentless pounding onto the dusty, dry earth, Bonnie and Ian glanced at each other as a green sedan came up the long driveway. Bonnie recognised it immediately. It was the detective's car from Ken's case. She stood immediately and watched with hope as it drew to a halt. The detective climbed out of the front seat and she waited tensely for her father to open the back door and join them – that he'd been found. But Ernie did not. And the look on the detective's face said it all.

Ernie's body had been found on a dirt track, lying in the hot Australian sun near some bushes and illegally dumped garden waste. His ute was found abandoned a short distance away. Foul play was suspected, but couldn't be proven at this point in time and so that information was withheld.

Bonnie's jaw dropped open and her heart stopped momentarily, chilling her skin. Ian slumped into a chair. There was no easy way for the message to be imparted.

'It seems your father had fallen and broken his femur, which caused internal bleeding. At his age, he would have succumbed to the blood loss in a short space of time. He probably wasn't in pain for long, but there are drag marks in the dirt that indicate he tried to crawl some distance for help. With this kind of injury and in this heat, he wouldn't have lasted long. I don't think … … ….'

Ian's loud moan of rage and despair filled the verandah. 'Why didn't you start looking for him when I told you?! How could you have let this happen!' he raged.

'With an injury like this, he would have been gone before you even knew he was missing.'

Ian's head dropped down, the loss of his vulnerable father, a man he loved more than life itself, taking its toll on him. Bonnie rested her hand on his head, consoling him, the news still yet to sink in fully.

'Sheila has done this. She preyed on him and Mum, tricked them, lied to her own flesh and blood to wreak havoc on this family. She's a cold-blooded killer!' Ian felt nauseous, bile threatening to rise to his throat. He didn't care what the police thought now. He rose to stave off the nausea, imagining the coroner would be looking after his father now. He shook his head again, unable to believe the warmth had left his father's body, that his father had been injured. His father was so agile for an old bloke, so active. Wild thoughts raged in his head.

'What was he doing out there? Why had he been left half dead and clearly in distress?' Tears streamed down Bonnie's face, her jaw locked, words unable to come out.

'We'll be looking into those issues, Mr Finch. We will be looking into those issues.'

Bonnie stood frozen, watching him return to his car. Her head started shaking. 'Ian, it's that Sheila. She's a monster.' She could hear herself becoming louder, verging on the point of hysteria. She kicked the verandah post as hard as she could, trying to find pain stronger than what she was feeling at her loss. She screamed, and her fists clenched at her sides. It was hard to believe, and she swore out loud, 'Fuck her! I want to kill her! I want to kill her!'

Once again, the coroner and a forensic pathologist were involved, and family members, including Sheila, were questioned. Words like 'motive' were absent from the language as the unthinkable lay dormant. The official report was Ernie had driven himself to Bridgewater, but deviated to dump the green waste off the ute, and somehow became separated from his vehicle. Falling, he suffered an injury that, combined with the extreme heat, proved fatal.

Then Bonnie started to rant, as if it would exonerate her pain. 'Why would he do that? Dad would never dump rubbish in the bush. Never!'

'I know,' Ian replied. 'That's not Dad at all. Something's definitely not right here.'

A quick thought flashed through Bonnie's mind as she deliberated on how she would break the news to her mother. She had to get back to the hospital as soon as she could.

*****

Sheila's alibi panned out. She had been at the hospital with Pat all afternoon. Staff remembered seeing her there, on and off. Mal, Ian and Bonnie, however, knew a serious crime had been committed and Mal suggested contacting his work colleagues in the police force, but Bonnie adamantly refused to allow it. She didn't want to explain the blackmail, or Zimbabwe.

'Bon, we need to explain all this to the police. We can nail Sheila and put her away.' Mal felt increasingly frustrated with Bonnie and lost count of how many times he'd told her to forget Sheila's threats, but Bonnie wouldn't budge. From experience, he knew that law was often about losing "unlosable" cases and winning "unwinnable" ones. There were no guarantees in law and a lot of evidence was hearsay. While Bonnie's drug situation in Africa was a living hell for her and could be proven untrue, he couldn't understand why she would still be so afraid of it being revealed.

Bonnie was no match for Sheila, regardless of the law. And Bonnie had been through enough, was on the verge of a breakdown and nothing they did was going to bring her father home. He felt like screaming out to her again that the African incident was irrelevant in a court of law in Australia. But hanging over all of it was Ken's death. Push the issue and it could be Sheila on the stand charged with murder, or Bonnie on the stand in a court of law trying to defend herself on the same charge. Which way would it go? That was the issue. Sheila would be very convincing and coherent while Bonnie would be in tears and a blubbering mess and one shade off of a nervous breakdown.

A large part of Mal certainly didn't want Bonnie to be considered again as a prime suspect because he'd bullied her into decisions against her better judgement. Her mental health was fragile at best. He couldn't stand the thought of her being cross-examined for Ken's death … and now her father had died under mysterious circumstances. Against his better judgement and his love of a good fight, he decided to let the matter drop, realising there were plenty of crazy psychopaths on the loose, and Sheila was one of them.

*****

After Pat's death a few months later, Sheila's claim for the Glenelg Homestead, *her home*, played out in the courts. She knew she had a strong case as she had lived in the house for some time. It was her only home. She was living in hardship. Had no job. No means of supporting herself. She'd given up her career to be Pat's carer. And even though the Will stated otherwise, she wasn't budging! She had new locks fitted to the house and, in the eyes of the law, it was her home. She knew she could use the collateral in the house to pay lawyers to fight her case. And if she had to, she could sell the house to pay lawyers; she would still have enough to buy another home. And so she played the victim who needed a home or she would be living on the streets – she knew the courts would avoid putting individuals out of their homes. She'd kept her precious paperwork from the lawyer, typed it on his formal letterhead, and drooled with pleasure when she read the words he'd dictated to the old, smelly secretary. As for Bonnie, she could always live in hospital accommodation or at Trevilly, the family home, so she had two prospects of somewhere to live.

Mal and Anne knew how the law functioned and that it would be difficult to prove Sheila's blackmail of Bonnie. It was all hearsay. And they wanted to avoid damaging Bonnie's professional reputation by casting a shadow of drug theft on her record, whatever the outcome. People could believe the strangest things.

And so Sheila took them on and won. After a lengthy court battle, she became the new legal owner of the Glenelg Homestead, and no member of the Finch family was welcome. Mal felt snookered – by the law, by the fabrication, by the fear of those involved. And so too did the rest of the Finch family, for years to come.

Chapter Thirty

Some Time Later

2018

'Unbelievable,' Ross exclaimed as the story came to an end. He sat in stony silence, a cold shiver enveloping him and, if he'd been a religious person, he'd have sworn he felt the spirit of Pat and Ernie sitting around the fire beside him. After all, he was on the property they'd once owned, where they'd breathed and raised a family. They'd been custodians of the land as no one really owned land in this timeless realm of life. He drew a deep breath in, stood and stretched his legs lest he felt an unwanted tap on the shoulder or any other kind of spiritual presence.

Ross had been so intrigued by Sandy's account of events over the recent days that he'd pulled his caravan into a paddock near the old man's dilapidated shack and begged him to continue with the story about the boss and his sister. Nights blended into days and the two men went about their daily business, eagerly anticipating the late afternoon so they could continue the sharing and hearing of the tale.

'But what about Ernie's Will?' Ross asked Sandy, trying to imagine the horror that had just unfolded; he could hardly believe this injustice was sanctioned by law.

'Well, the law doesn't always follow what a Will dictates. That much you'd better believe,' replied Sandy. He liked having his caravan guest who, each night, made a fire pit where they could boil the billy and make tea. Sandy loaded his cup with spoonfuls of sugar and sat back in his fancy caravan folding chair that Ross had provided for him. 'We'd better not let the fire get away. Boss would be furious. One fire for now is enough. Not quite sure how the fire in the hayshed started but nowadays firebugs are around, and pyromaniacs set fire to whatever they can for the pure pleasure of seeing things burn. Vandalism is most difficult to prove and some slippery fellows get away with it. Police have a hard time proving who committed arson … unless you got those new-fangled CCTV cameras.' Sandy kicked some dirt towards the flames to ensure they remained subdued and under control.

'So why is the sister here? Where does she live? Come on, Sandy. Get on with it!' Ross prodded; he was now thinking about this own Will with some concern. He could hardly believe what he was hearing and thought: *things are not what they used to be. Life is full of complexities, and values change.*

'Oh yes … soon after poor Ernie's death, Sarah had a stroke. We're talking about quite a few years ago now. It didn't kill her but she needed considerable care, so Bonnie offered to come to Trevilly to care for her. With Mal and Anne married, Bonnie returned home to give them space, and it gave her a purpose. Remember the court awarded the Glenelg Homestead to Sheila … can you believe it, despite it being bequeathed to Ernie and Pat's daughter. Incredible really! How does that happen? What kind of laws do we have in this country? Anyway, it did.'

Sandy stopped his narrative, contemplating his last words and shaking his head. He looked skywards as if hoping for divine intervention before he began again. When he did, he spoke quietly.

'Bonnie's spirit felt revived at Trevilly with all the perks of nature and the dairy. She'd always loved Carson. You could imagine how she felt after the ordeal of losing two important men in her life. She was devastated, and part of her died that Christmas. She and Sarah had always been good friends – both are quite gentle souls, really.'

Sandy became pensive as the bush sounds subsided and night intruded on Sandy's tale. 'Let's get those lamb chops from your fridge, Ross. You can cook them while I keep the fire under control. What do you say to that?'

Ross could hardly believe his good fortune of the last week or so. He'd stumbled onto an innocent country incident with people who had a seemingly benign life, but he had the time and energy to delve deeper, to discover a tale of woe. *There might still be more to come*, Ross thought as he retrieved the lamb chops from his fridge and took them out to Sandy.

'My wife hated lamb chops, but she passed away last year so now I have them regularly,' Ross said as he emerged from his caravan.

When Ross found himself alone, he decided to buy a caravan and travel around Australia, leaving his home in Murray Bridge. He intended to be away for a year or more. He'd assumed he'd have encounters with locals, such as this one here in Carson, but he didn't really expect to become so involved in the lives of its inhabitants. 'So, what happened to poor Ernie's wife?'

Ross watched his step to avoid a fall but he made haste to the fire with his lamb chops. He was hungry.

'Pat Finch lasted a few months after her husband died but she never regained her power of speech. She drifted in and out of a coma, on life support, until the family gave its support to turn the machines off. Then she passed away, oblivious of family drama. I think she lasted so long because she was a robust woman who had quite a few pounds around her waist so she would have been good in a famine. By the time her end came, she was very thin. Ian described her as 'a skeleton' but hey, old fella, that's how it goes. Actually, I don't even know your name! My name is Sandy and I've been living here for years. Did I tell you that? Anyway, the boss wanted to build me a new house but I told him I was quite happy living in this old shack. It's been here for years and got a bit of history, just near the boundary of Ian and Ron's properties. That way I can keep an eye on both places. Can't trust a lot of folks these days. First, us old fellas keep an eye out for the young ones and then, before you know it, they're looking out for us old blokes. Unbelievable! Now, you were saying? I do apologise for rambling.'

'I'm Ross. I'm a widower from Murray Bridge,' Ross reciprocated. It was almost dark and the sound of a vehicle could be heard approaching. 'Who is that coming?'

'That's bound to be Ron. He probably smelt our lamb chops cooking! Nahhh, I'm only kidding. He sometimes drives past, going somewhere, but he may have seen your caravan lights and is coming to check up on me.'

Soon the car approached and a middle-aged man emerged from the driver's seat. A dog followed Ron and Sandy went to speak to the newcomer. Before long, Ron joined them so Ross had to retrieve another chair from his caravan for a new member of the group. Ross figured this Finch family were good talkers who liked a yarn and soon Ron and Ross were engaged in conversation. Ron lived on his own now as his mother had passed away some years ago. He too had a loyal band of workers who ensured profits were made on the nearby dairy. Ron and Sandy discussed the happenings from the last few days.

According to Adam, a car had been found near the shed. He had seen the black smoke coming from the hay as he was talking to the local stock agent but soon, the shed was crackling, angry orange flames taking on a life of its own. Soon the smoke was billowing and huge, and looked like the devil himself. Then a big man with curly ginger hair – a friend of Adam's who regularly pops over – arrived as the fire took hold and began raging. After a quick discussion they decided there was nothing they could do but contain it to that area. By that stage, the person trapped inside the shed had no hope of being rescued alive. It was pointless getting the fire equipment organised as it had all happened so quickly. The spread of the fire raised suspicions of an accelerant being used.

Then out of the blue, the person inside the shed stumbled out and collapsed. Ironic really. It was the damn arsonist! What a shock for the paramedics when they arrived! They said the death was probably caused by smoke inhalation. Smoke normally gets you before the flames, they say. Later, when they looked inside the car, a syringe was found so the police were called. Adam recognised the vehicle as being Sheila's, and documents were found inside verifying her identity.

'So, what was the ambulance doing, Ron? I've been pottering around here, but it seems there's no one at the shed, so I've just been servicing the milking machines and keeping the cows coming through. Have you seen Ian?'

'Yeah,' Ron replied as he leaned forward and helped himself to a chop. It was lucky Ross's caravan was well equipped with extra cutlery and crockery. They even had barbeque sauce, pepper and salt too. A few tomatoes and a carrot had been cut up to accompany the meat, and each man believed his dietary needs had been well attended to. As Ron bit into his chop, he peeled the edge of fat from the meat and gave it to the dog that waited attentively nearby. 'Ian's home from Adelaide now. Pretty awful, really. He had to identify his daughter's body: It was Sheila who burnt down the hayshed. She must have been overcome by smoke or somehow tripped in her efforts to evade the fire and bang, she never made it. Or perhaps she did it intentionally. Honestly, one will never know.'

Silence hung in the air, and all that could be heard was the dog chewing on freshly cooked chop bones. Almost by instinct, the frogs and cicadas knew when to hush. 'What was she doing there?' Ross inquired, his jaw dropping open.

'Who knows? She was seen here on the odd occasion, snooping rather than coming out with anything to say. Then she'd just leave without a word. Rather odd really. No one actually saw what happened. The next thing we know the hay shed was on fire. Bonnie smelt the smoke and when she went to investigate, she saw a strange figure stumbling around so she phoned the ambulance. I'd say they went straight through to Adelaide.'

Ron replaced his knife and fork on his plate as though he'd just dined at a Michelin restaurant and enjoyed a five-course meal.

Ross's curiosity peaked, intrigued by the nonchalance of the men. 'So, no one knew the identity of the fire victim?'

'Well, no. Though I've got a feeling Ian wasn't surprised. He knew his estranged daughter had paid unannounced visits over many years, and disappeared just as promptly as she arrived. Apparently, in her job, she was a chemicals auditor or something like that, so she could easily have started a fire, and a good one at that. But really, anyone can start a fire. Well, it looks like this fire took on a life of its own. We all know that once a fire starts in a hayshed, there's no stopping it.'

'We'd better put some dirt over this fire pit. I don't really want Ian coming down here. You know how he's always talking about trusting people, particularly his workers.' Sandy stood up and kicked dirt onto the fire, and soon it was just a smoulder of smoke and coals.

'Well, he must be trusting of you, Sandy. How long have you been here now? No, don't start counting up the years. All that'll lead to is some more historical stories and that'll make me feel old. I can see now why Mal and Anne have retired. They're living the good life travelling and relaxing.' Sandy stroked his chin and prepared to roll a cigarette, without responding to the comments. 'Ross, where are you going next? How long have you had your caravan?'

It was a good question, one Ross wasn't quite sure how to answer. He spoke briefly of his life, which he felt had been quite inconsequential compared with what he'd been hearing. After a comfortable cup of billy tea, Ron and his dog left. Sandy took the plates into his shack and began to wash the dishes. The moon shone, creating an eerie light in the southeast of South Australia. The summer warmth was a comfort as he moved in his chair and relaxed. Ross could hear the rattle of dishes being washed and waited until Sandy brought them back. 'Sandy, I think I'll move on in the morning.'

'Righto, mate.'

The men bid each other a good night and retired, each to their separate abodes. Ross couldn't sleep that night as his mind kept thinking about the story he'd just heard. He was astounded how the sight of the boss and his sister had led to an interpretation of events Ross would never have expected. He made a mental note to check his Will with his lawyer when he returned home, and perhaps, he may need to make an appointment sooner rather than later. He kept thinking about all the unexpected twists and turns in the lives of the people he'd just heard about and how situations could go horribly wrong. As he thought about each of them, he felt sorry for the way life had treated them. He dreamt strange things that night and was relieved when morning came.

As he swallowed his last piece of toast, he thought about hitching up his caravan and checking to ensure nothing was out of place. His tired body ached, and he missed his wife. She would have been able to comfort him, particularly now that he wanted to talk to his lawyer about his Will. He'd thought he had left all that behind him as the last year had been full of details about death and dying. Now he felt in the midst of it again.

He drove his vehicle towards the road away from Sandy's shack and, as he neared the next corner, he hesitated before turning towards Murray Bridge and home again. He was going to phone his lawyer to ensure his Will would stand up in a court of law. He just wanted to be sure, then he could set off in his caravan again without any more of these burning issues.

About the Author

Leah MacGuire grew up in Australia and spent her early years engaged in the routines of farm life. After a short time in Africa, Leah realised the many injustices and developed a social conscience. With a working life as a teacher, like Sarah's character in the novel, Leah focused on writing narratives with her students over three decades. Towards the end of her teaching career, Leah was offered a role by Edith Cowan University in Western Australia, where her focus was on mentoring undergraduate teachers.

Burning Issues is her first fiction novel.

Leah MacGuire